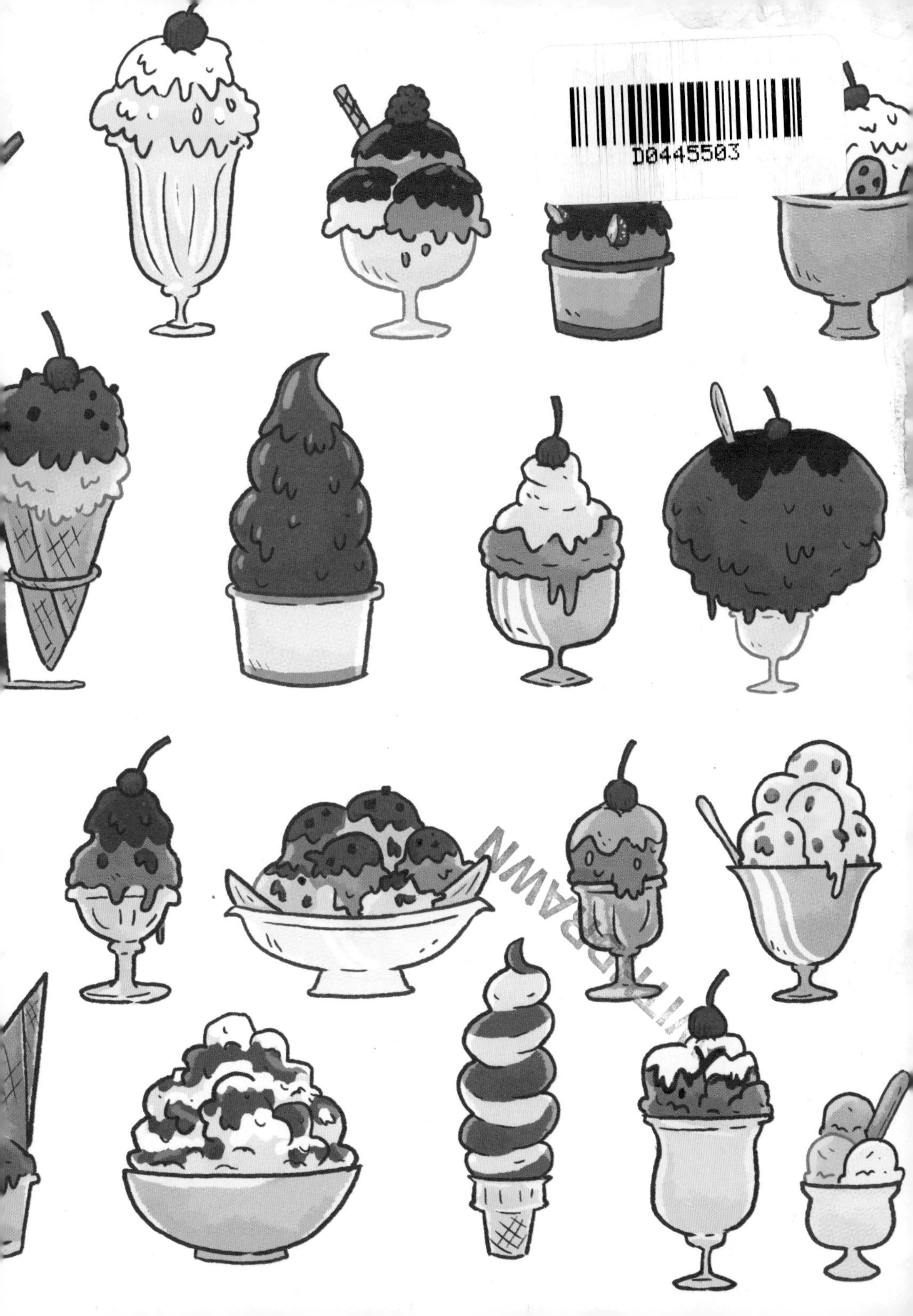

Blue, Barry & Pancakes

DANGER ON MOUNT CHOCO

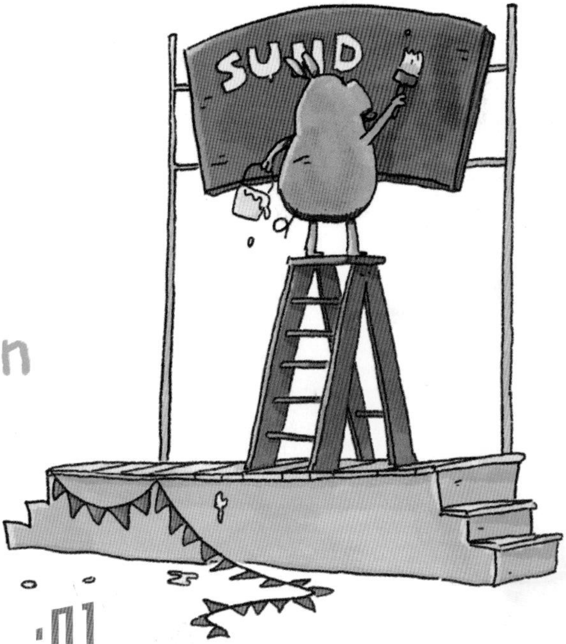
SUND

by

Dan & Jason

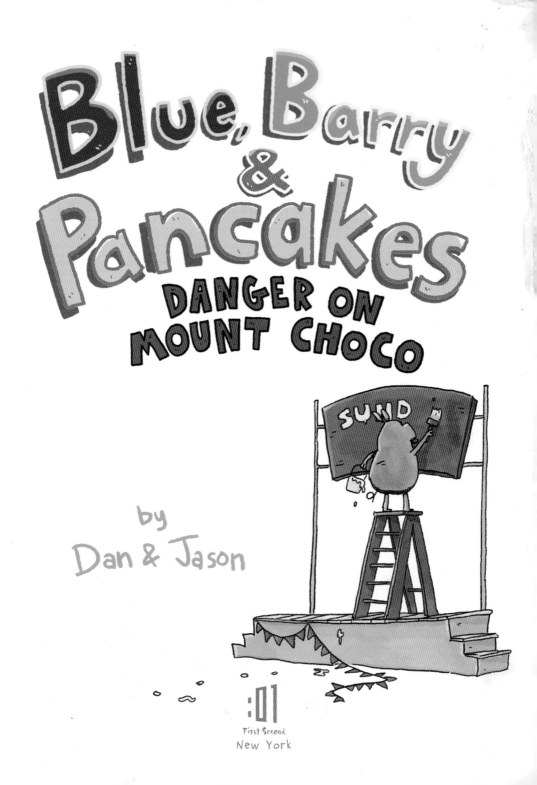

:01
First Second
New York

FOR:

My mom, Susan, who never once questioned drawing cartoons for a living. —D.A.

June. She always believed I could scale the highest peaks. Even the ones with yetis. It meant the world to have someone rooting for me. —J.P.

First Second

Published by First Second
First Second is an imprint of Roaring Brook Press,
a division of Holtzbrinck Publishing Holdings Limited Partnership
120 Broadway, New York, NY 10271
firstsecondbooks.com
mackids.com

© 2022 by Daniel Rajai Abdo and Jason Linwood Patterson
All rights reserved.

Library of Congress Control Number: 2021900595

Our books may be purchased in bulk for promotional, educational, or business use. Please contact your local bookseller or the Macmillan Corporate and Premium Sales Department at (800) 221-7945 ext. 5442 or by email at MacmillanSpecialMarkets@macmillan.com.

FIRST
EDITION

First edition, 2022
Edited by Calista Brill and Alex Lu
Cover and interior book design by Sunny Lee

This book was drawn mostly on a Wacom Cintiq and iPad Pro. Dan & Jason write, draw, color, and letter together in Photoshop and Procreate. The font is a unique Blue, Barry & Pancakes typeset created specifically for this book.

Printed in January 2022 in China by RR Donnelley Asia Printing Solutions Ltd., Dongguan City, Guangdong Province

ISBN 978-1-250-25557-0
10 9 8 7 6 5 4 3 2 1

Don't miss your next favorite book from First Second! For the latest updates go to firstsecondnewsletter.com and sign up for our enewsletter.

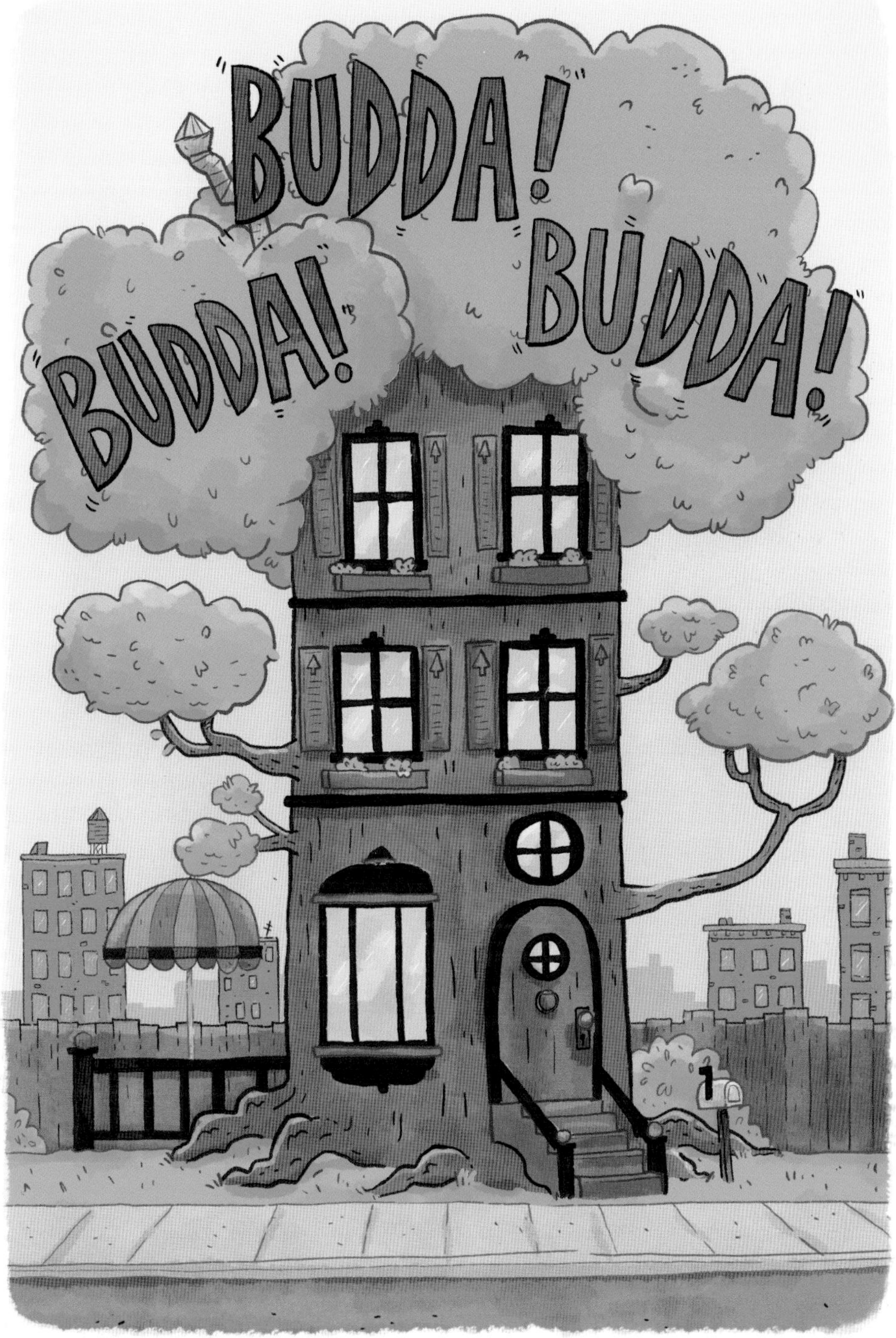
BUDDA!
BUDDA!
BUDDA!

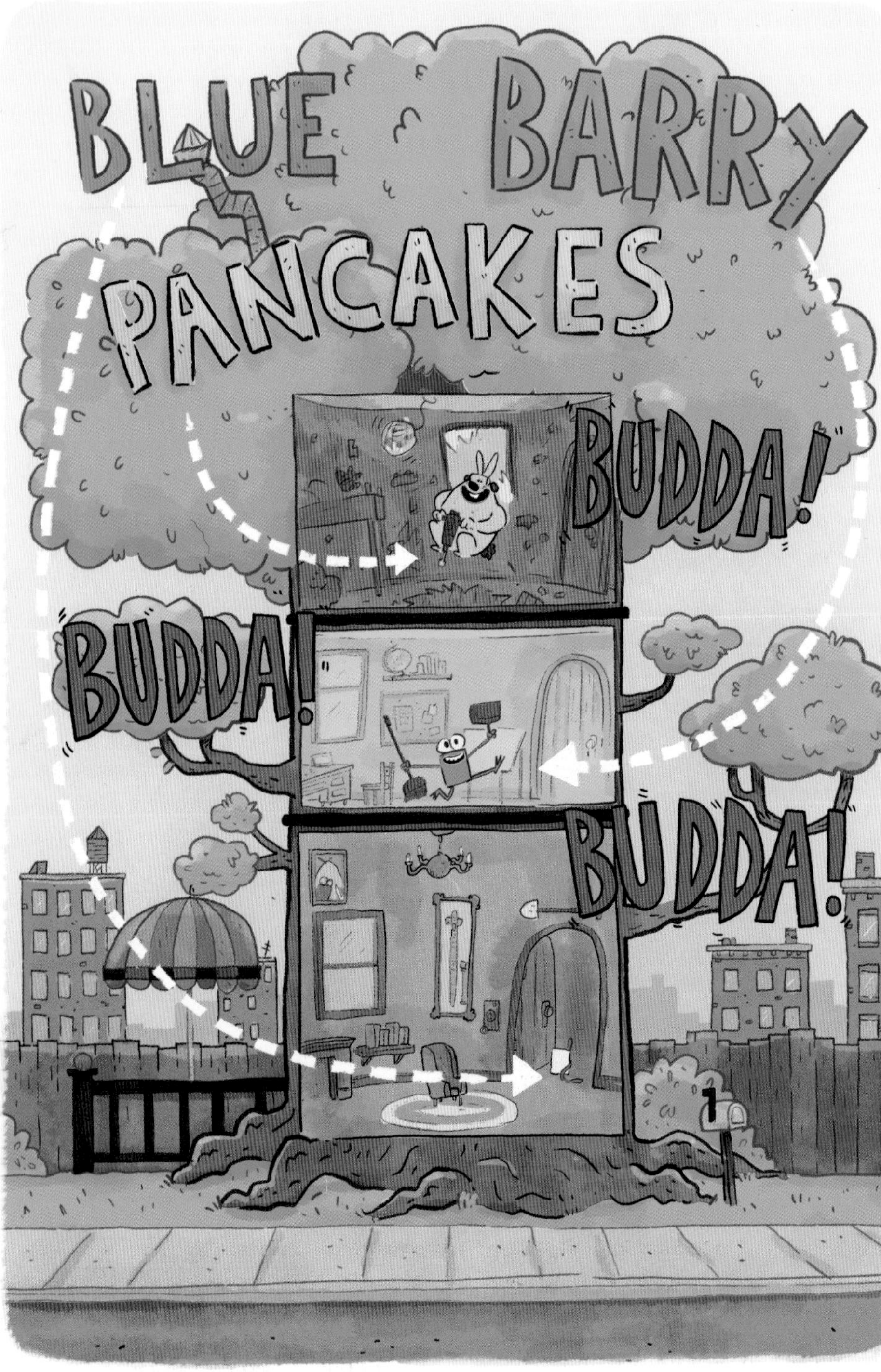
BLUE BARRY PANCAKES
BUDDA!
BUDDA!
BUDDA!

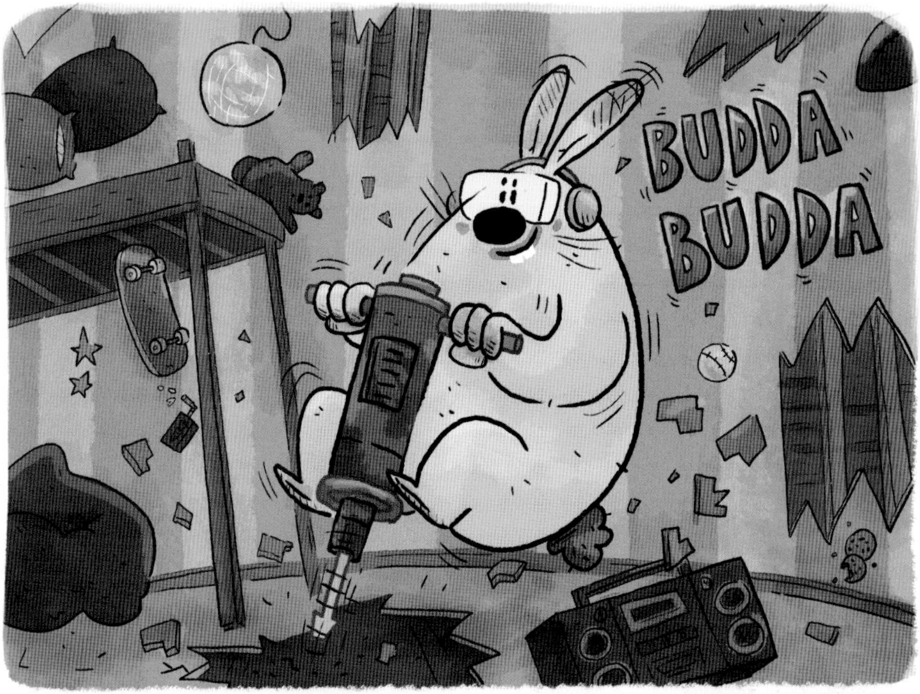
BUDDA
BUDDA

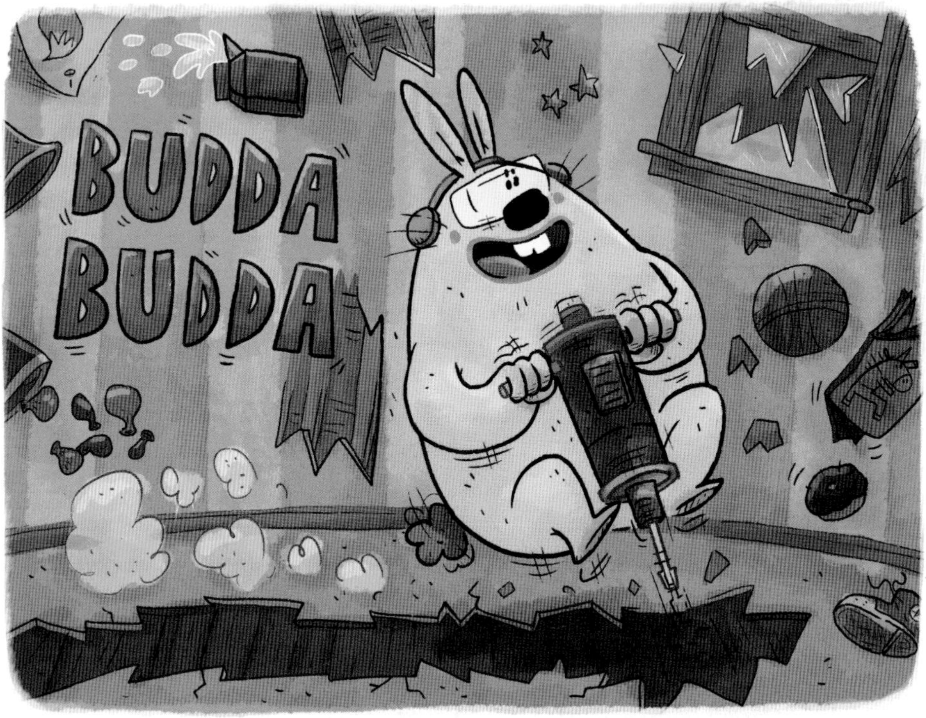
BUDDA
BUDDA

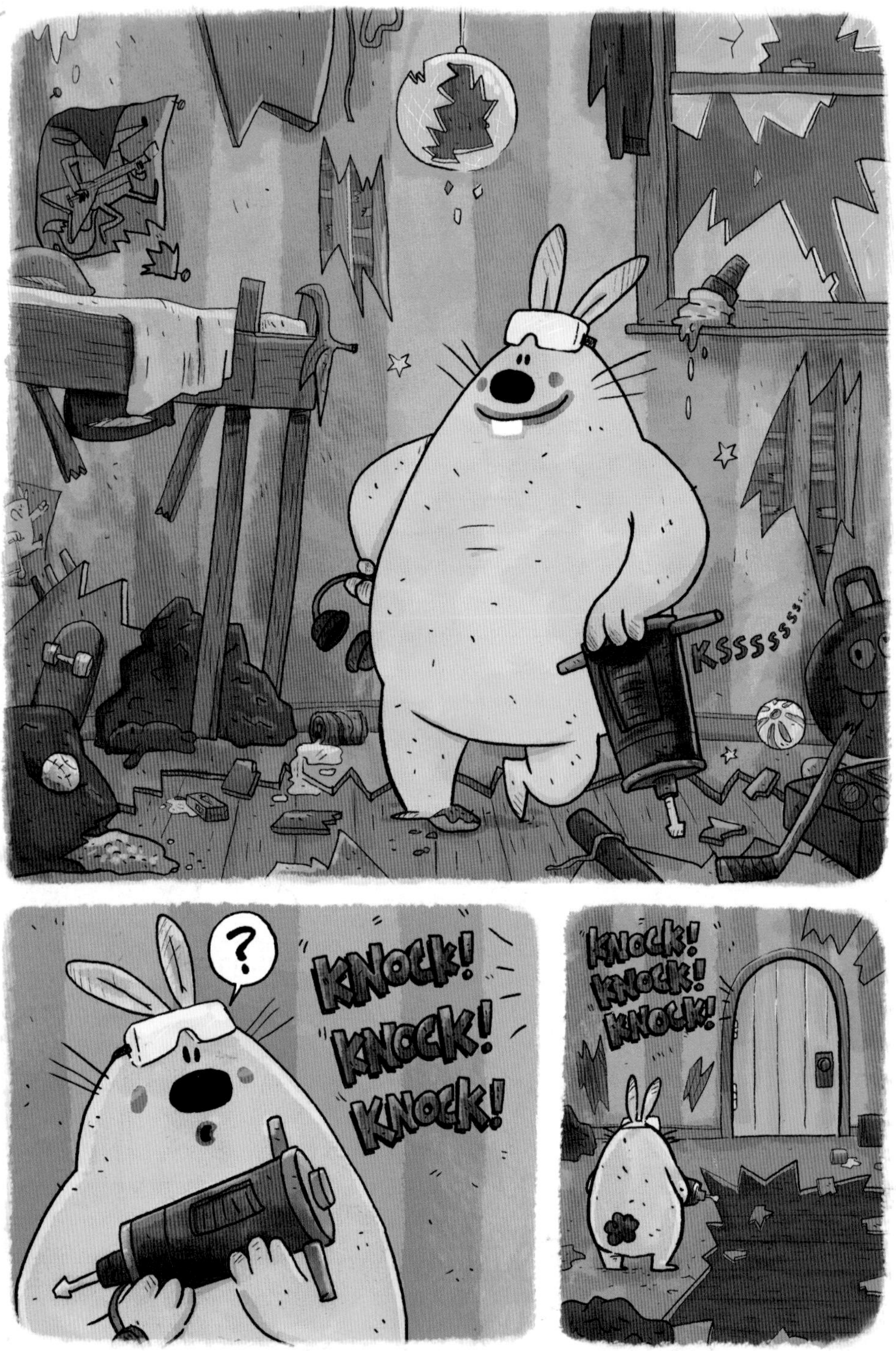
KSSSSSSSS...
?
KNOCK! KNOCK! KNOCK!
KNOCK! KNOCK! KNOCK!

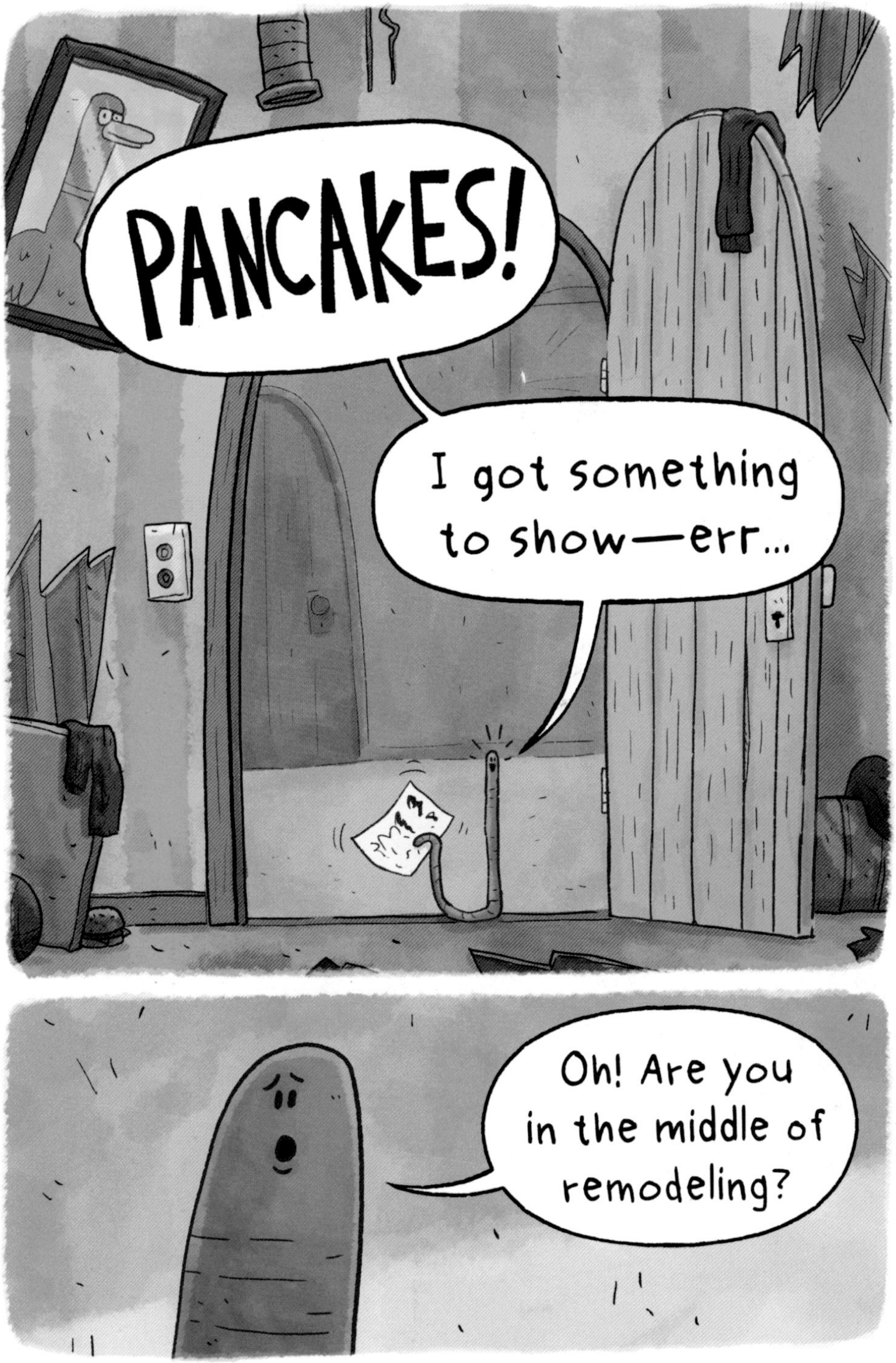
PANCAKES!
I got something to show—err...
Oh! Are you in the middle of remodeling?

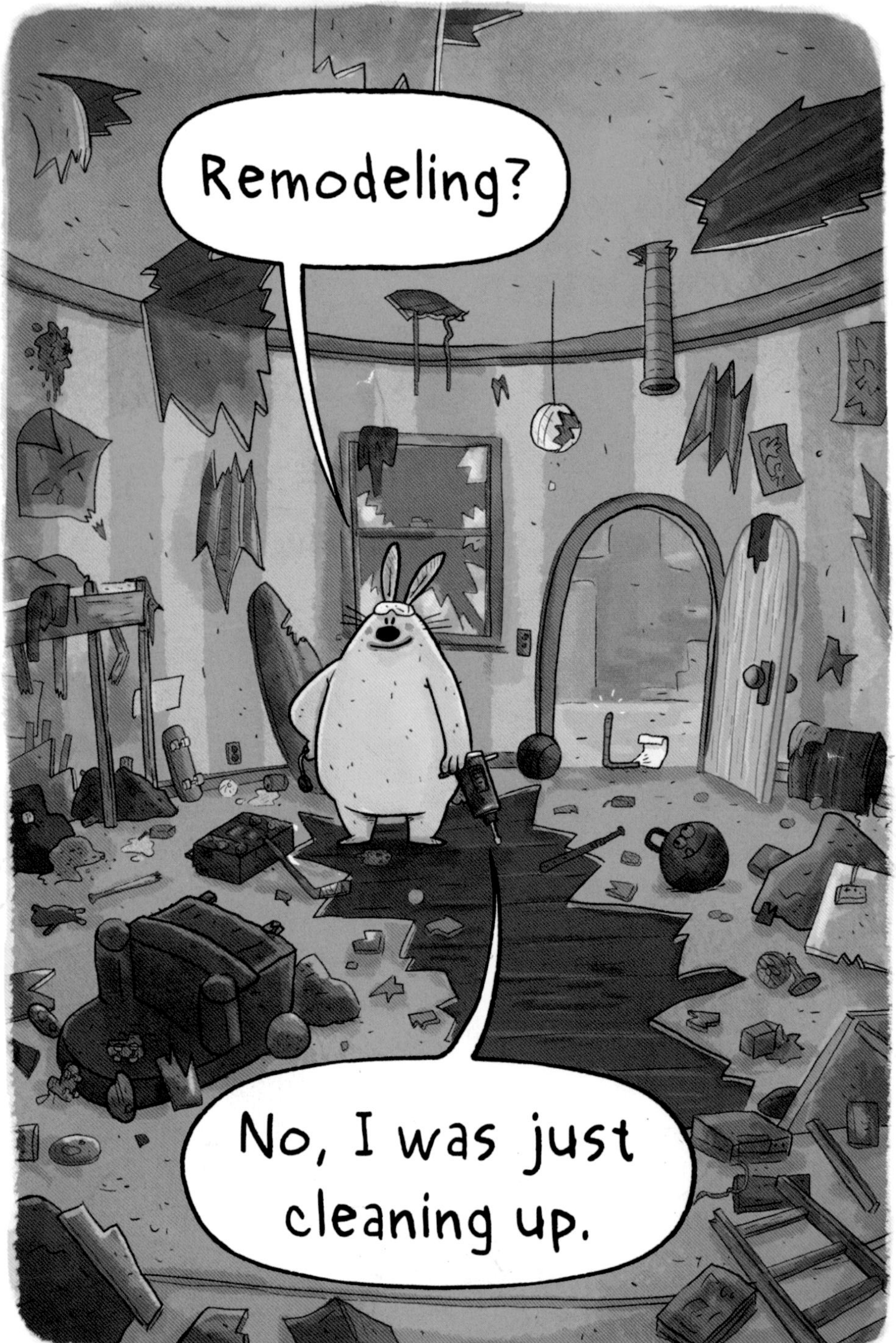
Remodeling?
No, I was just cleaning up.

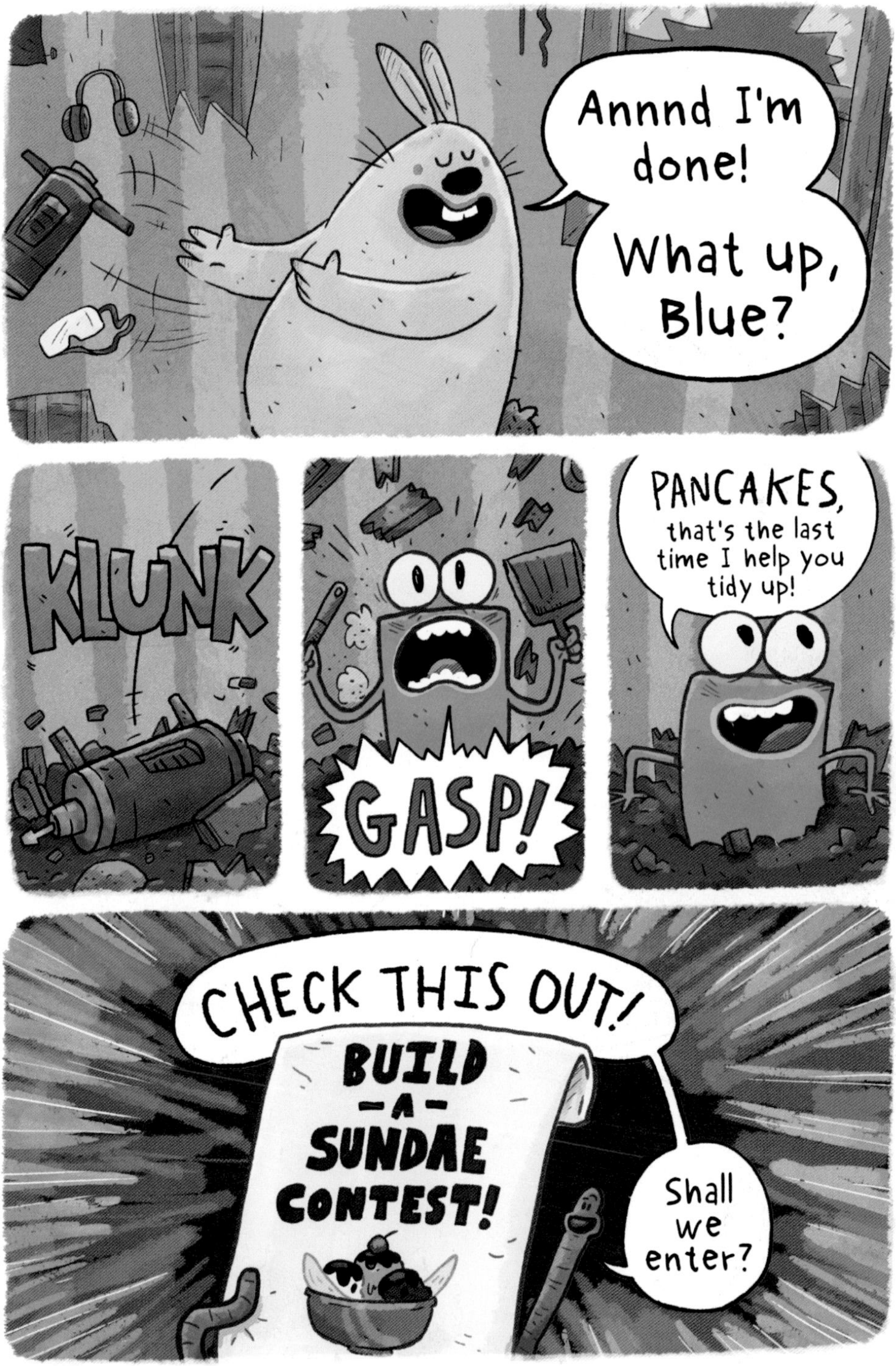
Annnd I'm done!
What up, Blue?
KLUNK
GASP!
PANCAKES, that's the last time I help you tidy up!
CHECK THIS OUT!
BUILD -A- SUNDAE CONTEST!
Shall we enter?

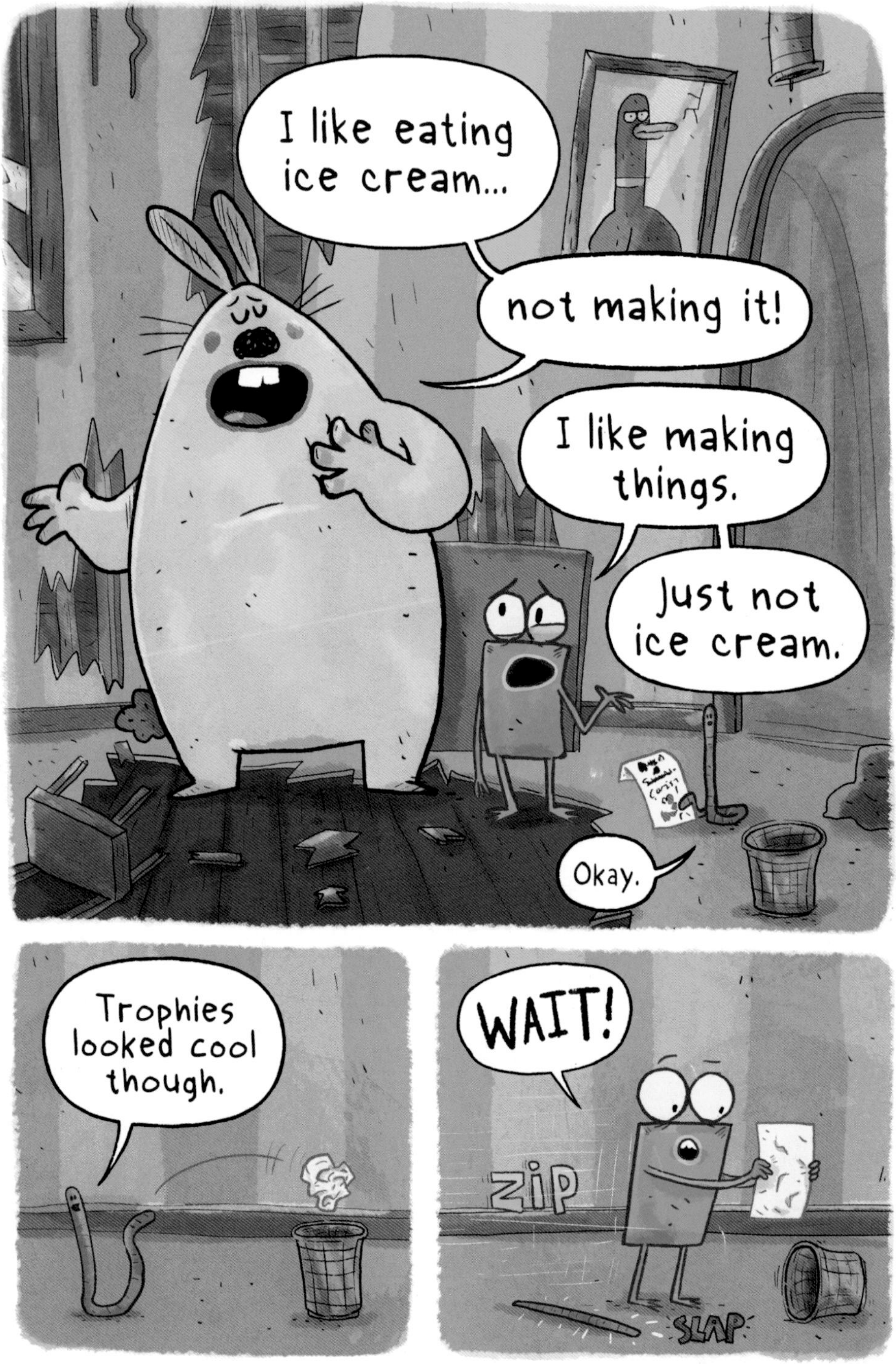
I like eating ice cream...
not making it!
I like making things.
Just not ice cream.
Okay.
Trophies looked cool though.
WAIT!
ZIP
SLAP

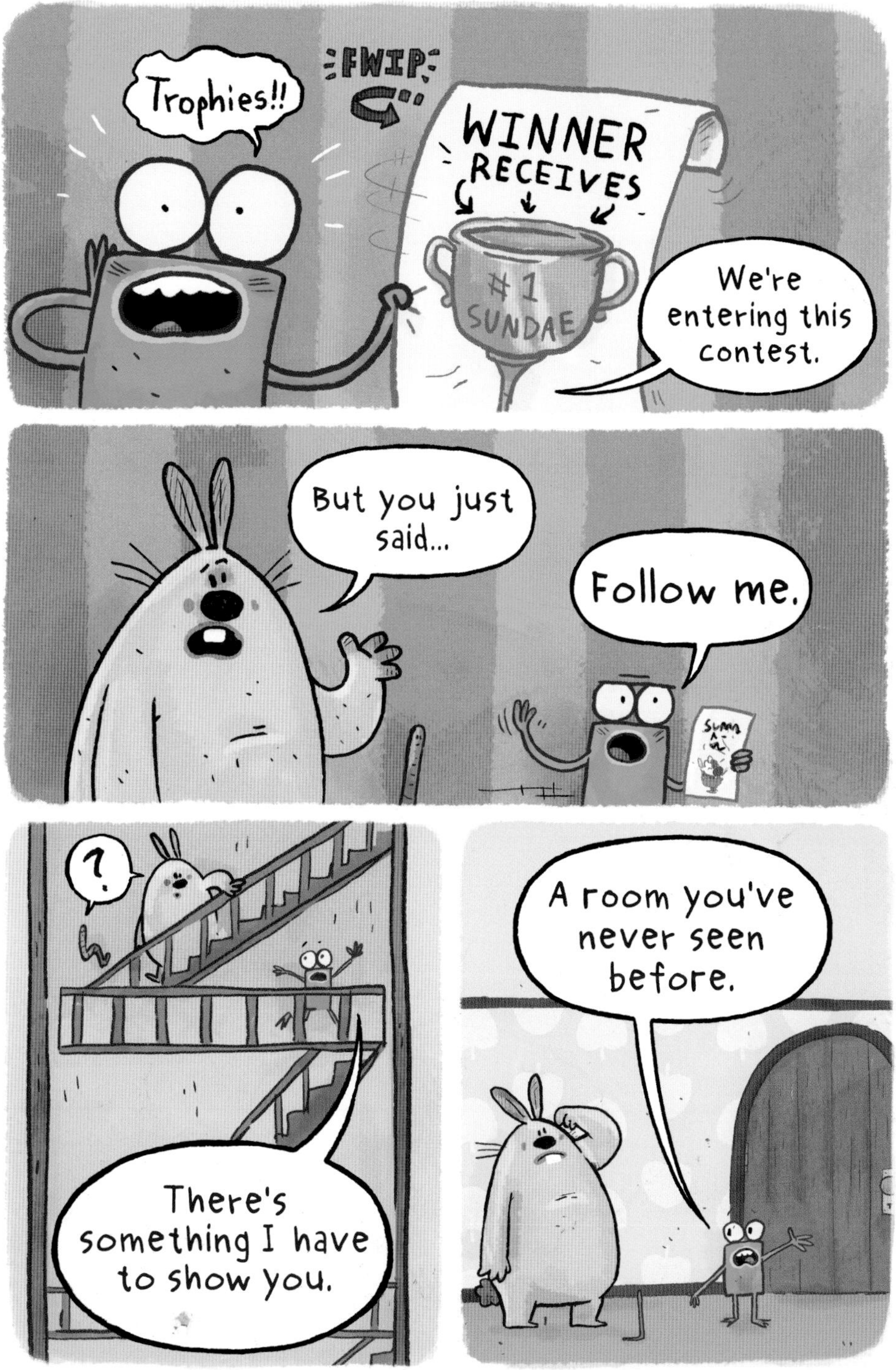

Trophies!!
FWIP
WINNER RECEIVES
#1 SUNDAE
We're entering this contest.
But you just said...
Follow me.
?
There's something I have to show you.
A room you've never seen before.

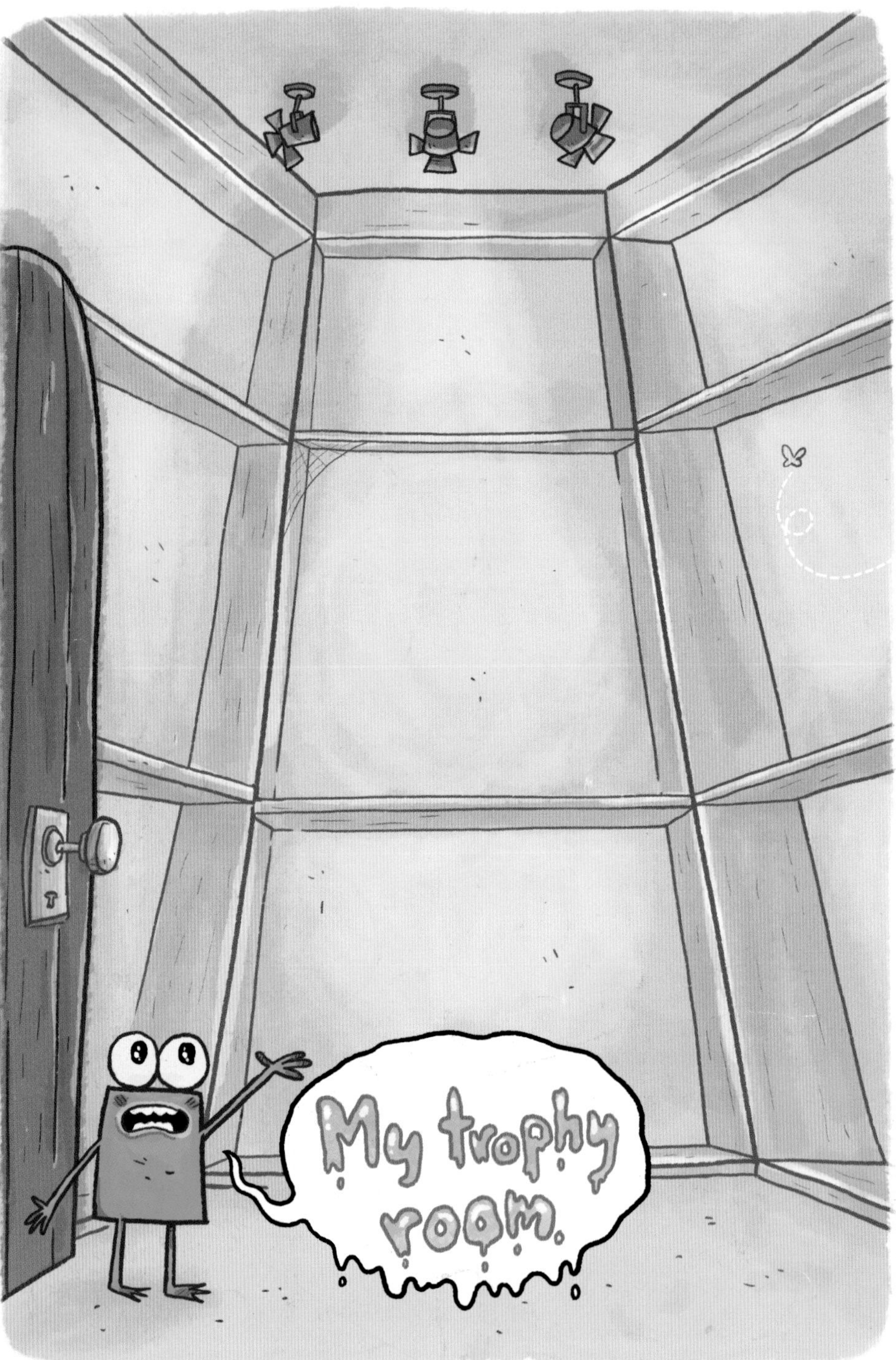
My trophy room.

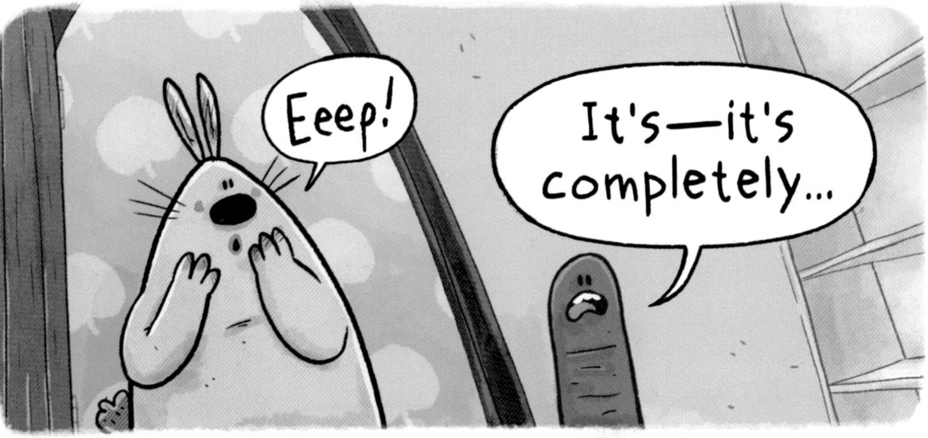
Eeep!
It's—it's completely...

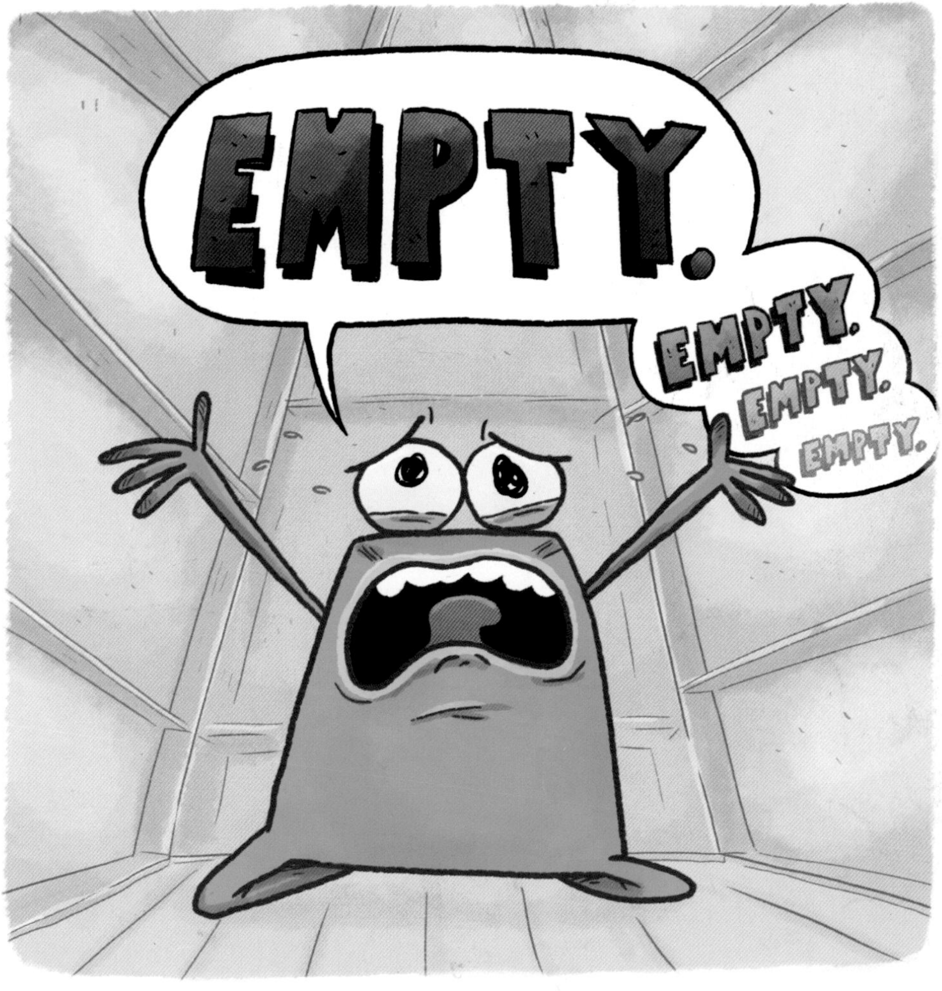
EMPTY.
EMPTY. EMPTY. EMPTY.

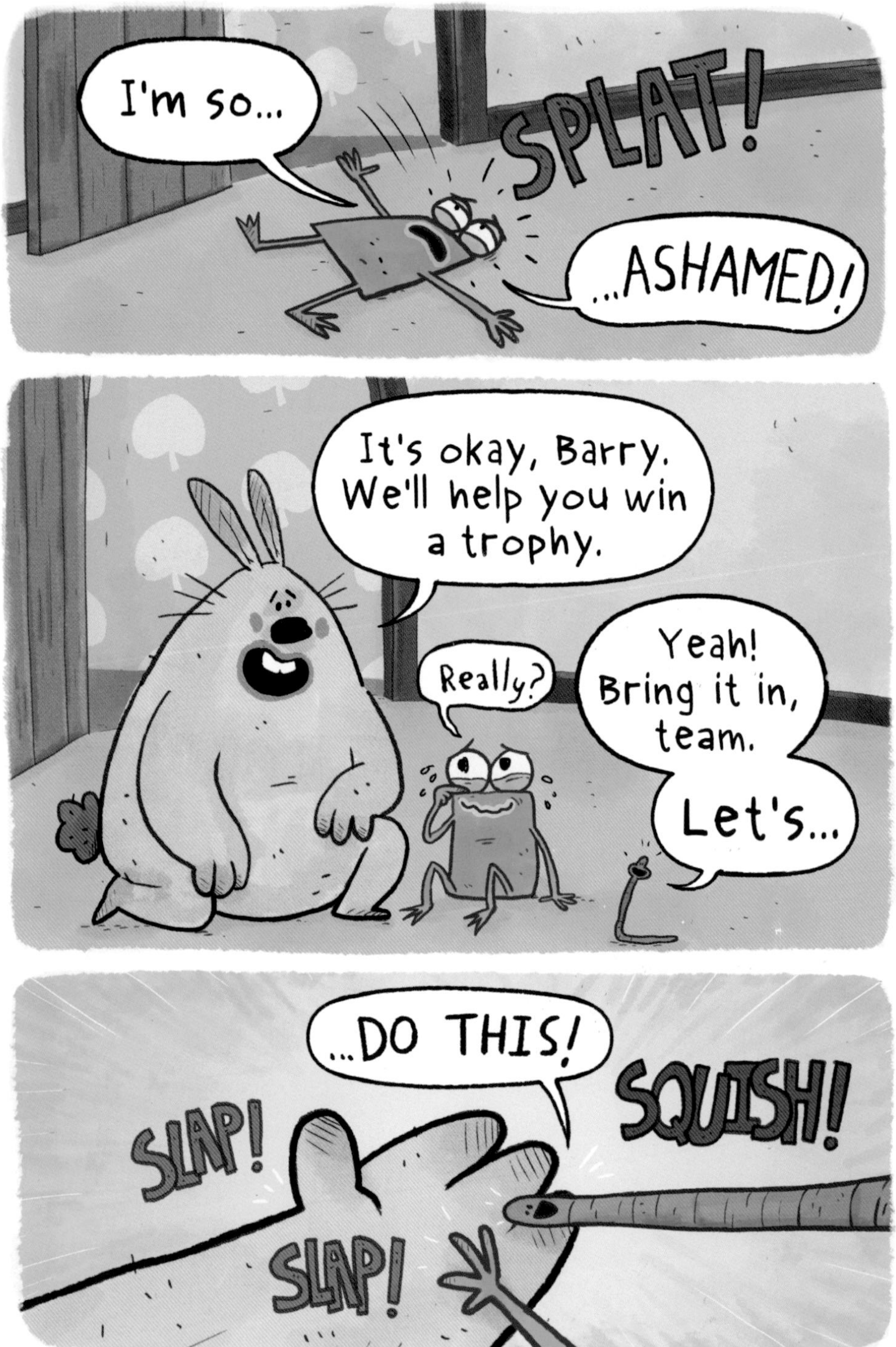
I'm so...
SPLAT!
...ASHAMED!
It's okay, Barry. We'll help you win a trophy.
Really?
Yeah! Bring it in, team.
Let's...
...DO THIS!
SLAP!
SQUISH!
SLAP!

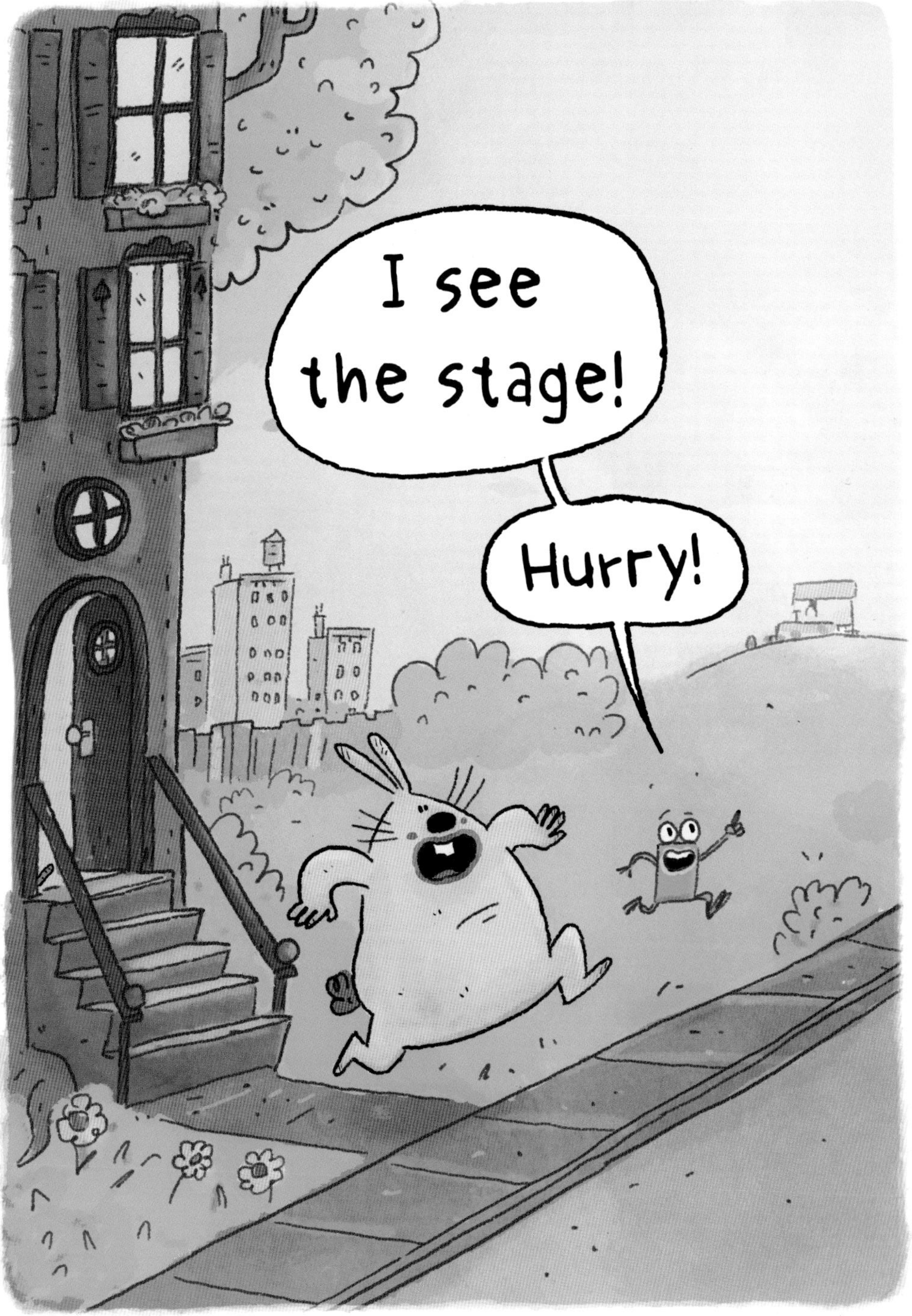
I see the stage!
Hurry!

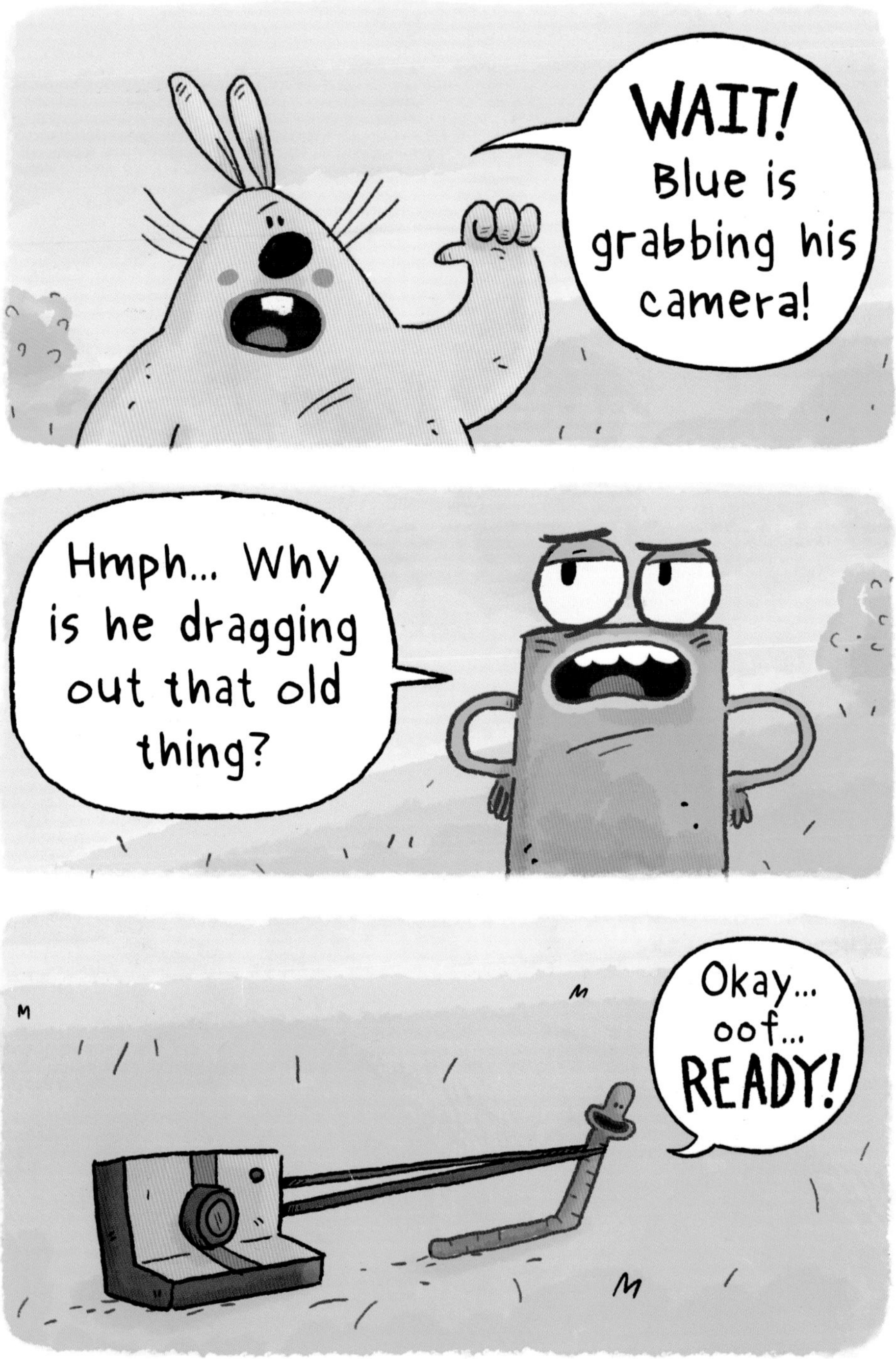
WAIT! Blue is grabbing his camera!
Hmph... Why is he dragging out that old thing?
Okay... oof... READY!

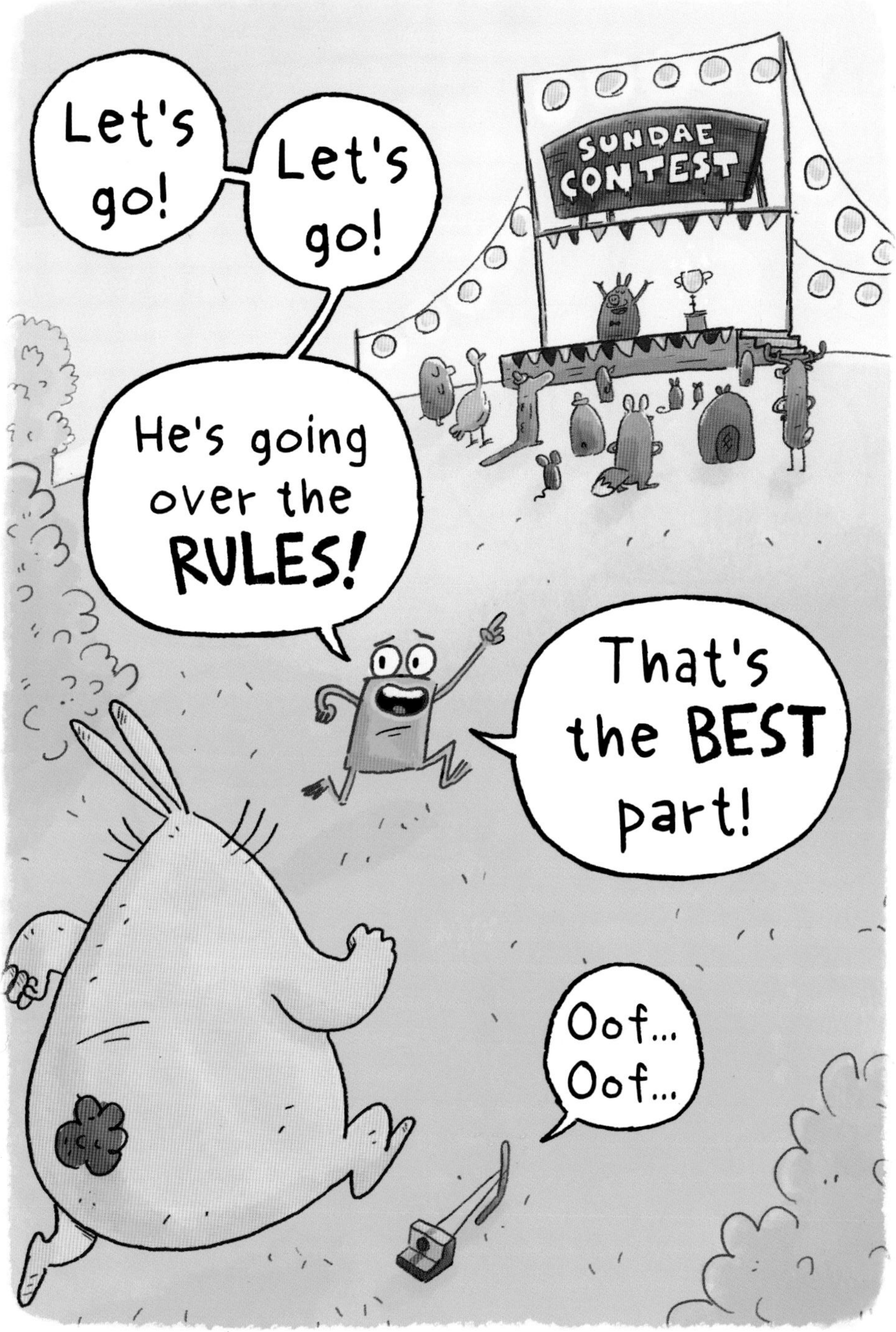
SUNDAE CONTEST
Let's go!
Let's go!
He's going over the **RULES!**
That's the **BEST** part!
Oof... Oof...

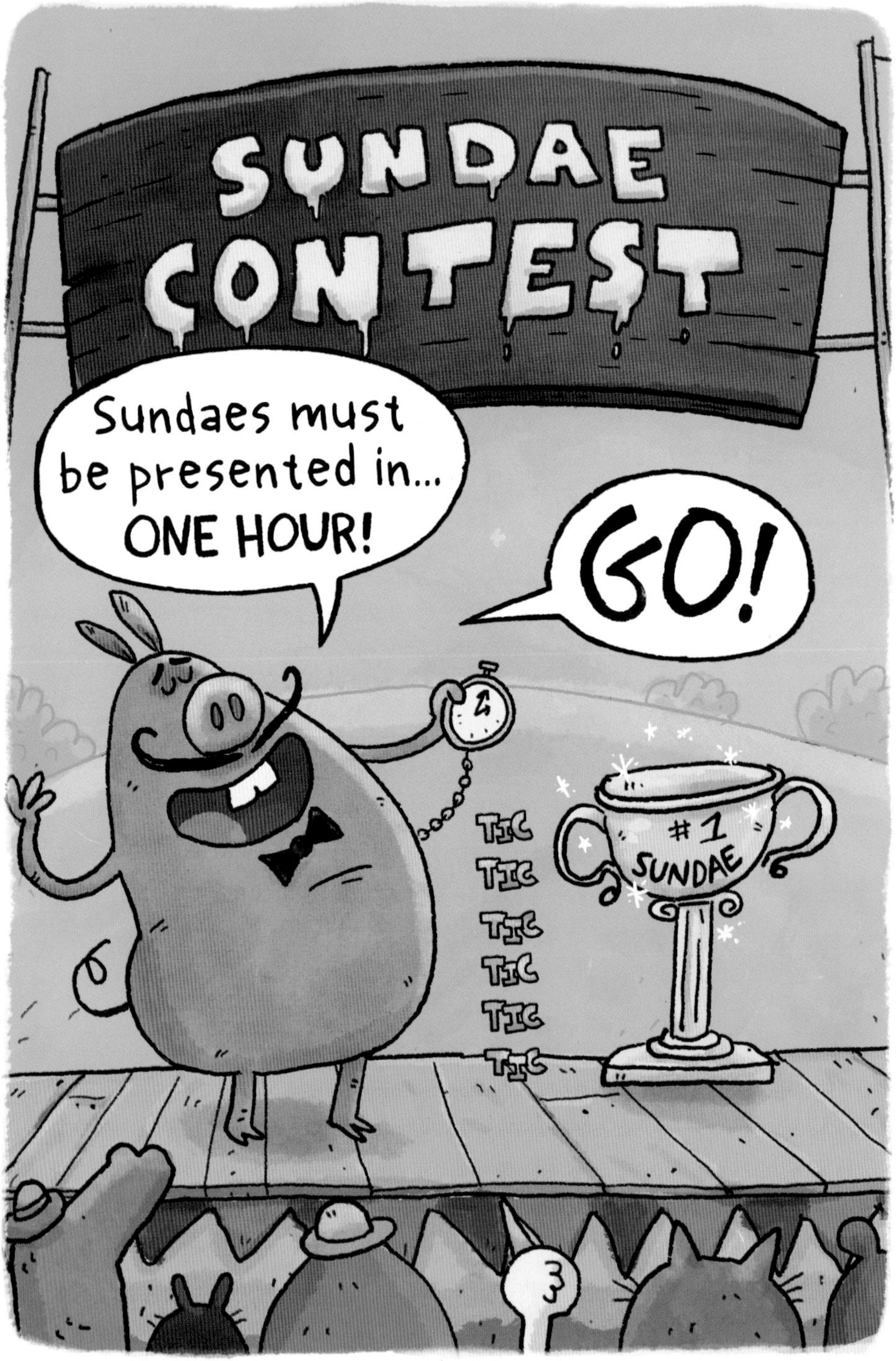
SUNDAE CONTEST
Sundaes must be presented in... ONE HOUR!
GO!
TIC
TIC
TIC
TIC
TIC
TIC
#1 SUNDAE

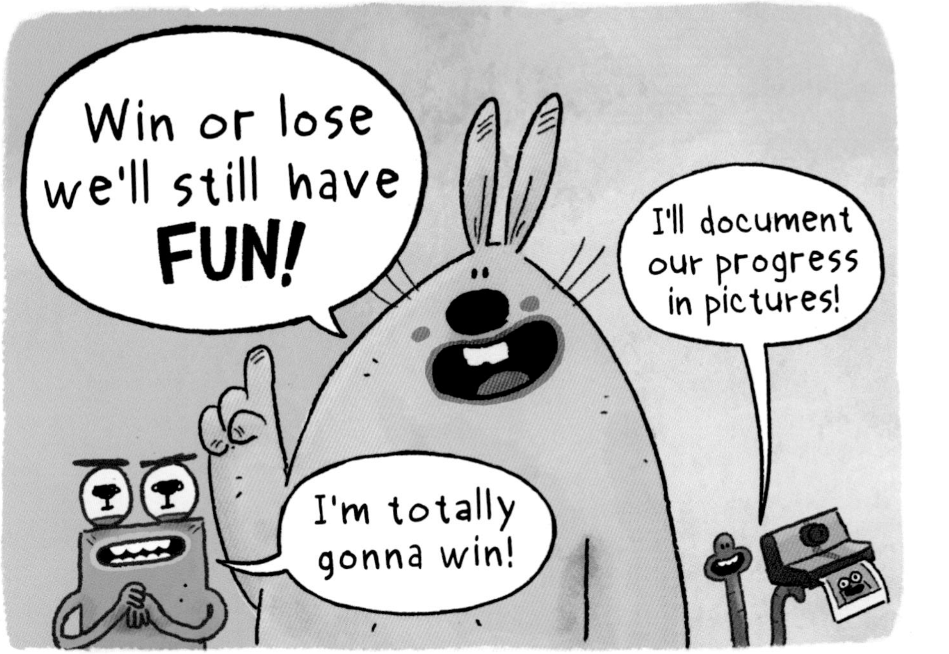
Win or lose we'll still have FUN!
I'll document our progress in pictures!
I'm totally gonna win!

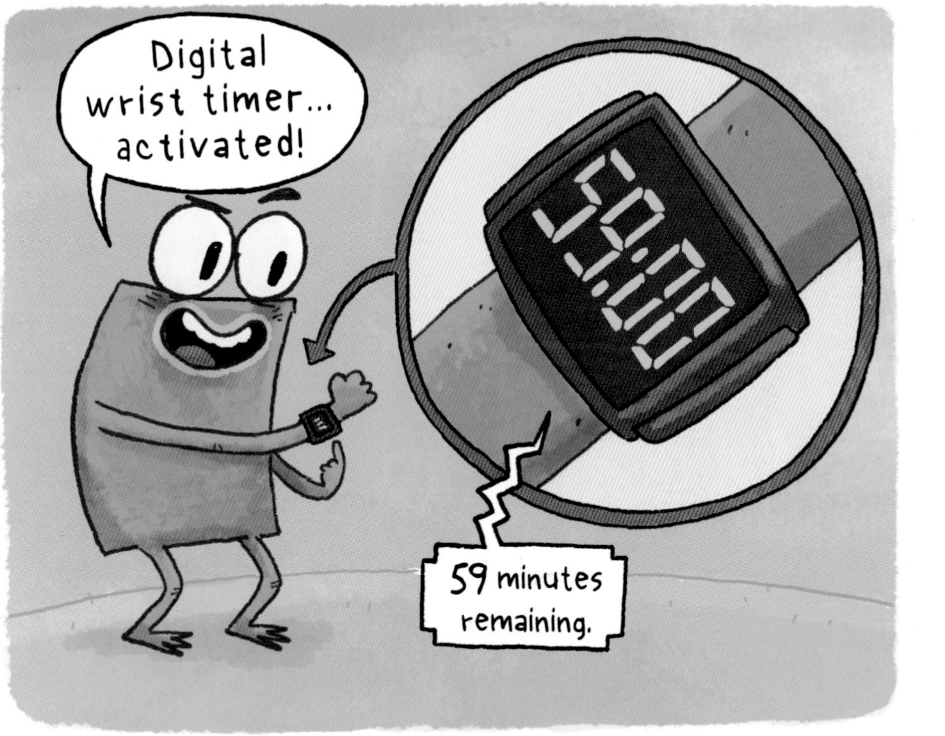
Digital wrist timer... activated!
59:00
59 minutes remaining.

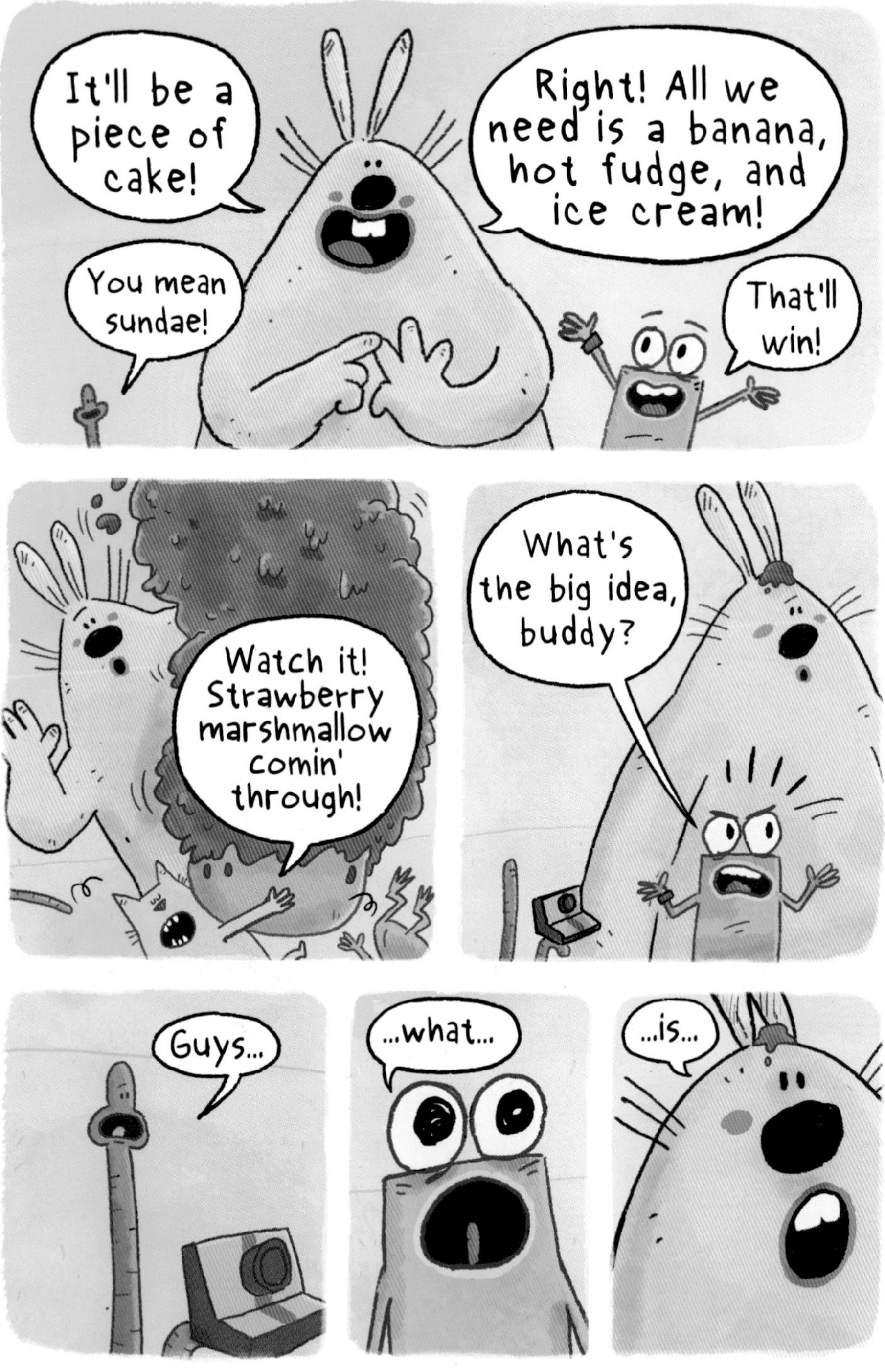
It'll be a piece of cake!
Right! All we need is a banana, hot fudge, and ice cream!
You mean sundae!
That'll win!
Watch it! Strawberry marshmallow comin' through!
What's the big idea, buddy?
Guys...
...what...
...is...

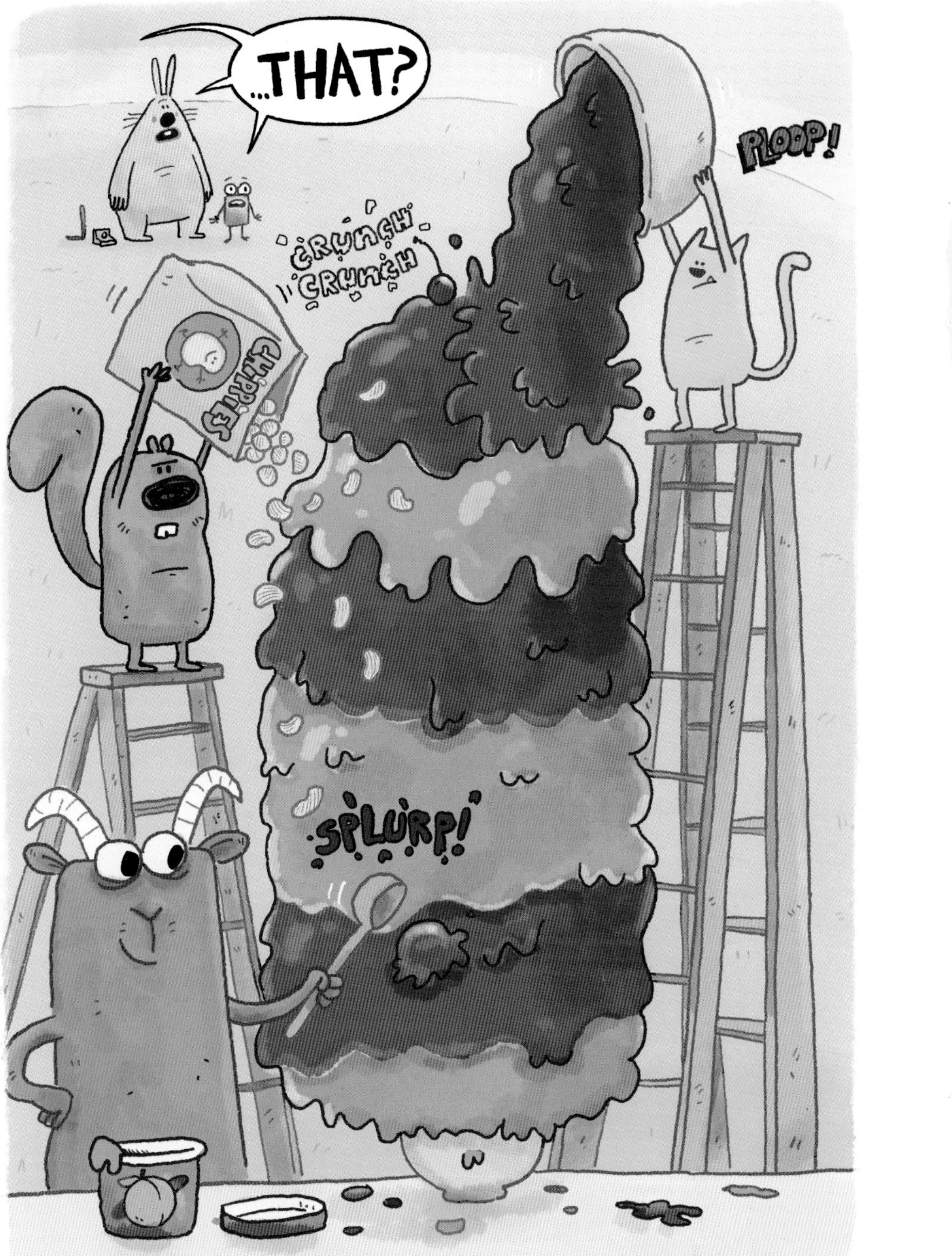
...THAT?
PLOOP!
CRUNCH
CRUNCH
CHIRPIES
SPLURP!

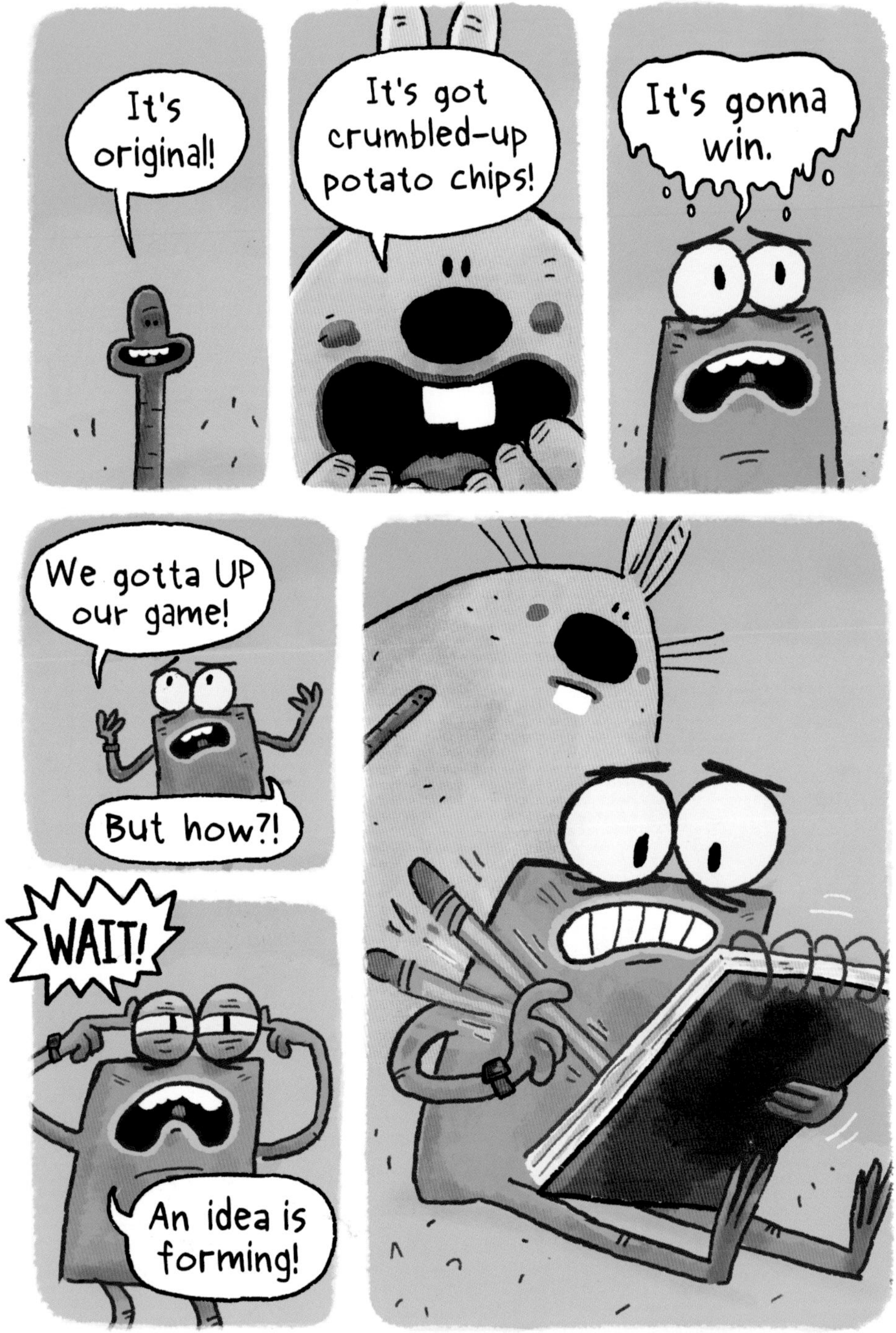
It's original!
It's got crumbled-up potato chips!
It's gonna win.
We gotta UP our game!
But how?!
WAIT!
An idea is forming!

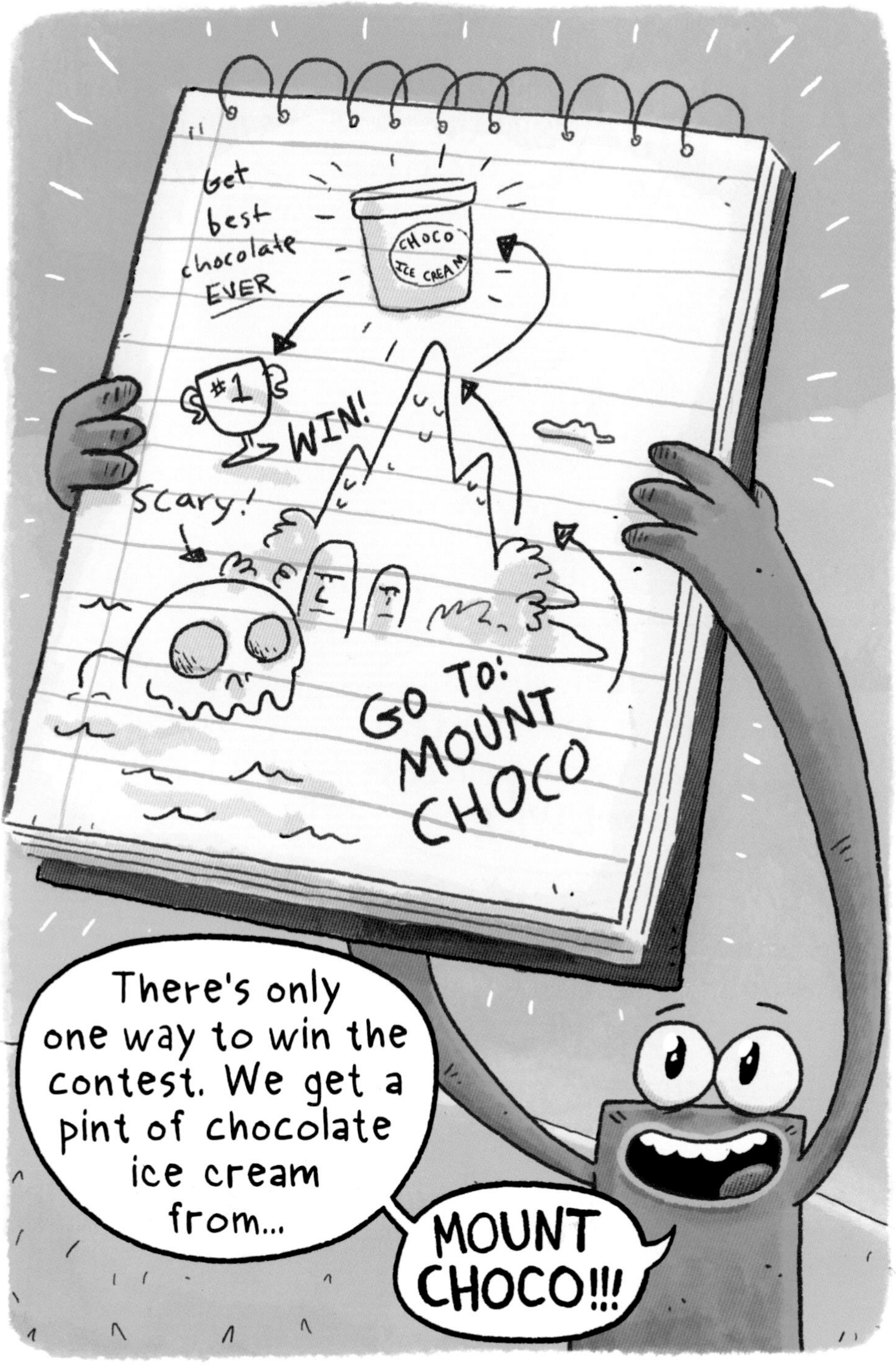
Get best chocolate EVER
CHOCO ICE CREAM
#1
WIN!
Scary!
GO TO: MOUNT CHOCO
There's only one way to win the contest. We get a pint of chocolate ice cream from...
MOUNT CHOCO!!!

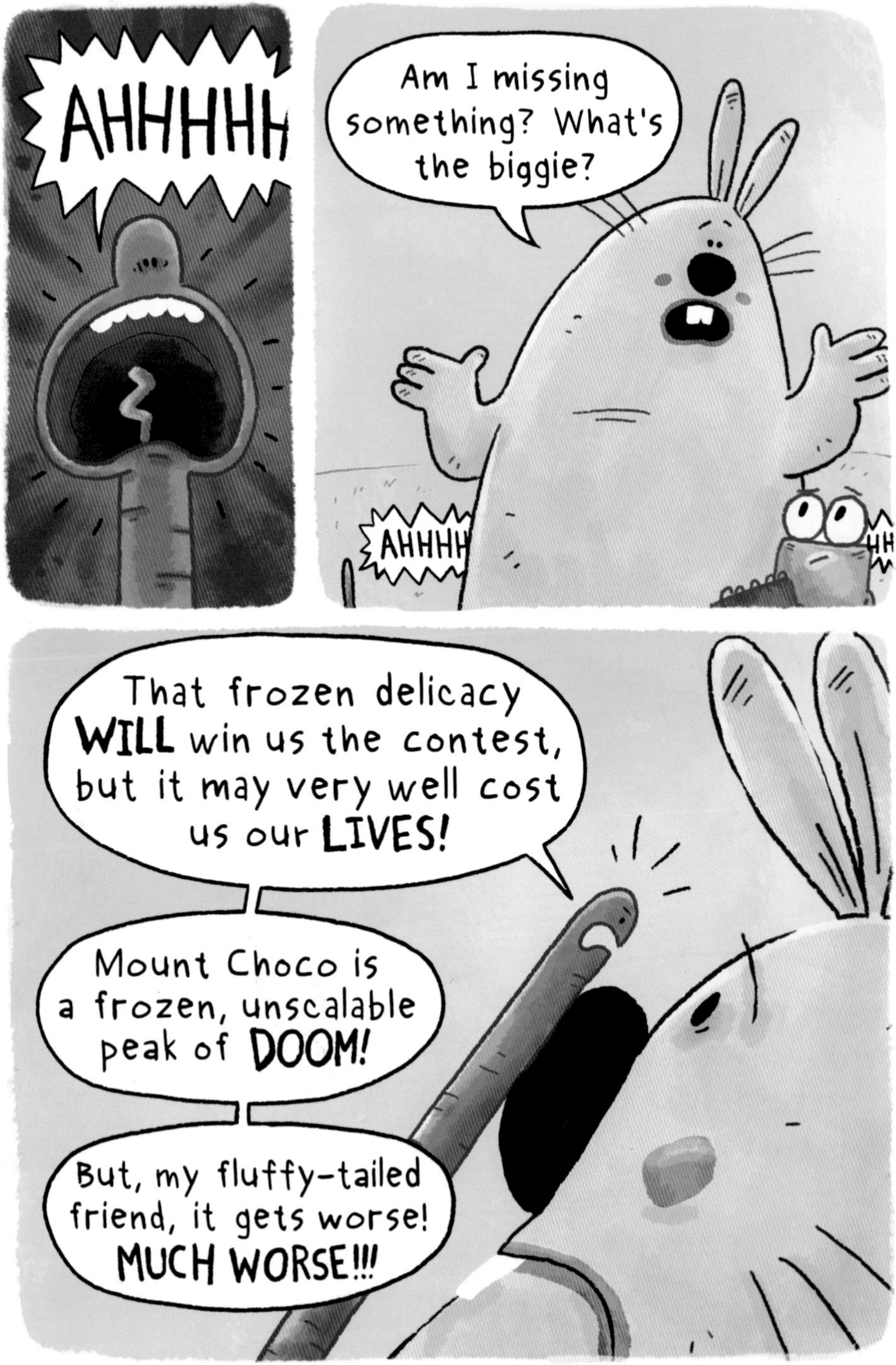
AHHHHH
Am I missing something? What's the biggie?
AHHHH
That frozen delicacy **WILL** win us the contest, but it may very well cost us our **LIVES!**
Mount Choco is a frozen, unscalable peak of **DOOM!**
But, my fluffy-tailed friend, it gets worse! **MUCH WORSE!!!**

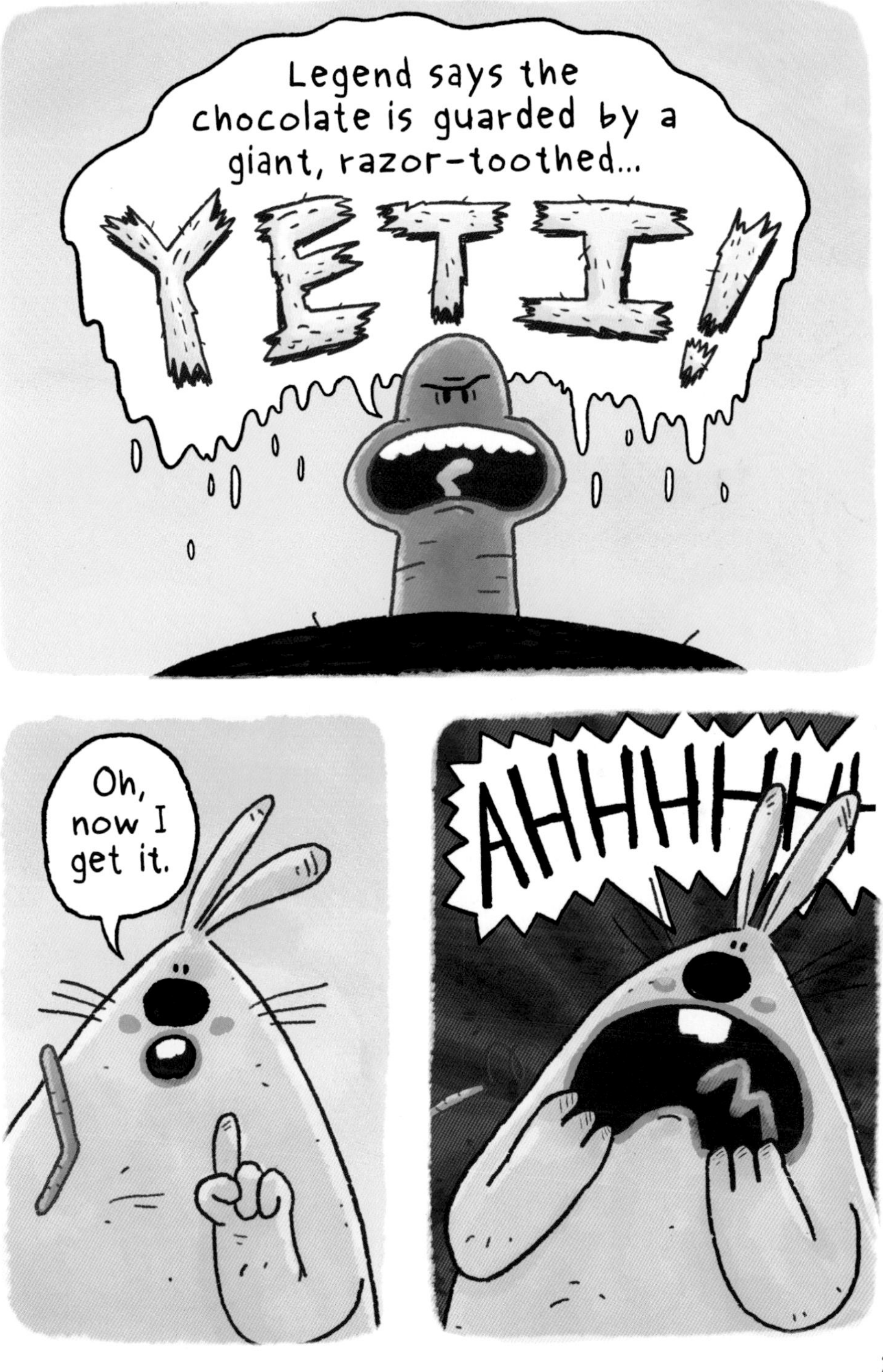

Legend says the chocolate is guarded by a giant, razor-toothed...
YETI!
Oh, now I get it.
AHHHHH!

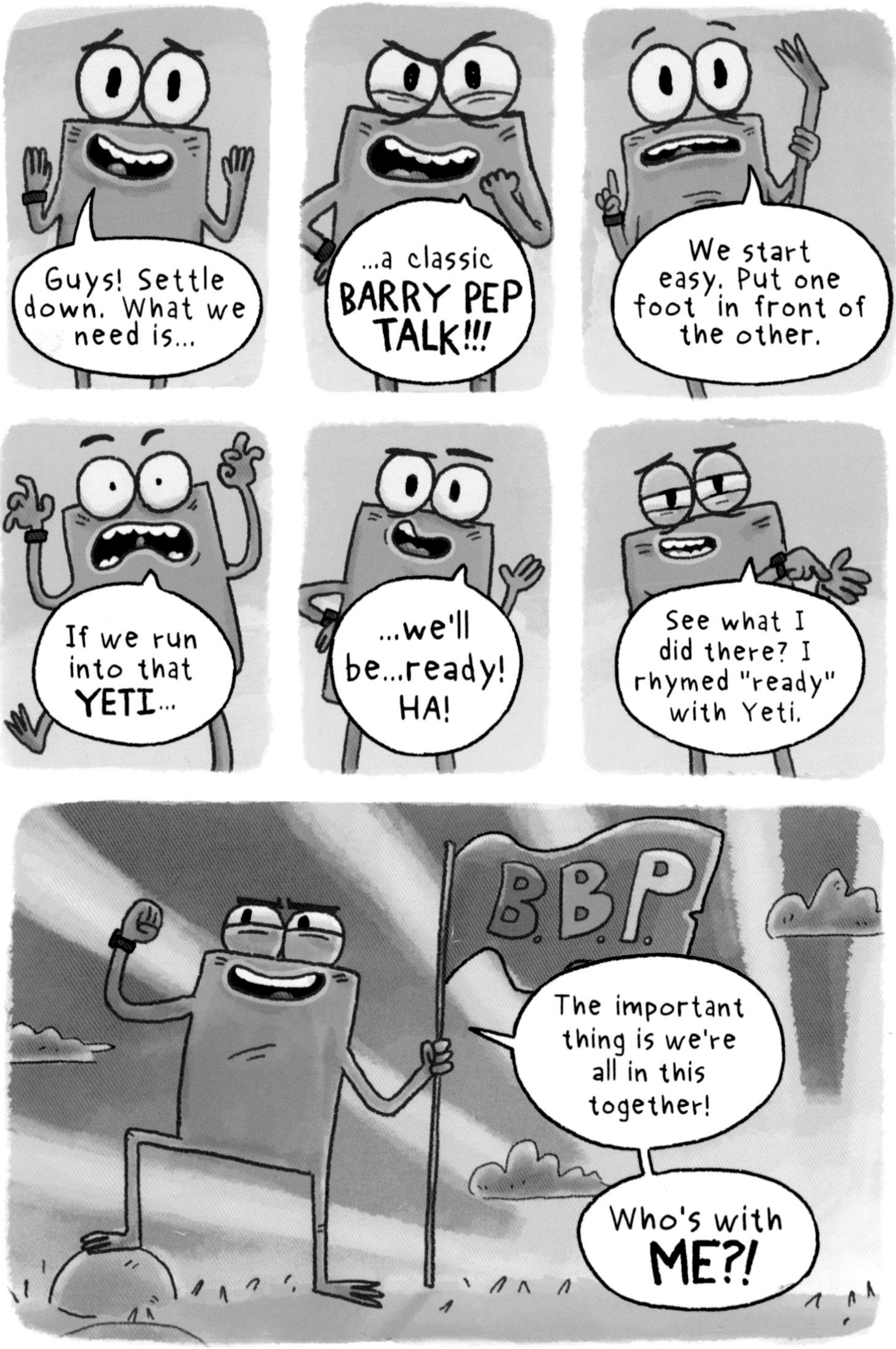
Guys! Settle down. What we need is...
...a classic BARRY PEP TALK!!!
We start easy. Put one foot in front of the other.
If we run into that YETI...
...we'll be...ready! HA!
See what I did there? I rhymed "ready" with Yeti.
B.B.P.
The important thing is we're all in this together!
Who's with ME?!

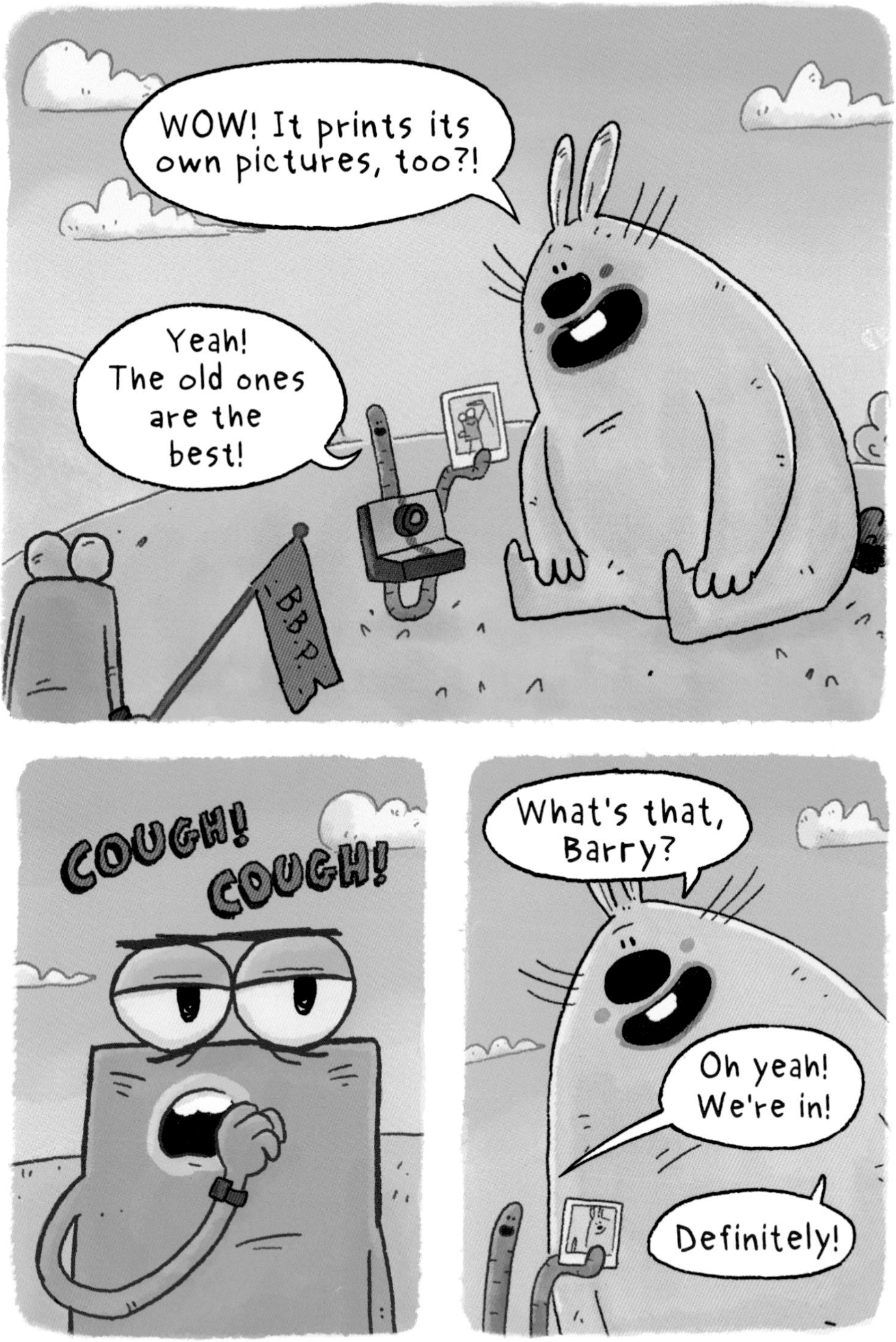
WOW! It prints its own pictures, too?!
Yeah! The old ones are the best!
B.B.P.
COUGH! COUGH!
What's that, Barry?
Oh yeah! We're in!
Definitely!

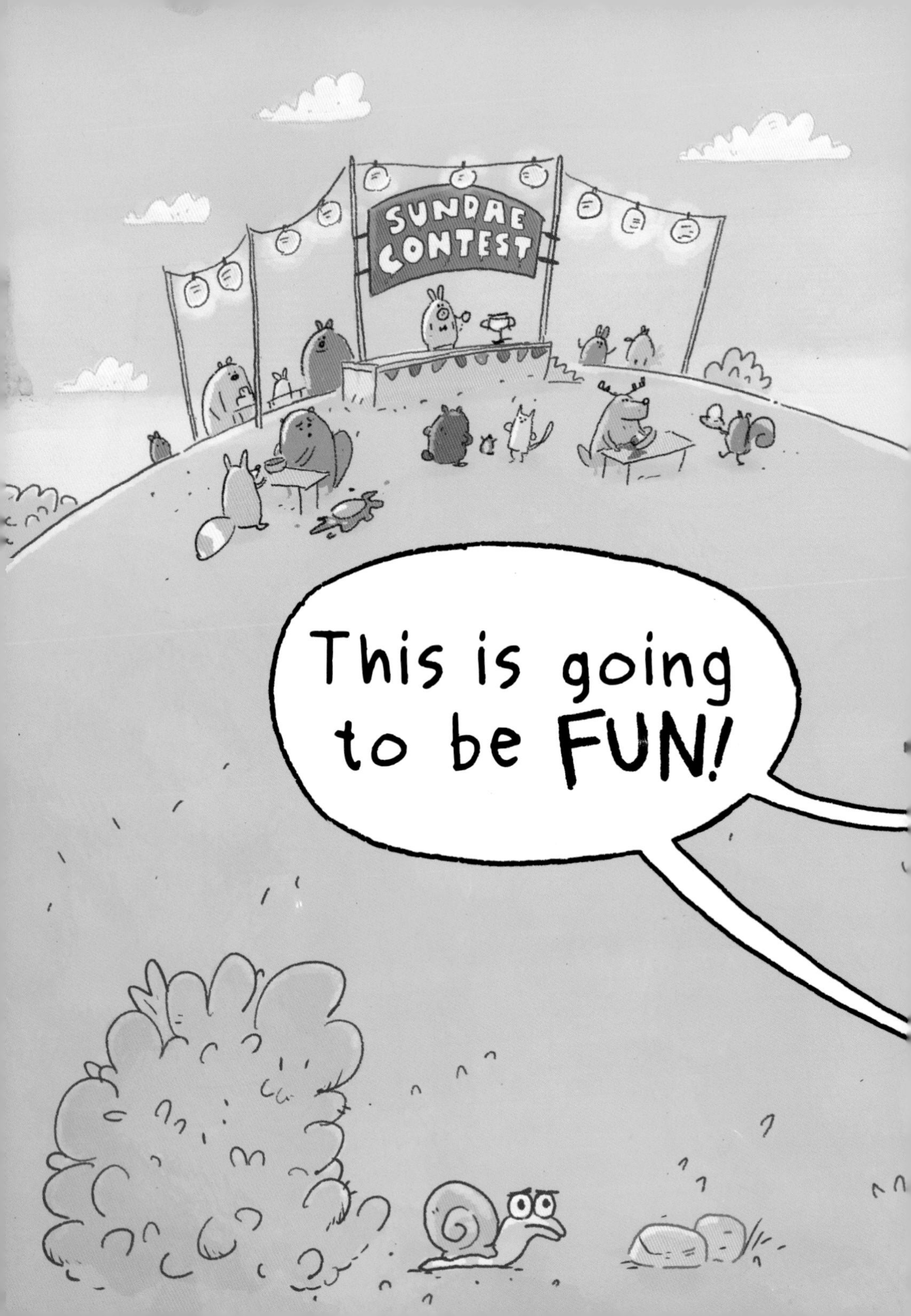
SUNDAE CONTEST
This is going to be FUN!

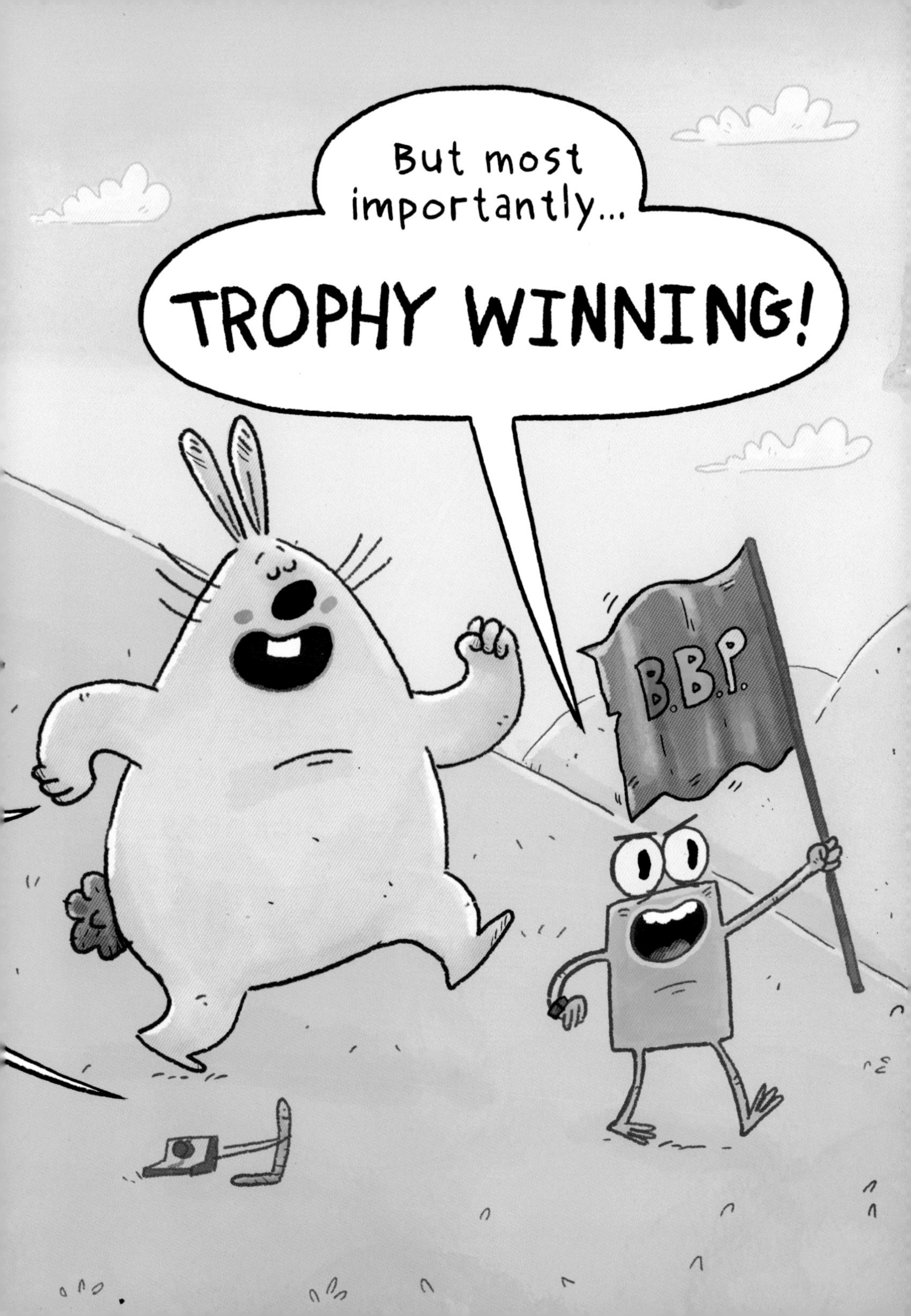
But most importantly...
TROPHY WINNING!
B.B.P.

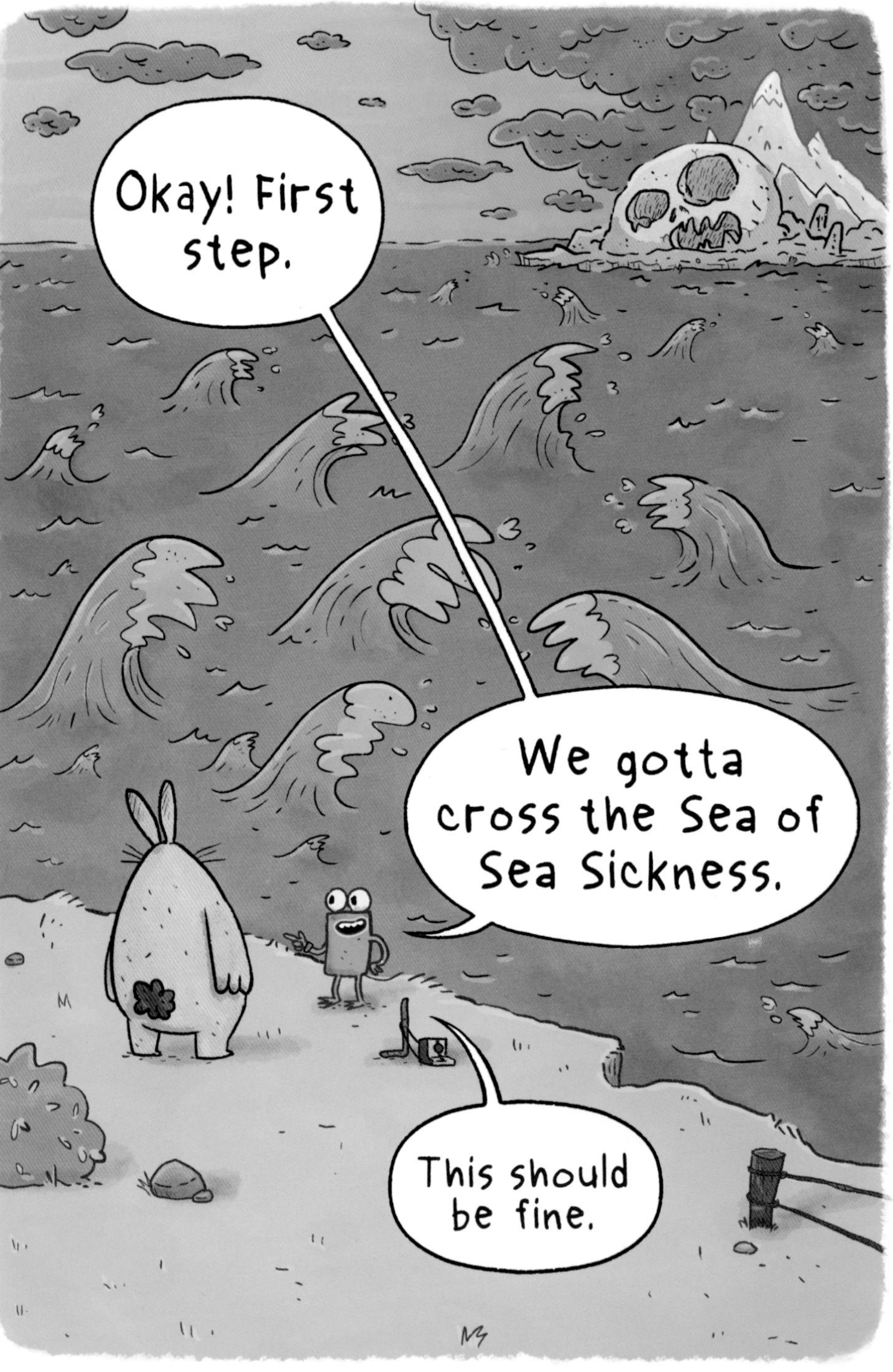
Okay! First step.
We gotta cross the Sea of Sea Sickness.
This should be fine.

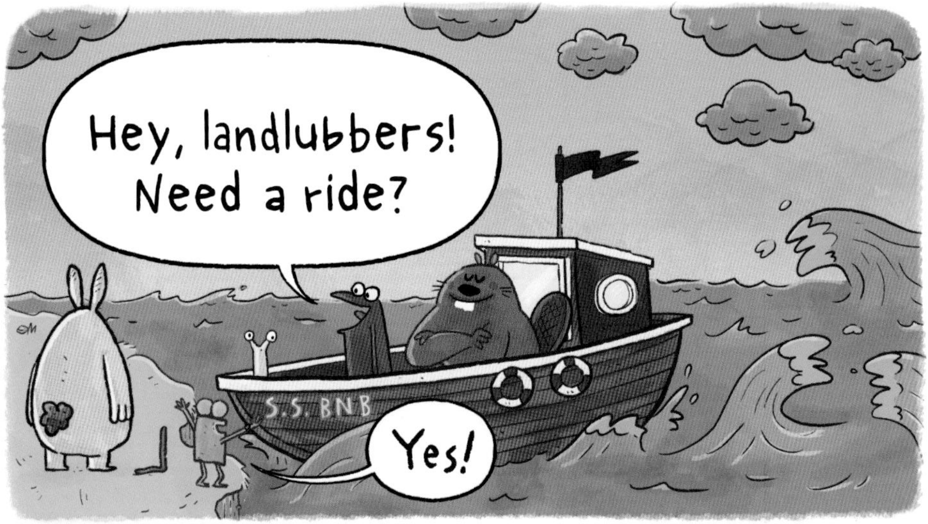
Hey, landlubbers! Need a ride?
S.S. BNB
Yes!

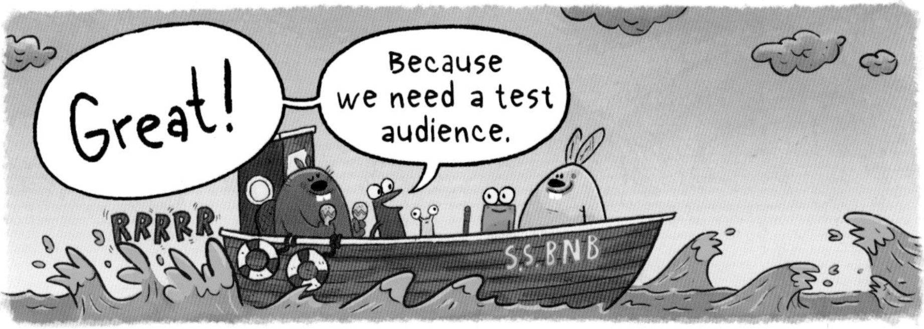
Great!
Because we need a test audience.
RRRRR
S.S. BNB

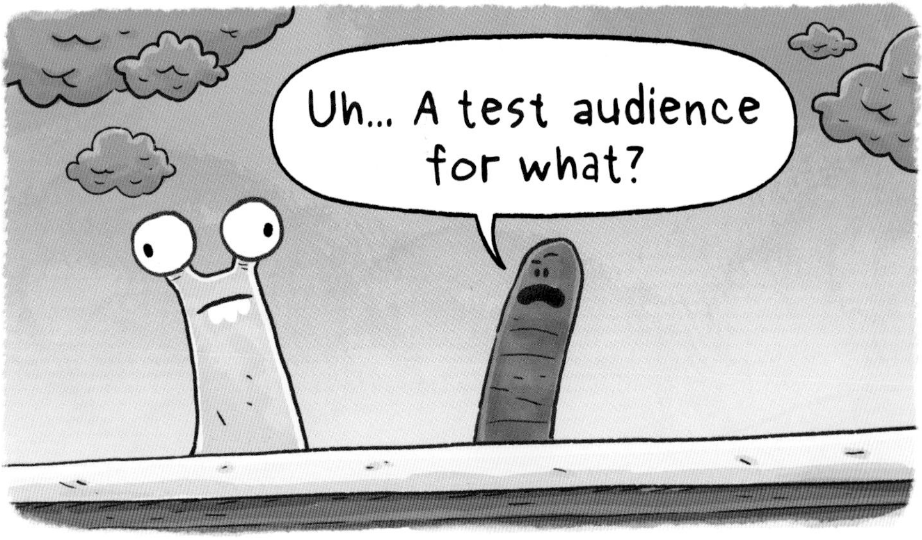
Uh... A test audience for what?

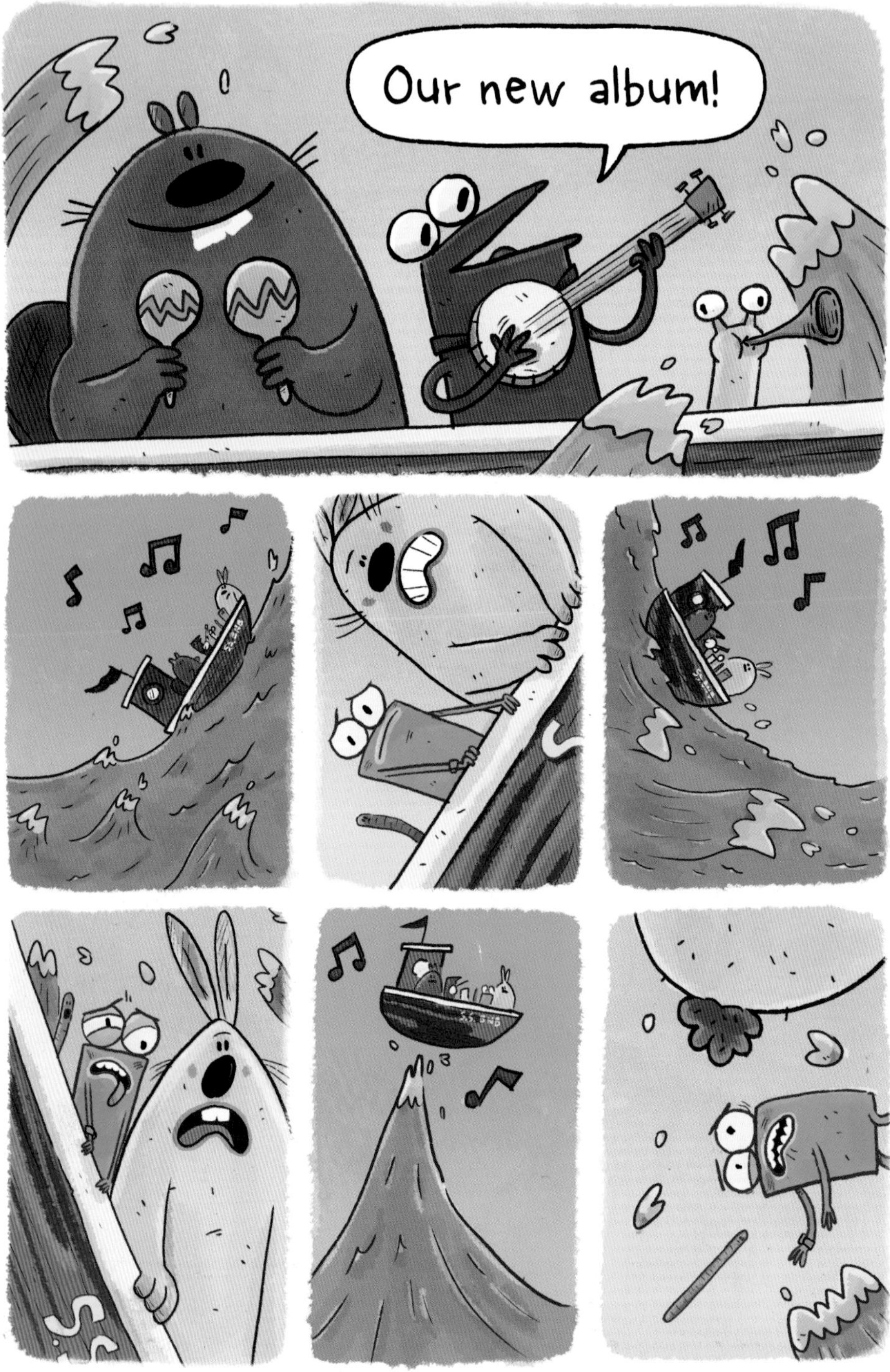
Our new album!

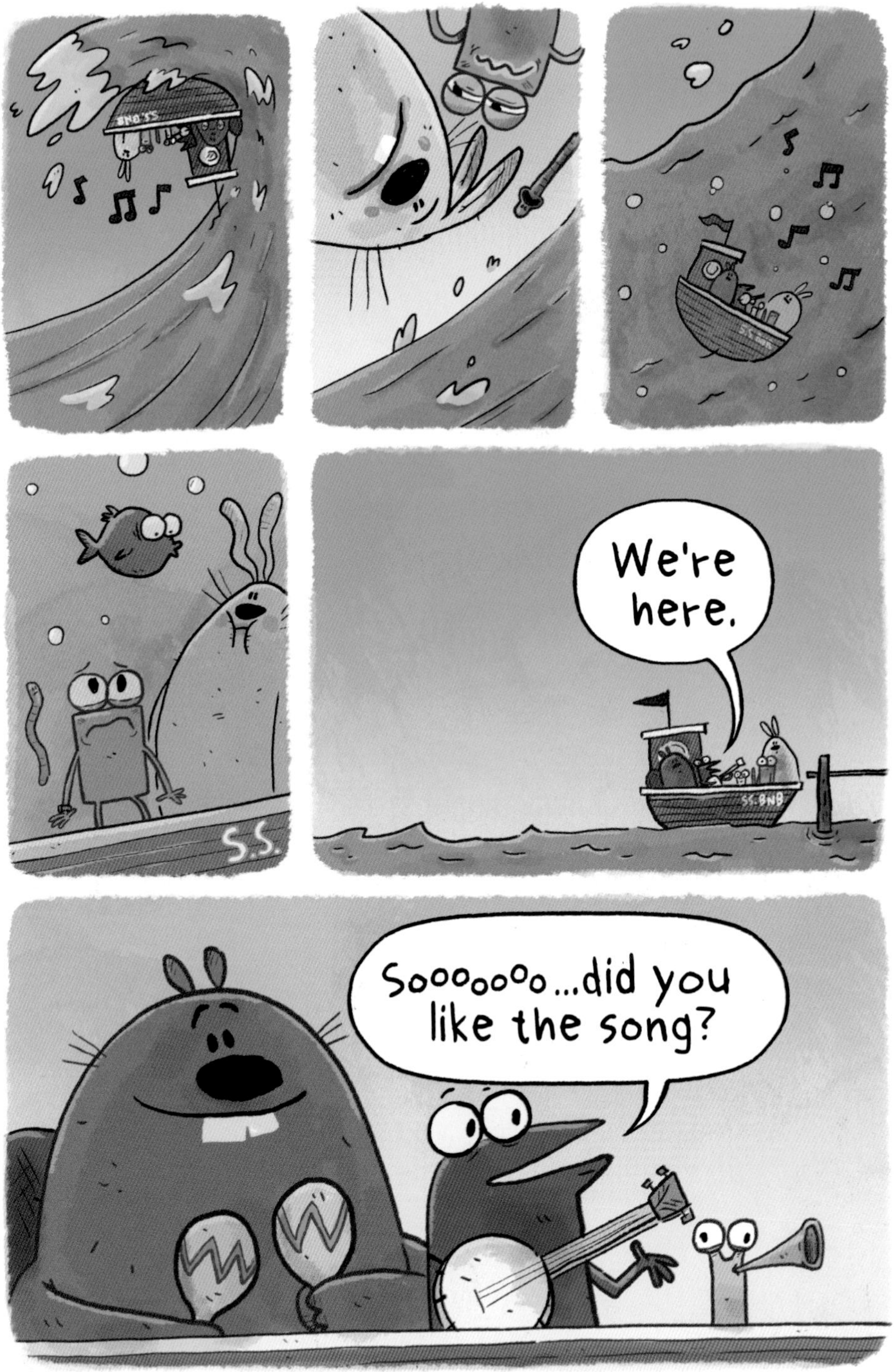
S.S.BNB
S.S.BNB
S.S.
We're here.
S.S.BNB
Sooooooo...did you like the song?

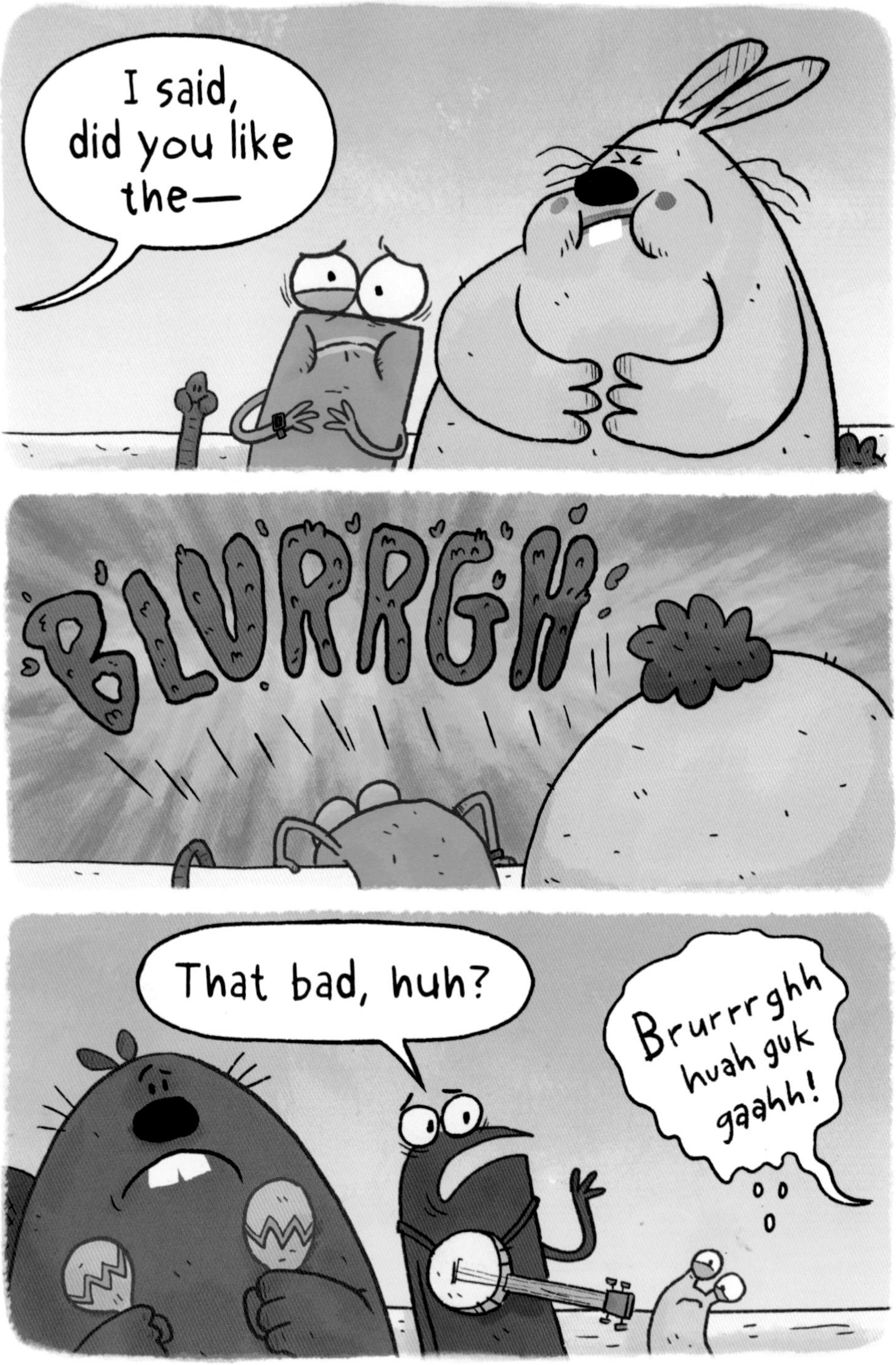
I said, did you like the—
BLURRGH
That bad, huh?
Brurrrghh huah guk gaahh!

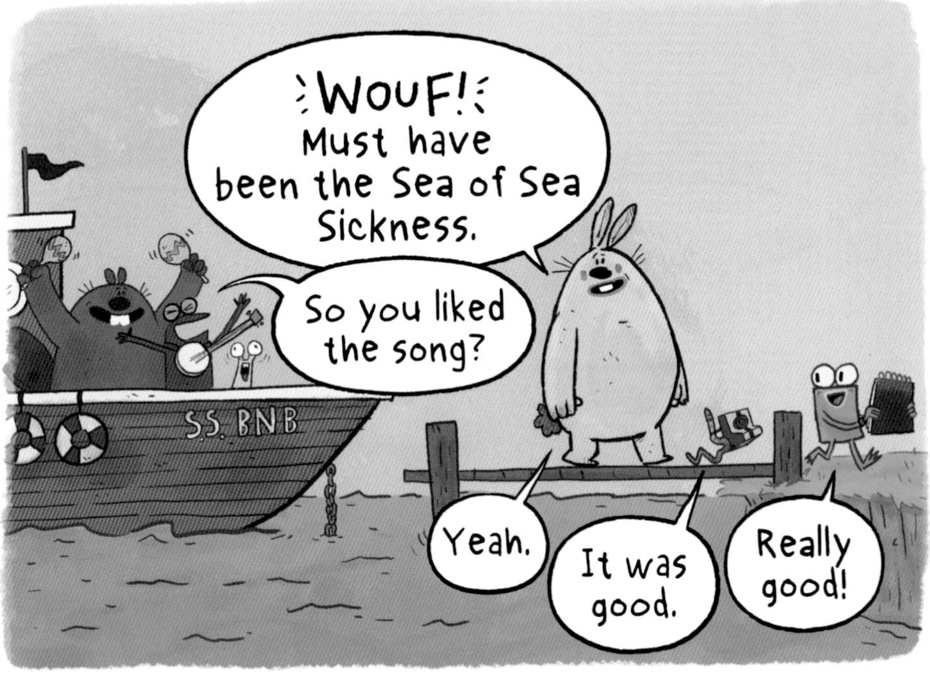
WOUF!
Must have been the Sea of Sea Sickness.
So you liked the song?
S.S. BNB
Yeah.
It was good.
Really good!

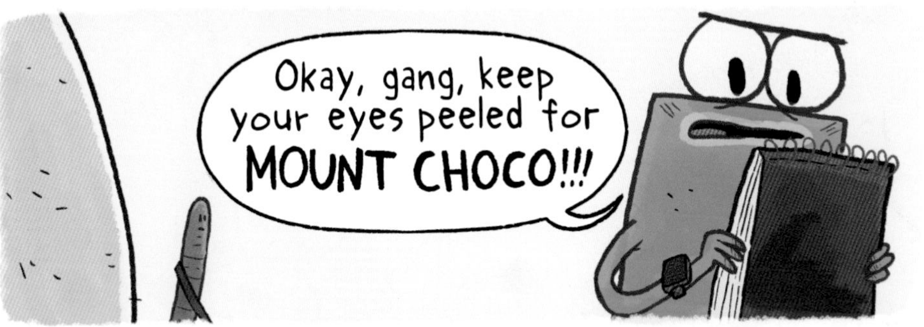
Okay, gang, keep your eyes peeled for MOUNT CHOCO!!!

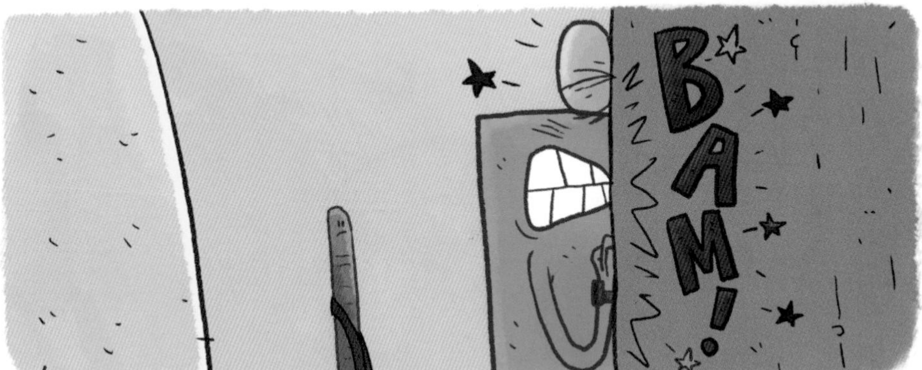
BAM!

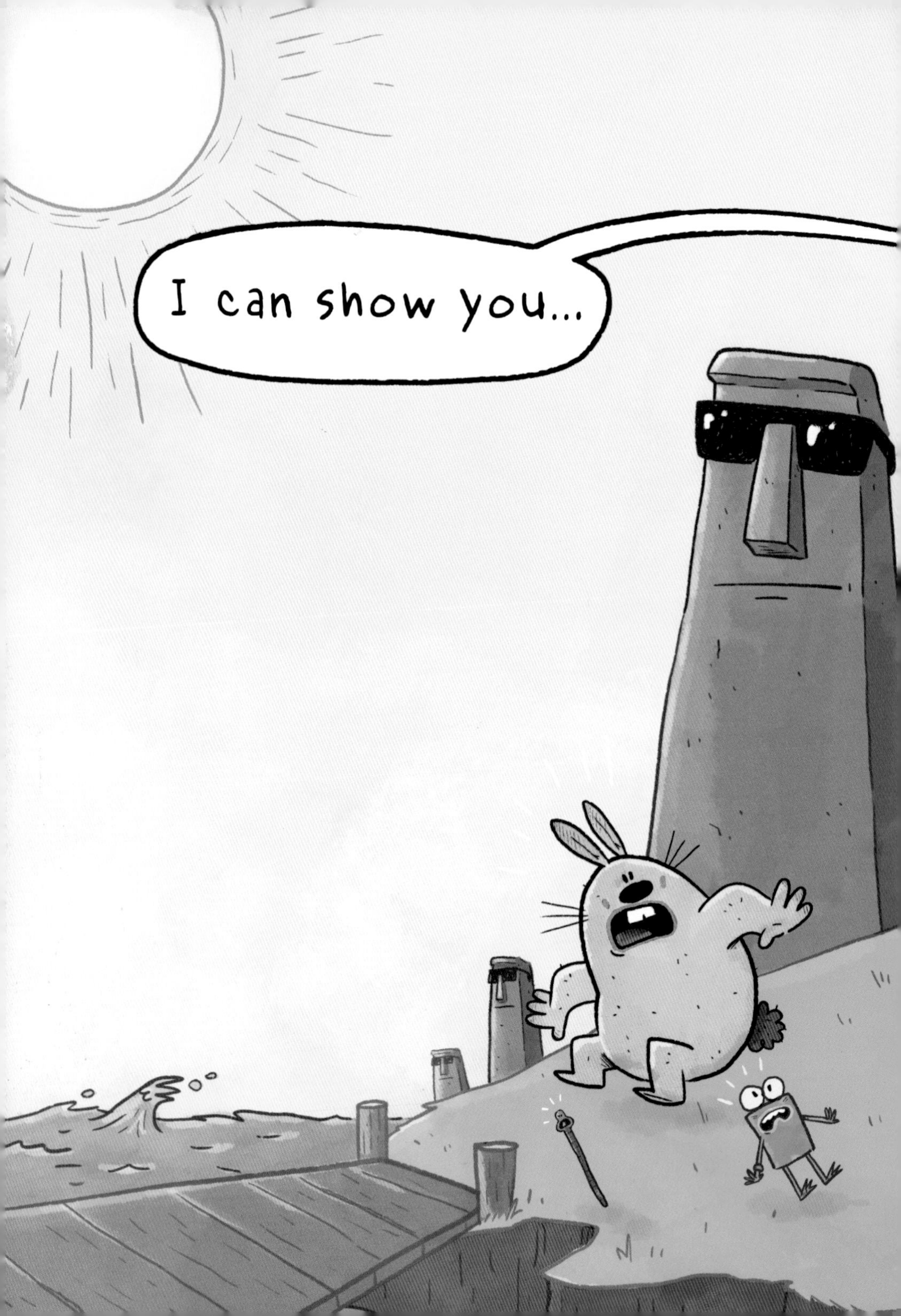
I can show you...

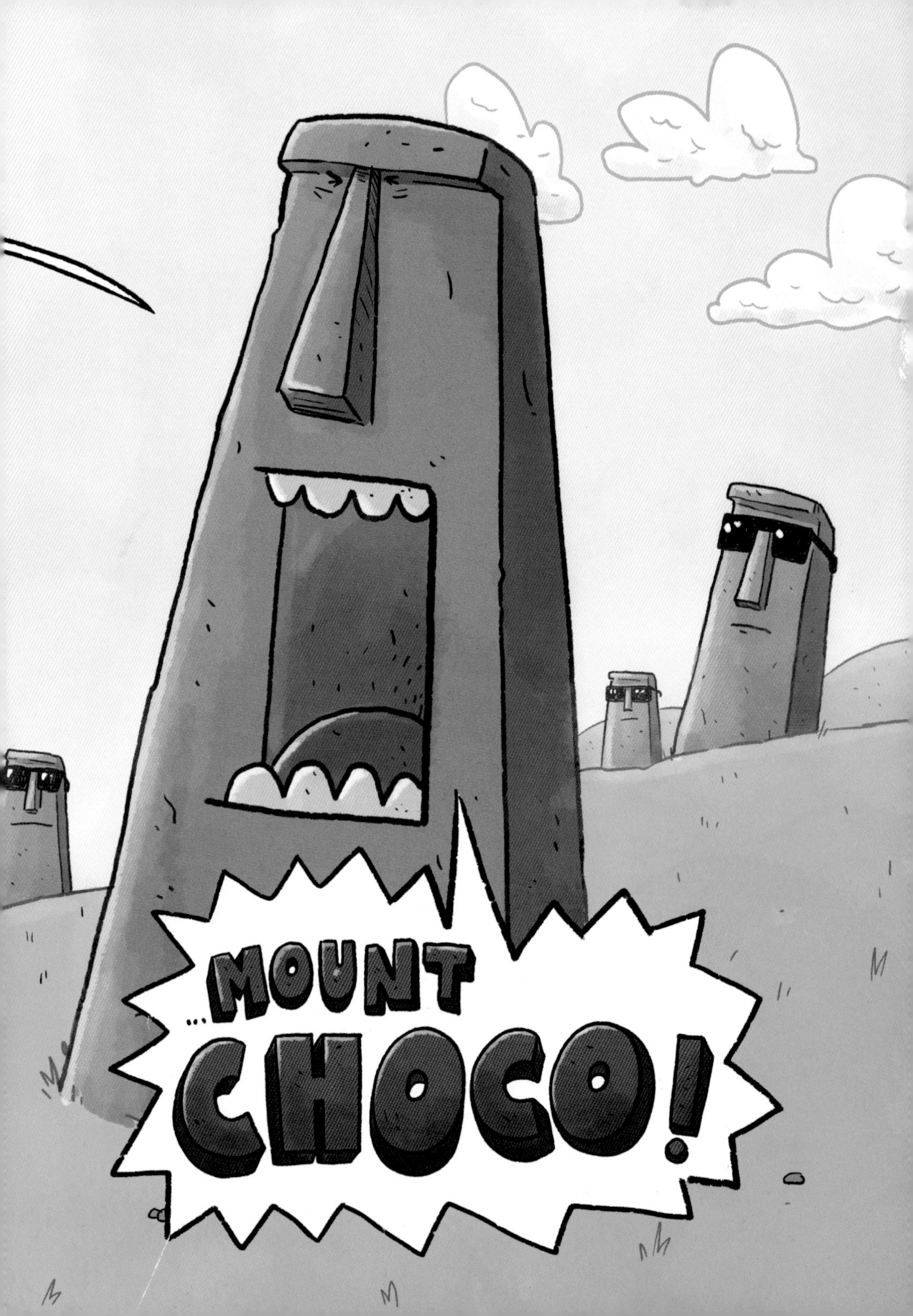
...MOUNT CHOCO!

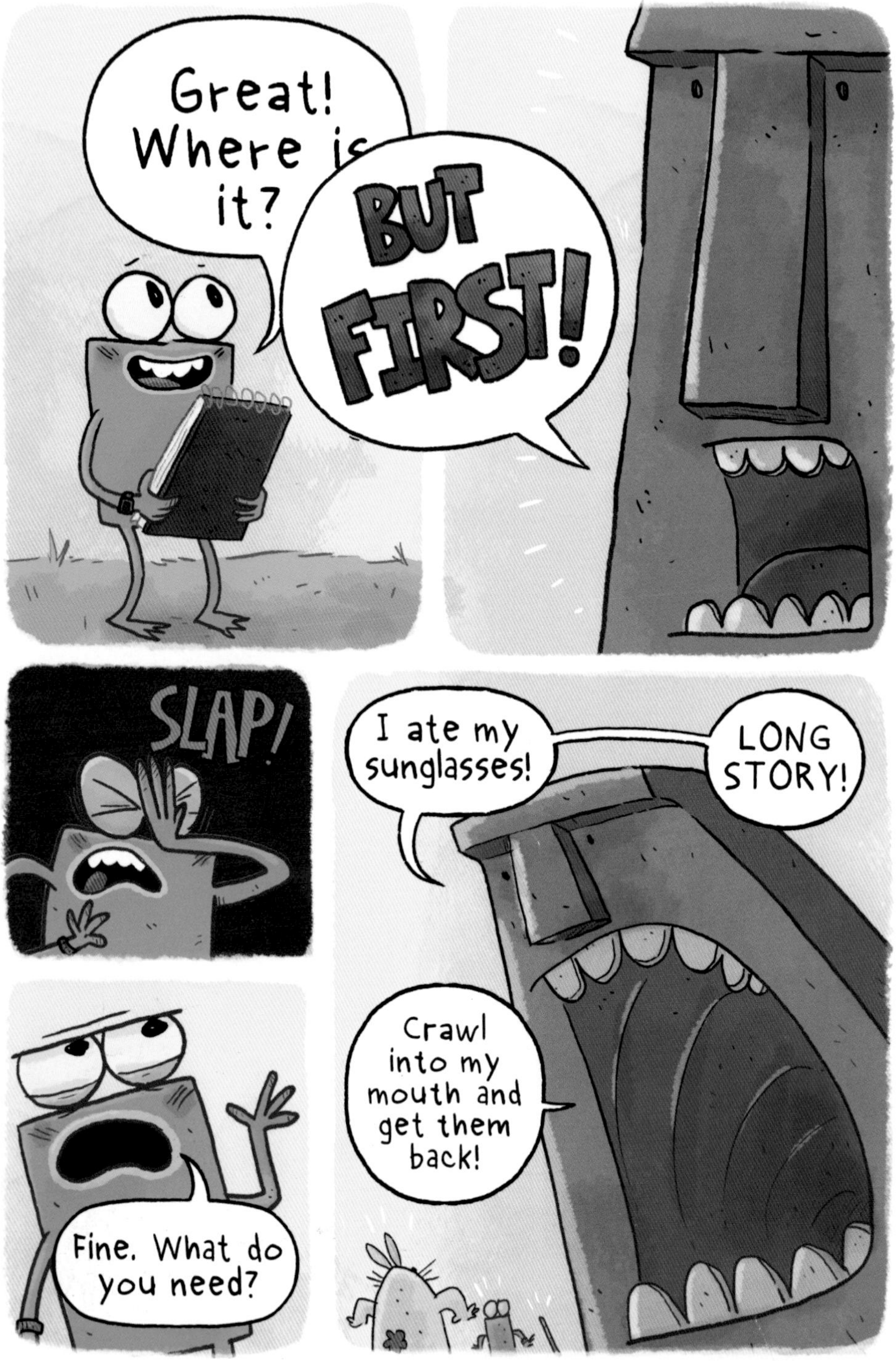

Great! Where is it?
BUT FIRST!
SLAP!
I ate my sunglasses!
LONG STORY!
Fine. What do you need?
Crawl into my mouth and get them back!

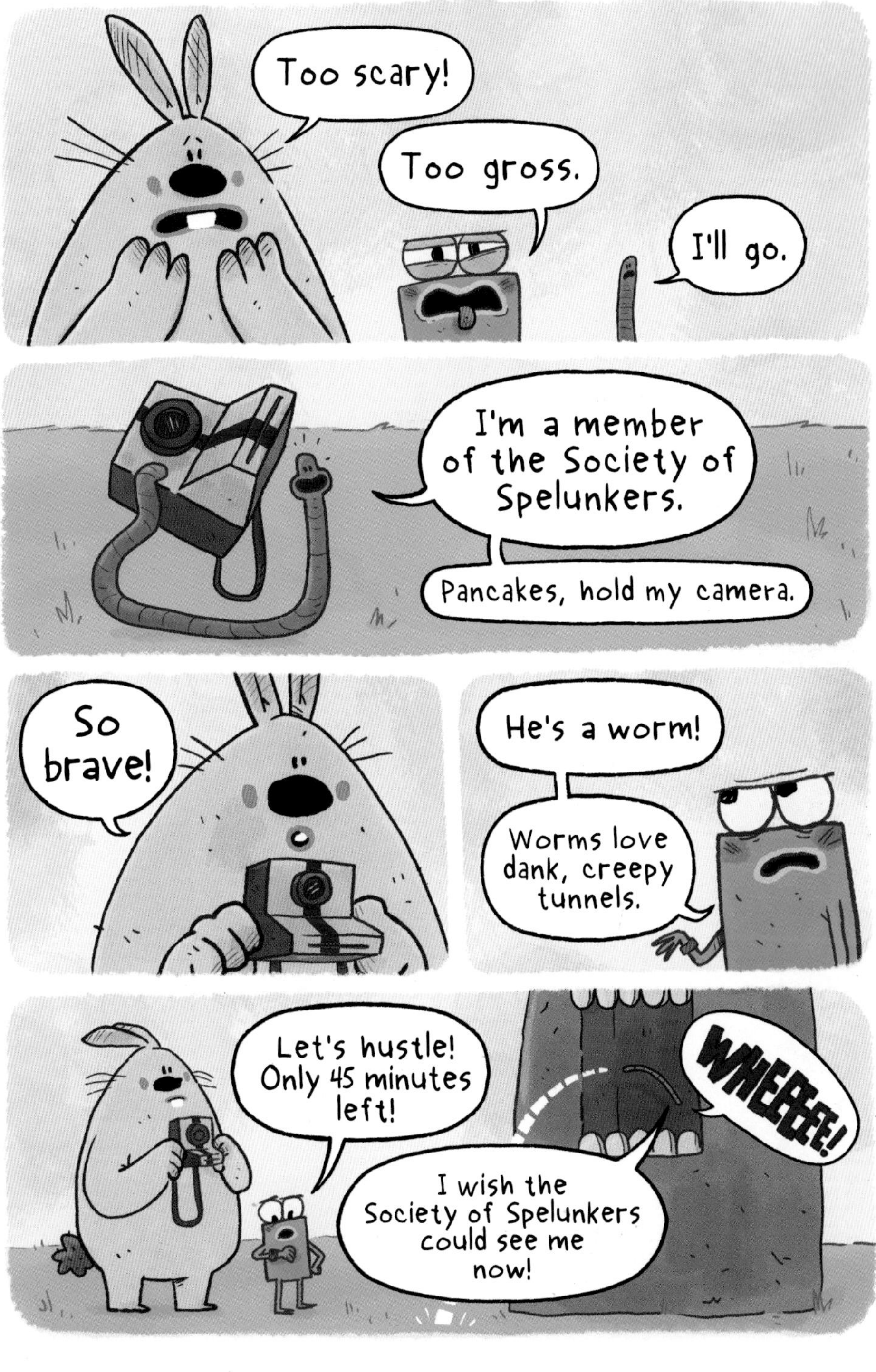

Too scary!
Too gross.
I'll go.
I'm a member of the Society of Spelunkers.
Pancakes, hold my camera.
So brave!
He's a worm!
Worms love dank, creepy tunnels.
Let's hustle! Only 45 minutes left!
WHEEEEE!
I wish the Society of Spelunkers could see me now!

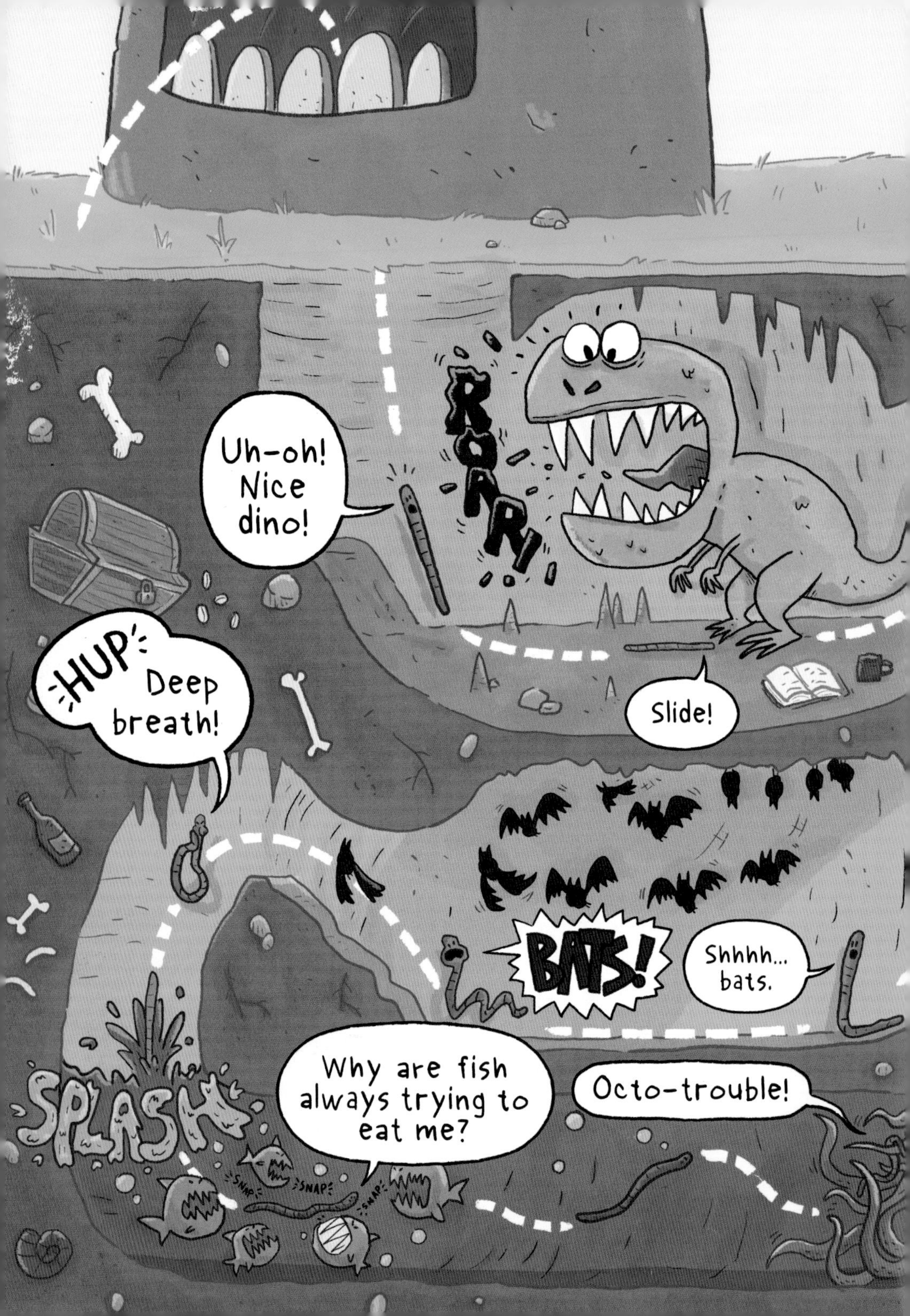

ROAR!
Uh-oh! Nice dino!
HUP Deep breath!
Slide!
BATS!
Shhhh... bats.
SPLASH
Why are fish always trying to eat me?
SNAP SNAP SNAP
Octo-trouble!

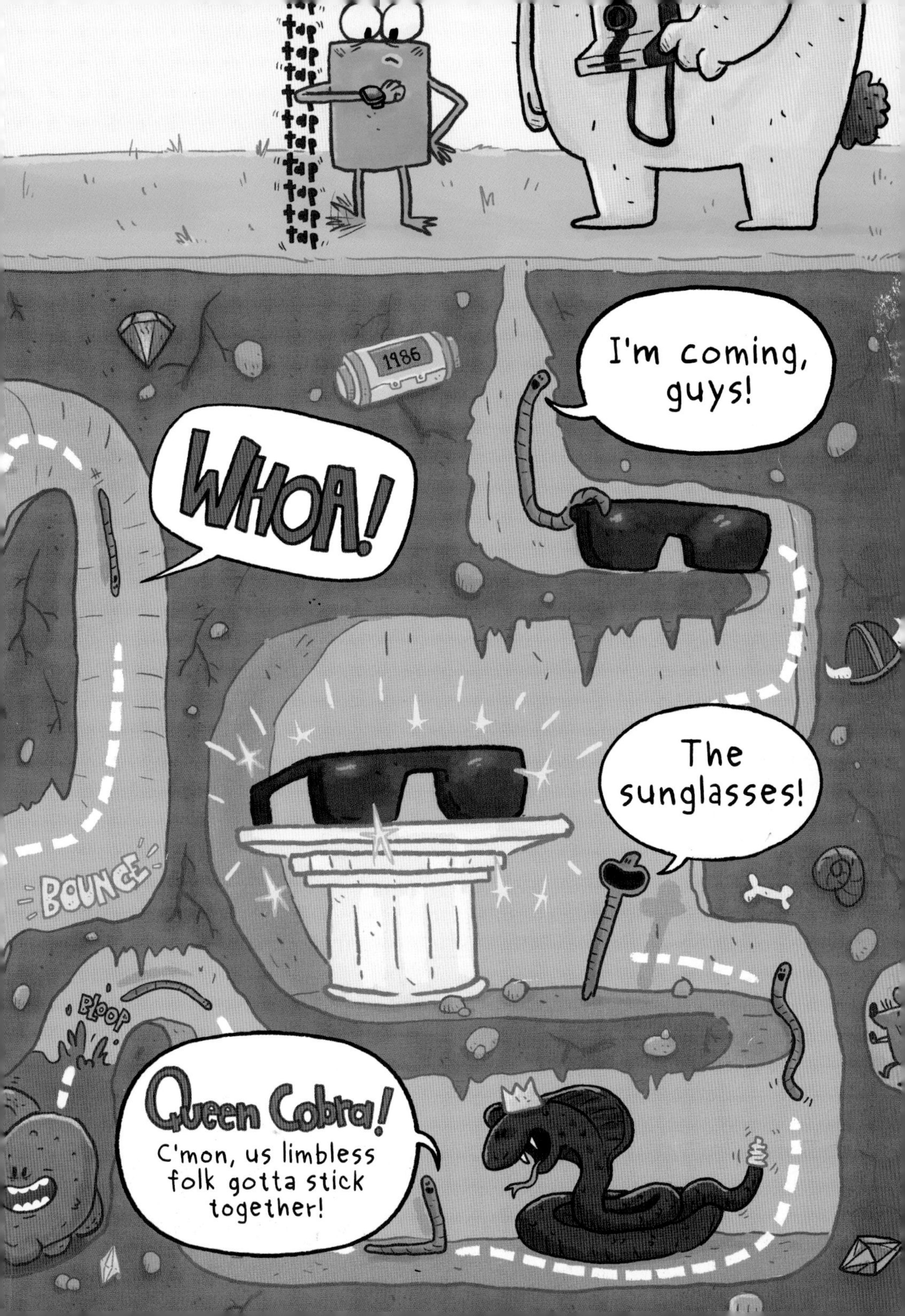
tap tap tap tap tap tap tap tap tap tap tap
1986
I'm coming, guys!
WHOA!
The sunglasses!
BOUNCE
BLOOP
Queen Cobra! C'mon, us limbless folk gotta stick together!

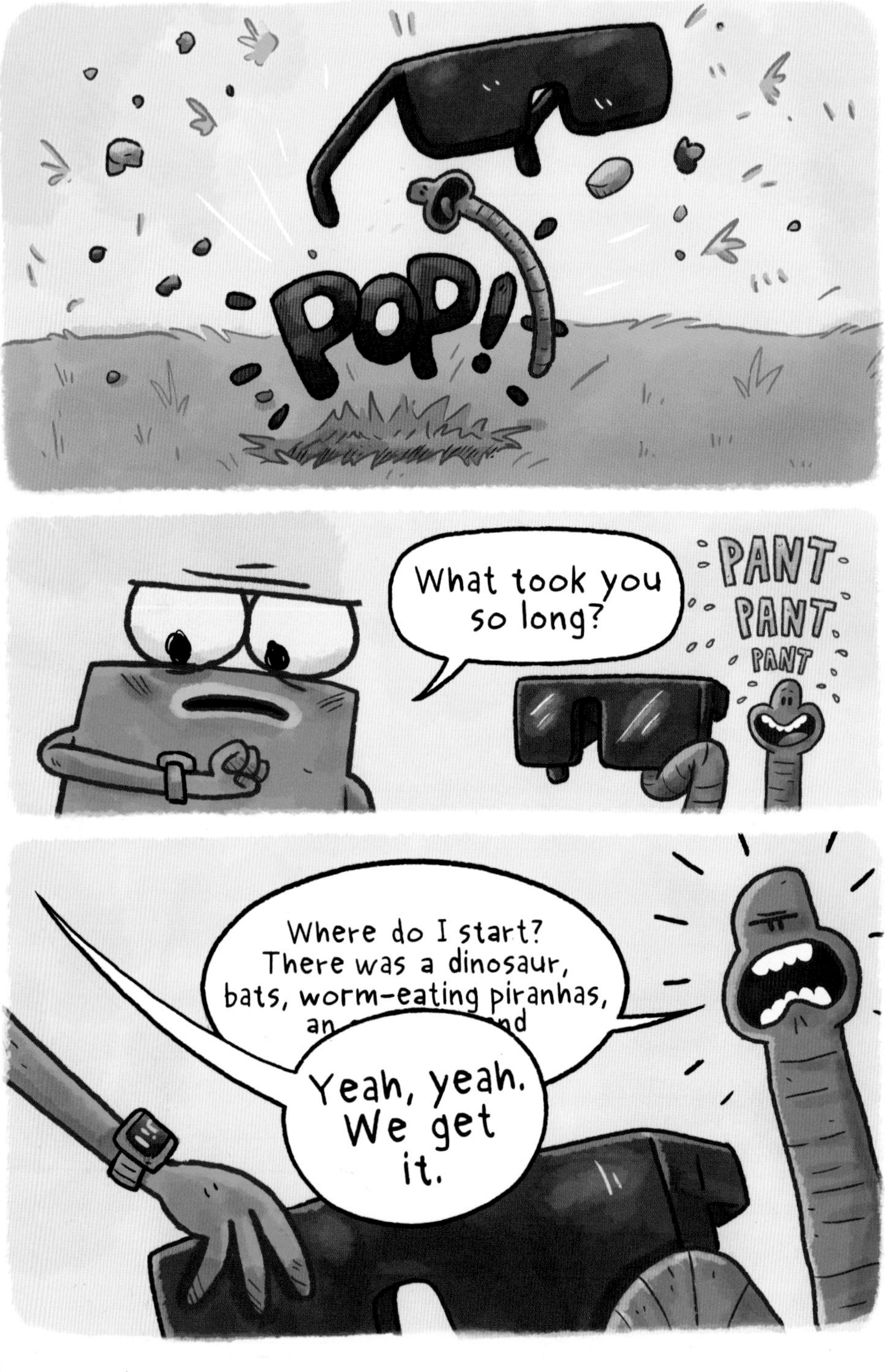
POP!
What took you so long?
PANT
PANT
PANT
Where do I start? There was a dinosaur, bats, worm-eating piranhas,
Yeah, yeah. We get it.

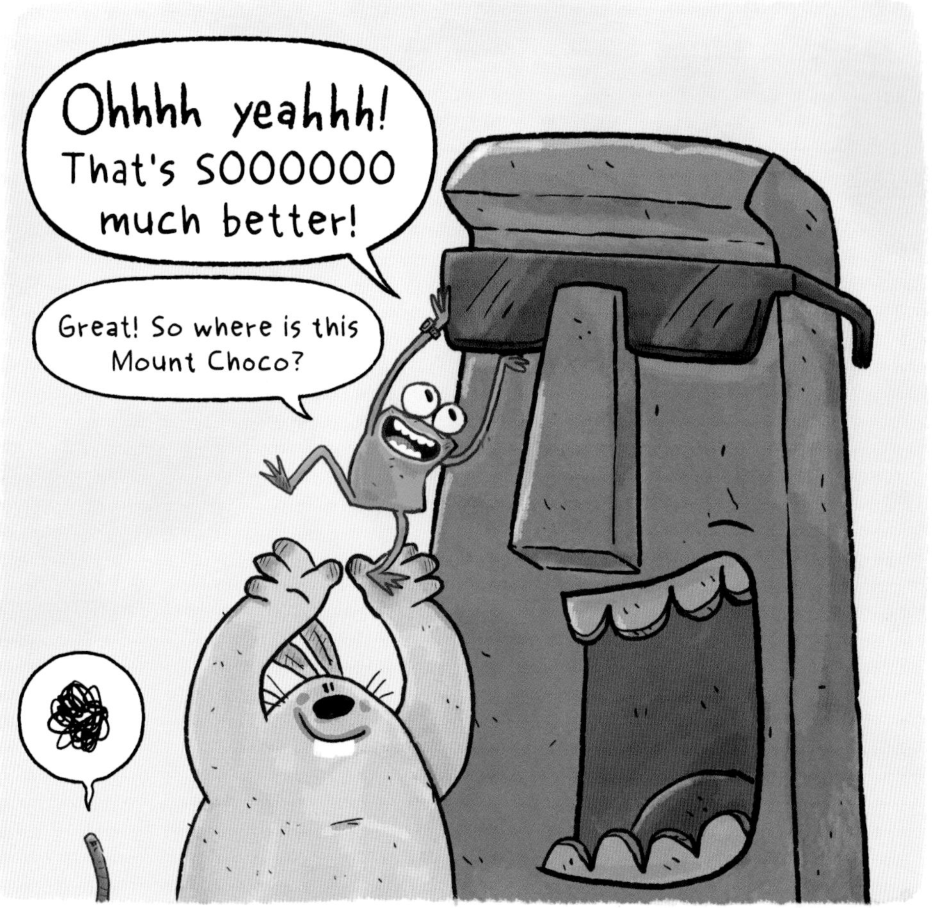
Ohhhh yeahhh! That's SOOOOOO much better!
Great! So where is this Mount Choco?

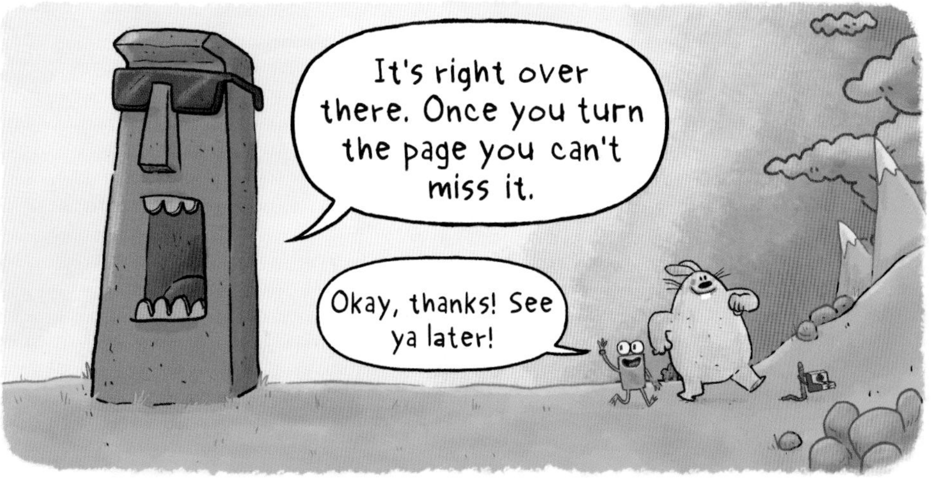
It's right over there. Once you turn the page you can't miss it.
Okay, thanks! See ya later!

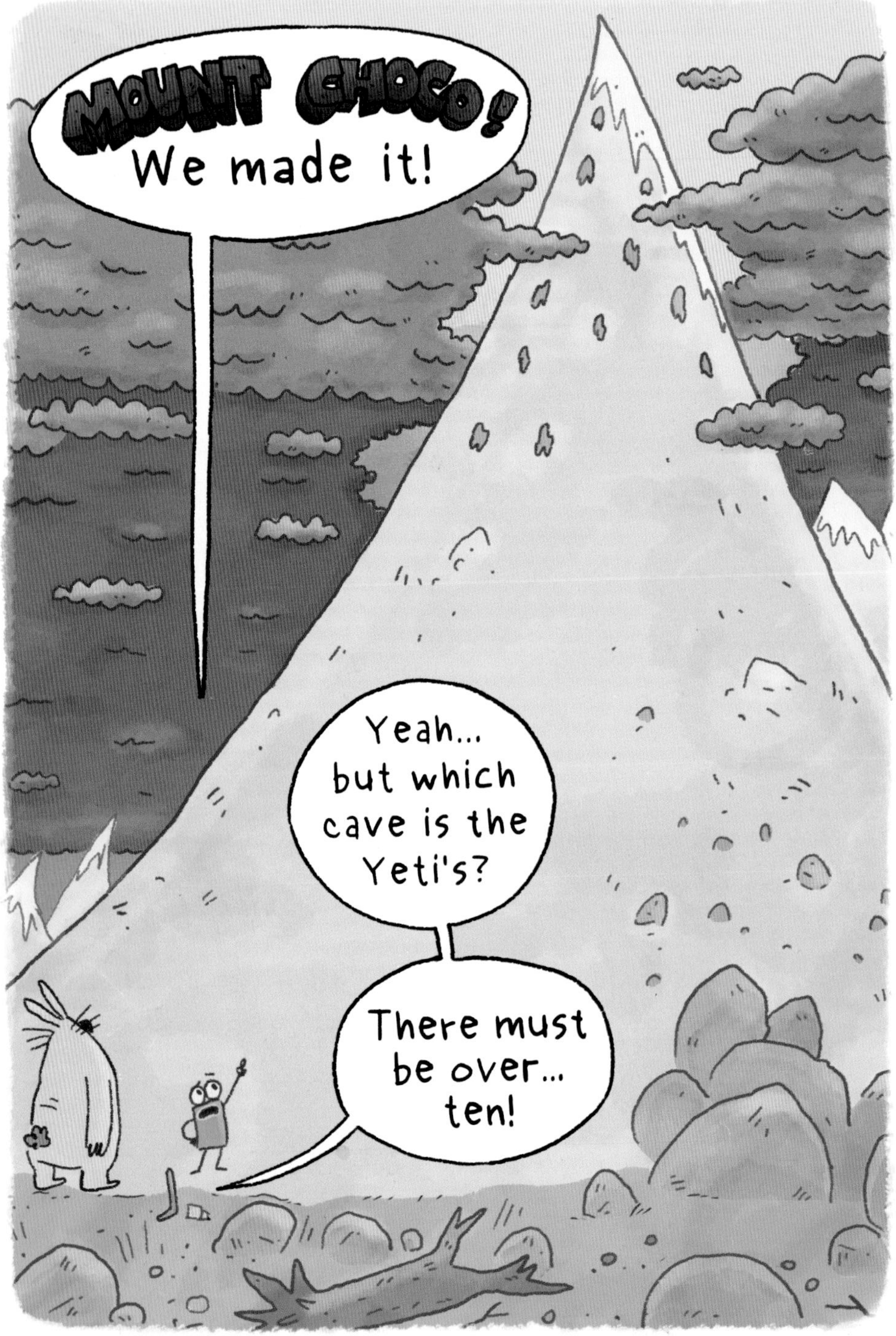
MOUNT CHOCO! We made it!
Yeah... but which cave is the Yeti's?
There must be over... ten!

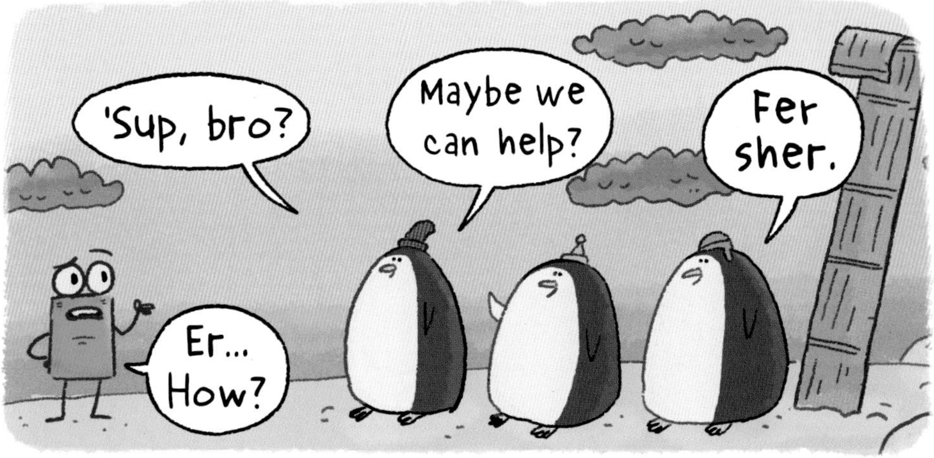
'Sup, bro?
Maybe we can help?
Fer sher.
Er... How?

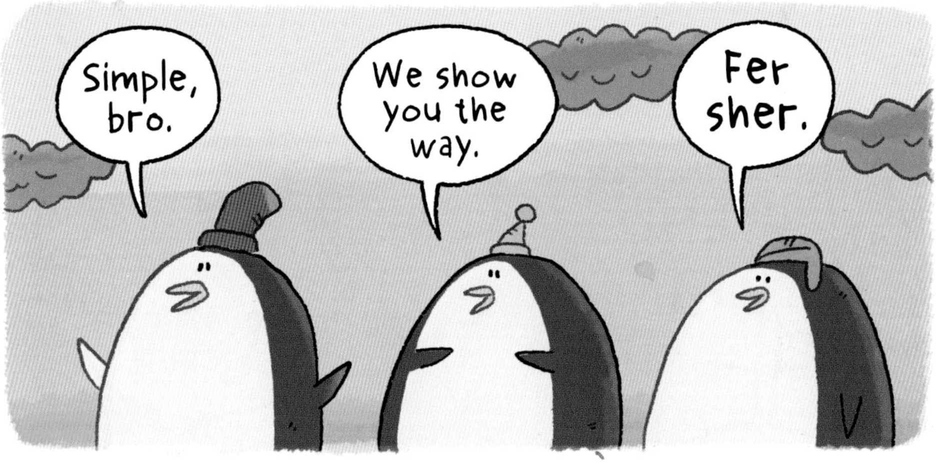
Simple, bro.
We show you the way.
Fer sher.

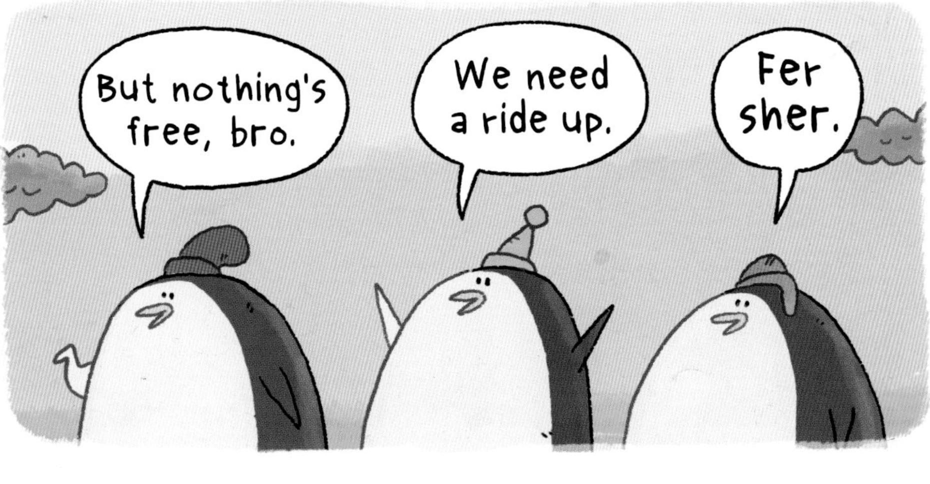
But nothing's free, bro.
We need a ride up.
Fer sher.

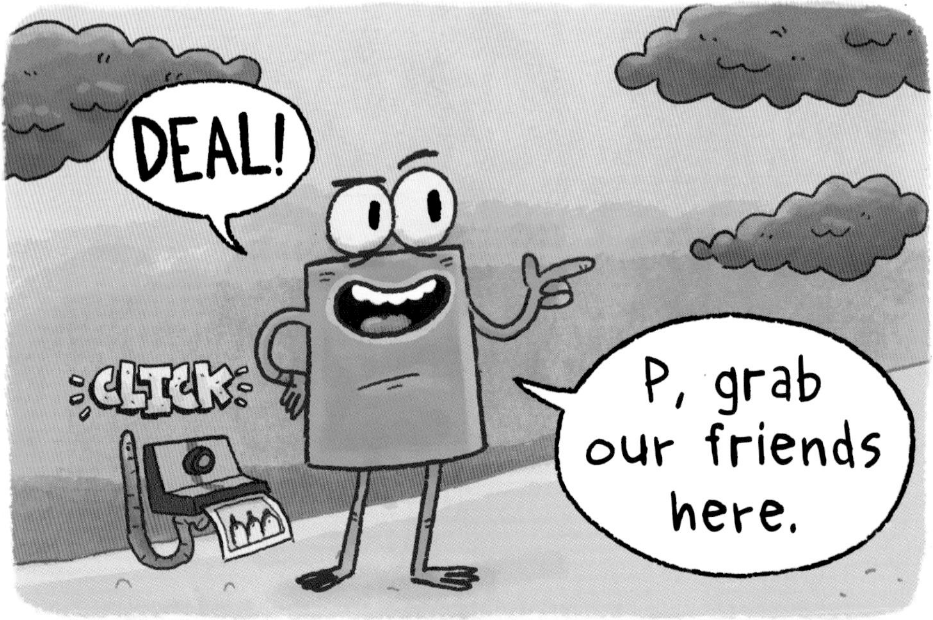
DEAL!
CLICK
P, grab our friends here.

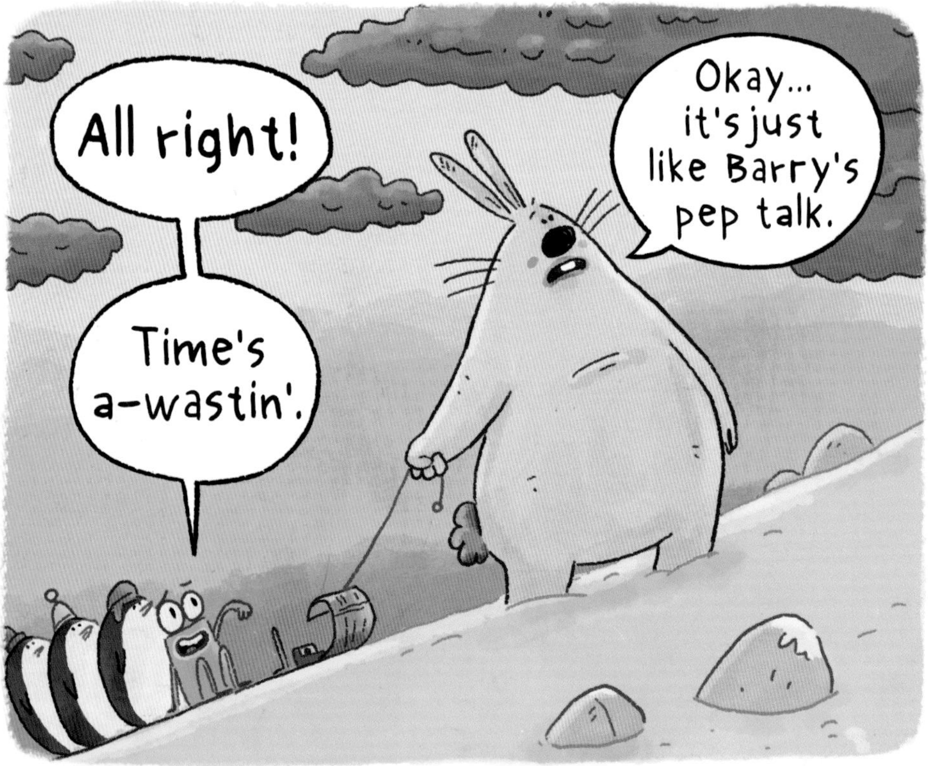
All right!
Time's a-wastin'.
Okay... it's just like Barry's pep talk.

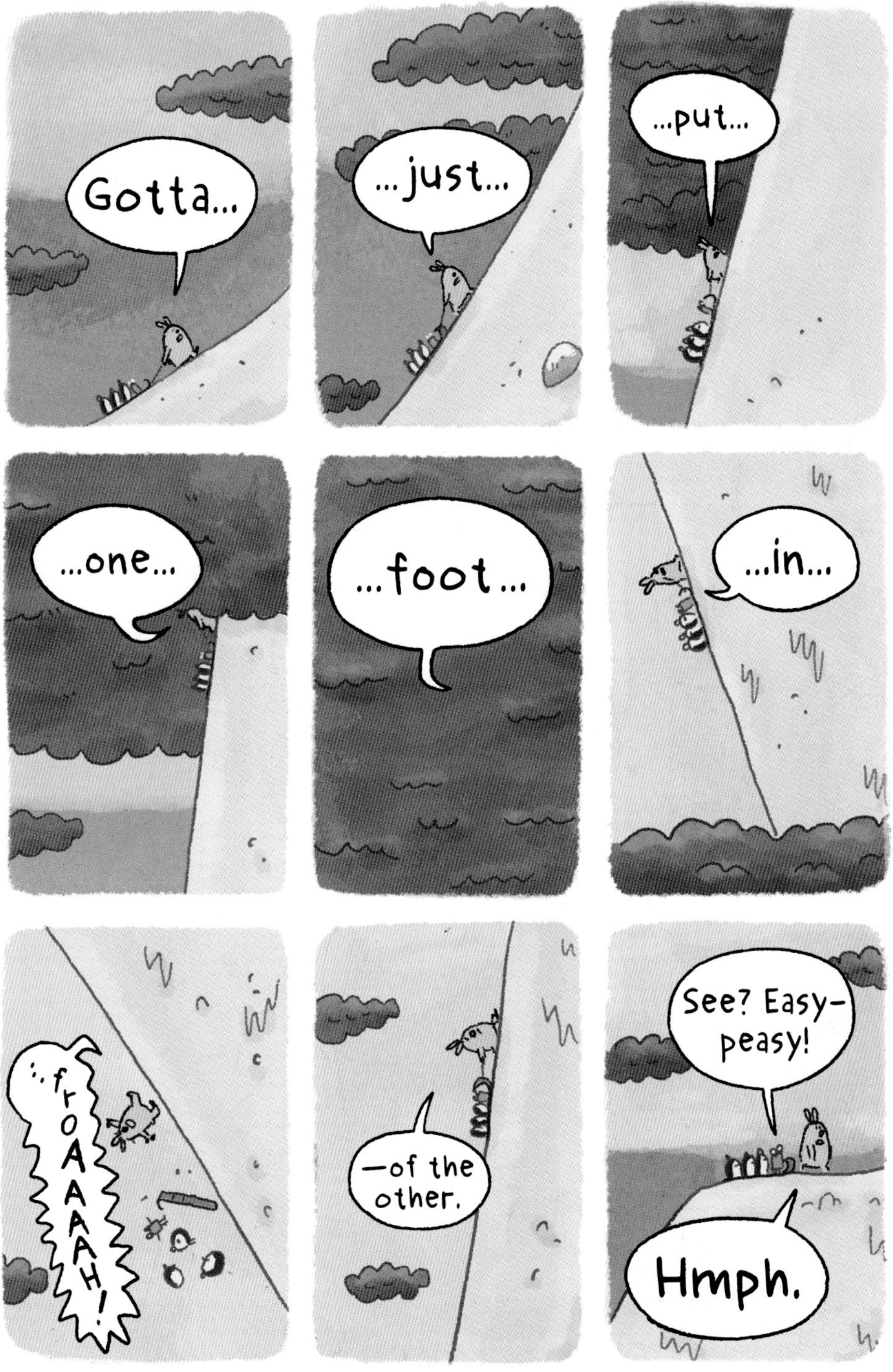
Gotta...
...just...
...put...
...one...
...foot...
...in...
...froAAAAAH!
—of the other.
See? Easy-peasy!
Hmph.

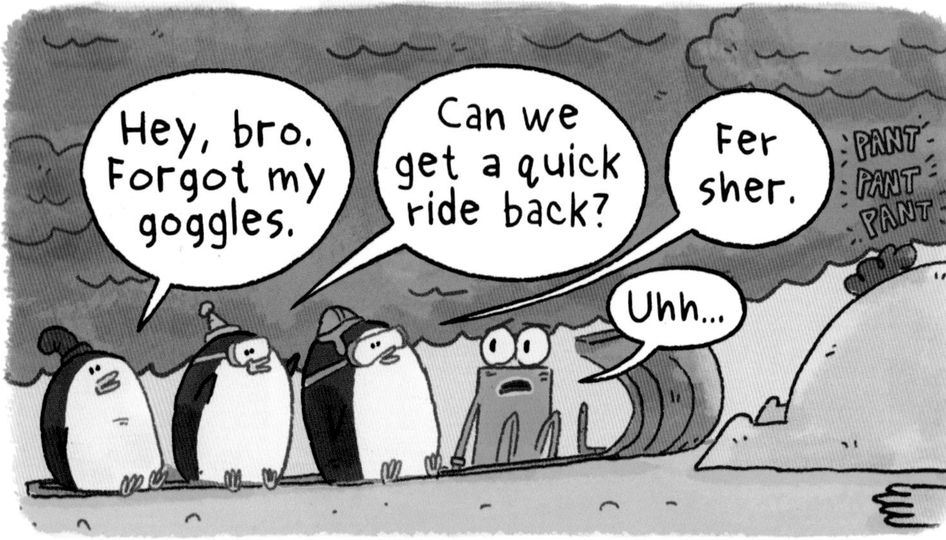
Hey, bro. Forgot my goggles.
Can we get a quick ride back?
Fer sher.
PANT PANT PANT
Uhh...

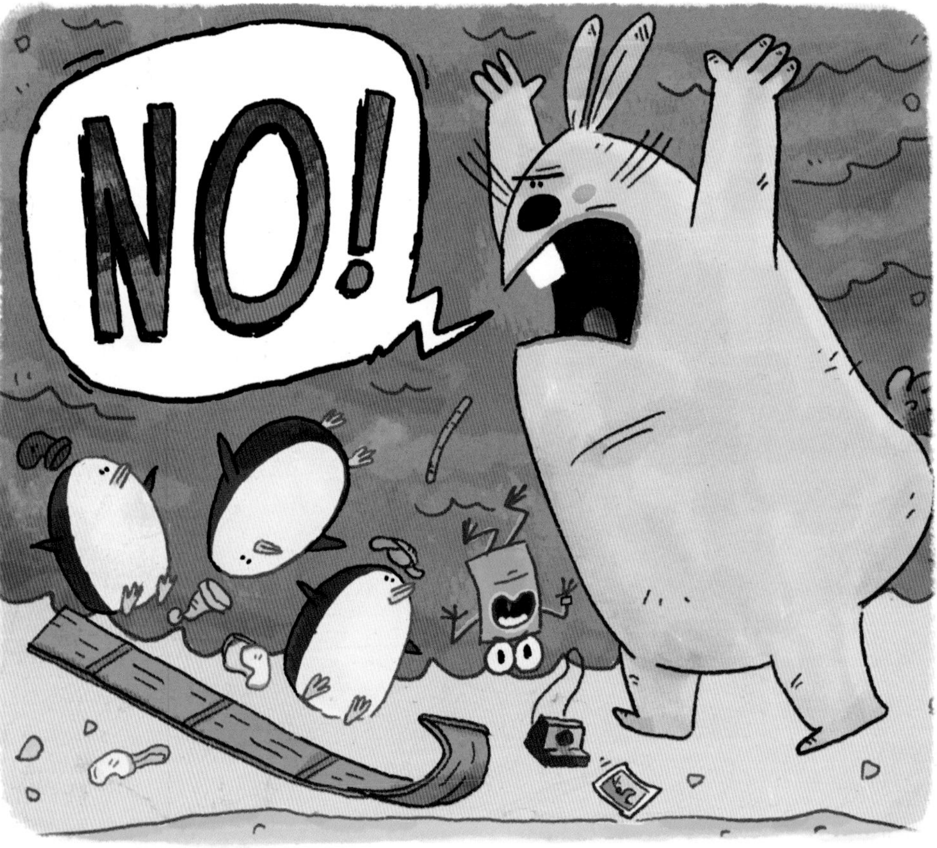
NO!

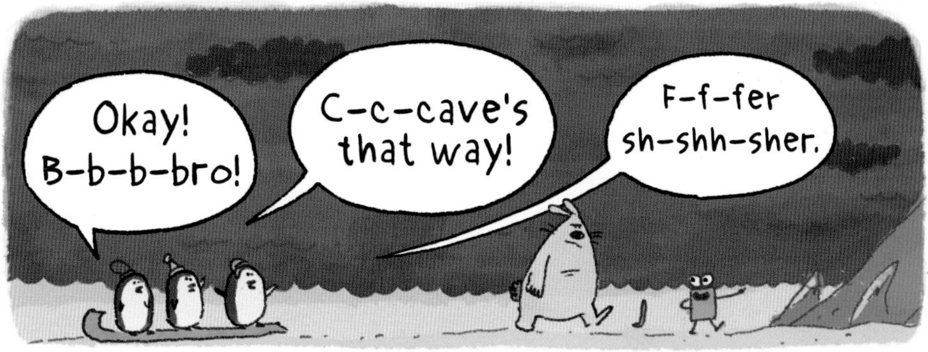
Okay! B-b-b-bro!
C-c-cave's that way!
F-f-fer sh-shh-sher.

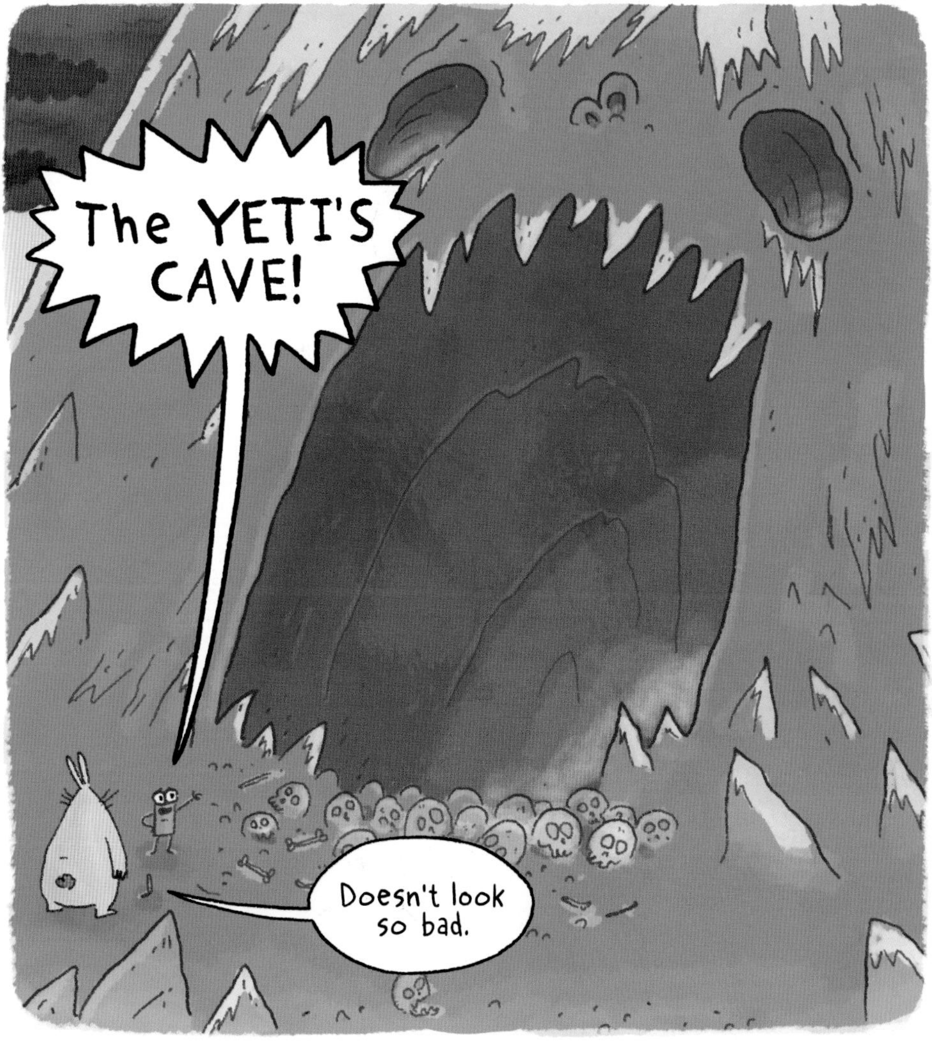
The YETI'S CAVE!
Doesn't look so bad.

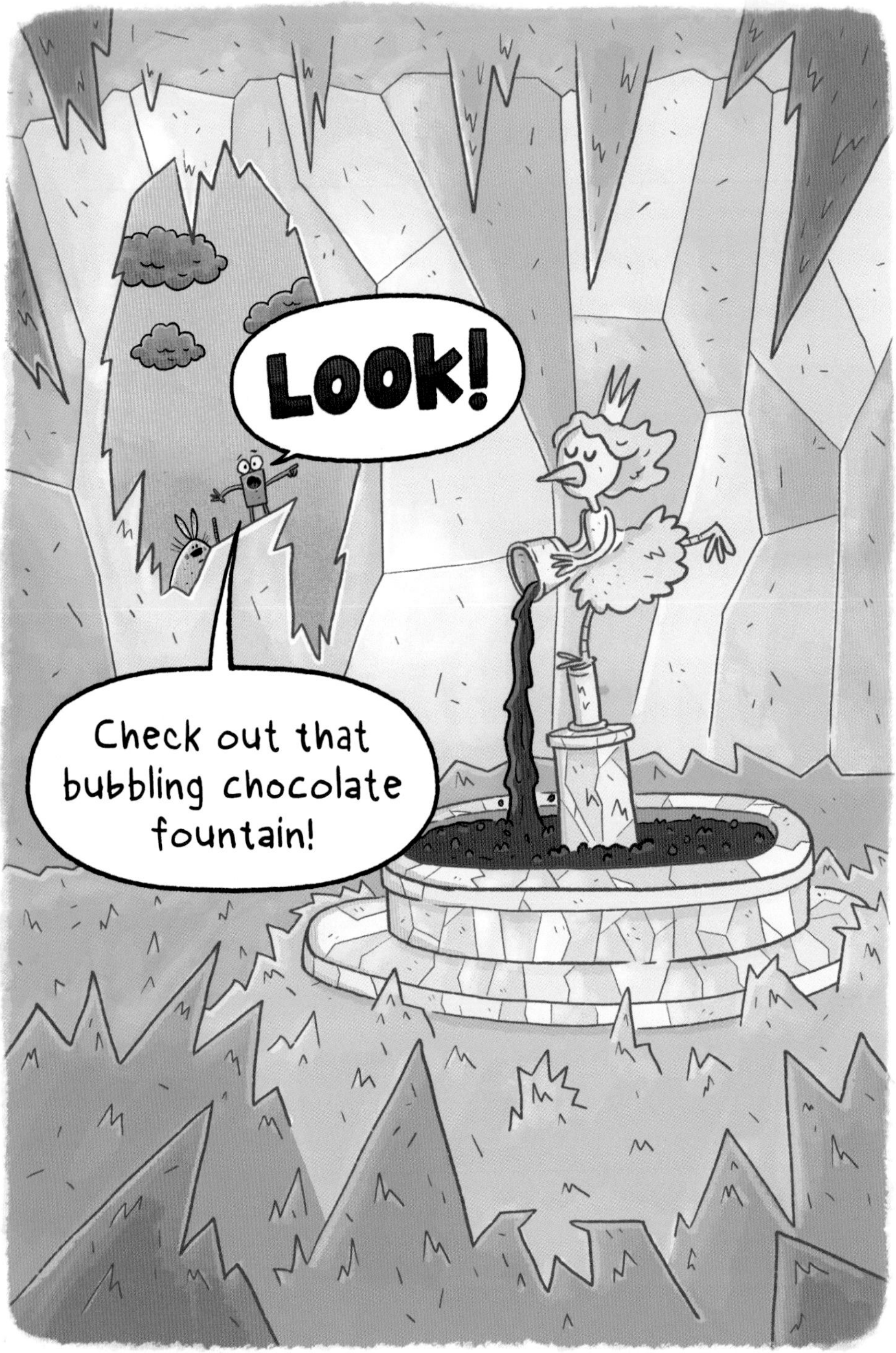
LOOK!
Check out that bubbling chocolate fountain!

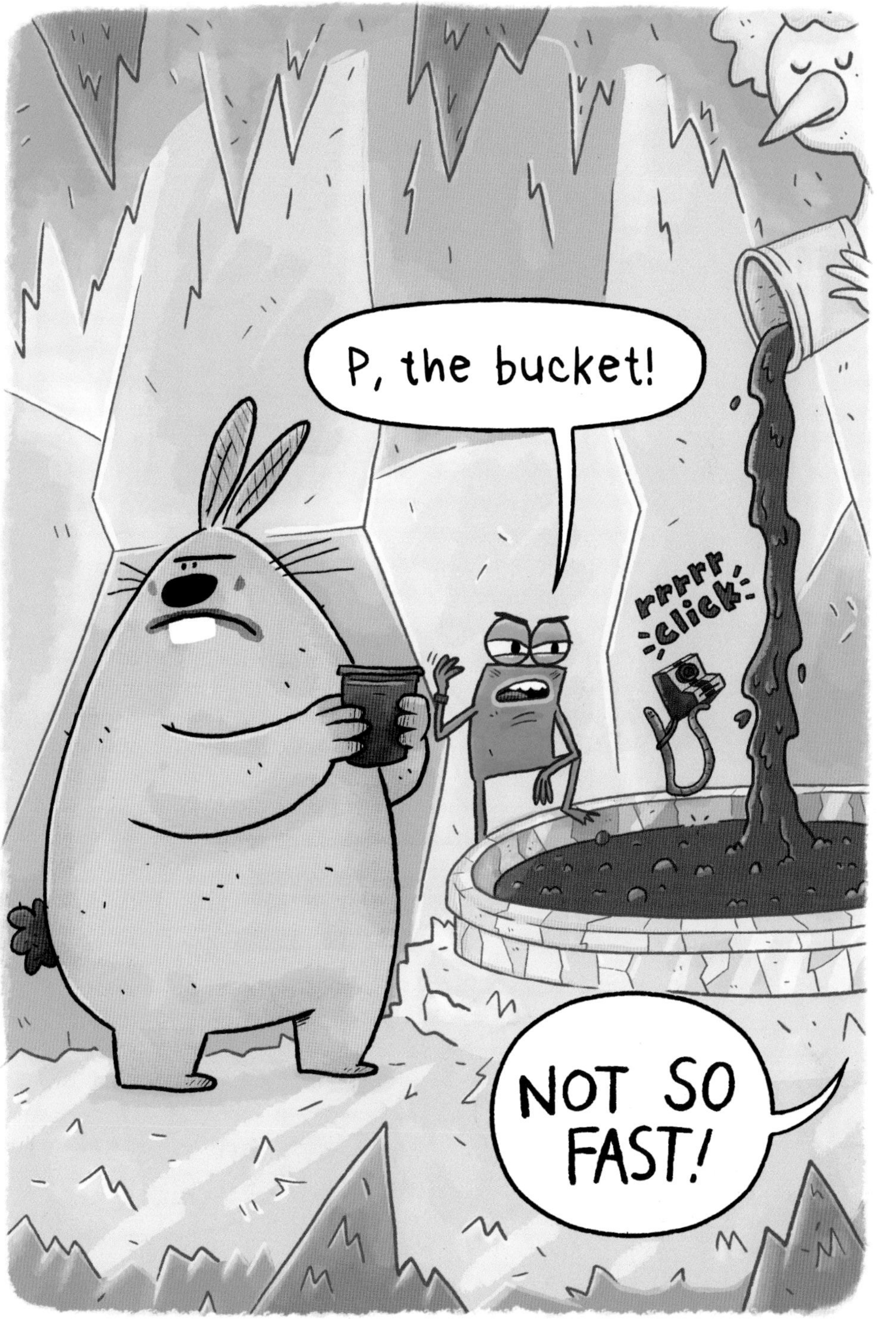
P, the bucket!
rrrrr
click
NOT SO FAST!

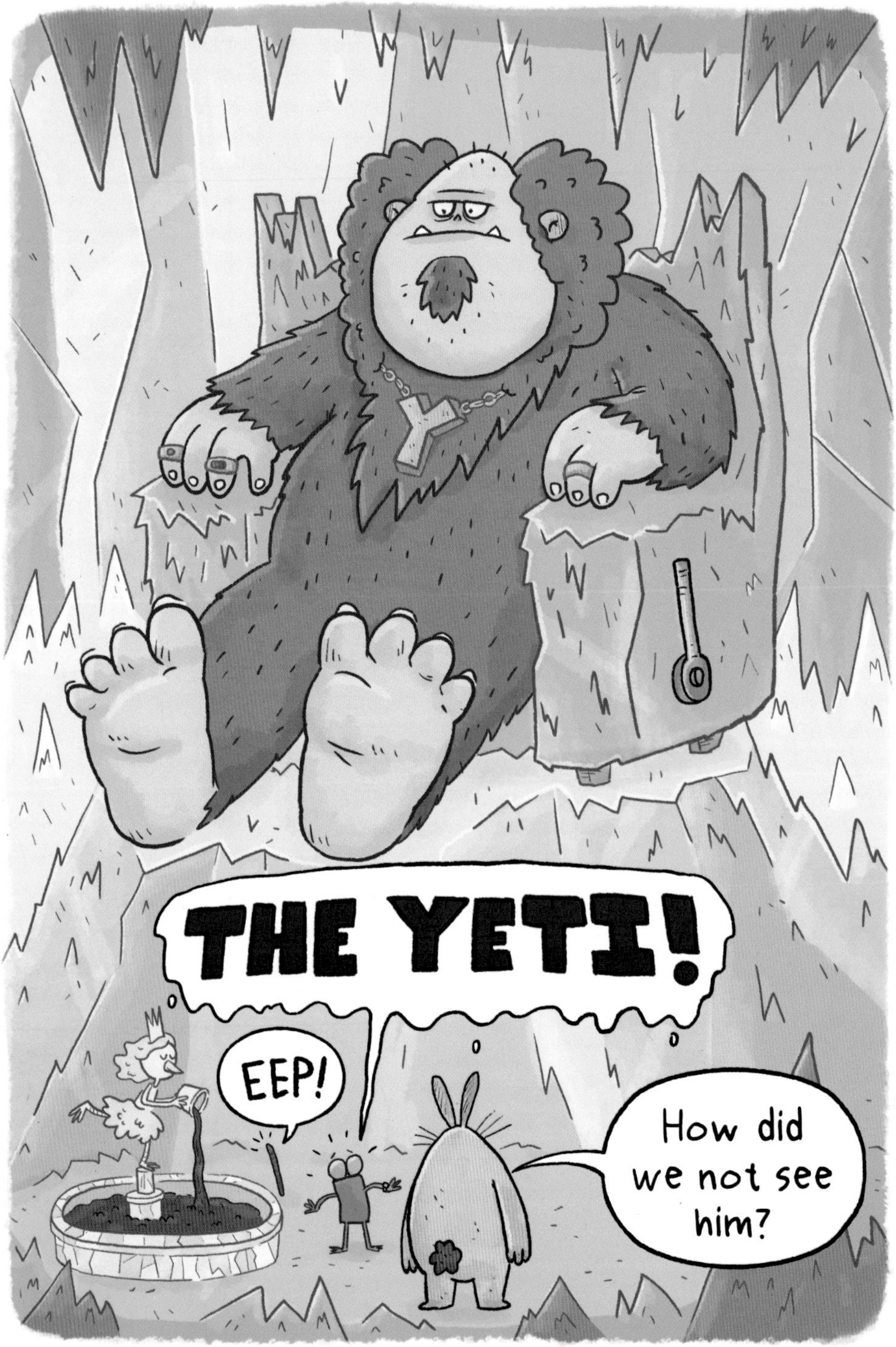
THE YETI!
EEP!
How did we not see him?

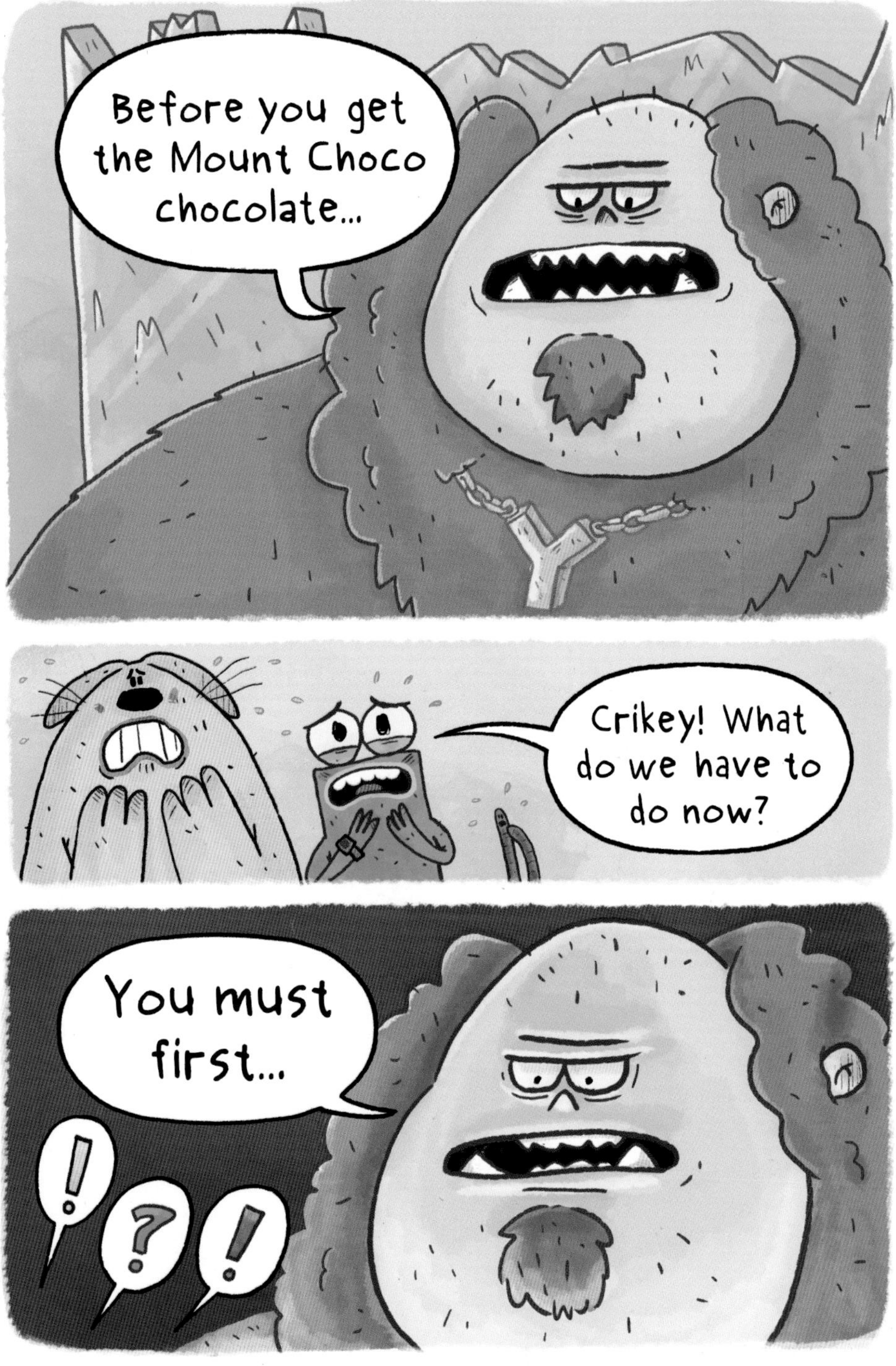
Before you get the Mount Choco chocolate...
Crikey! What do we have to do now?
You must first...
!
?
!

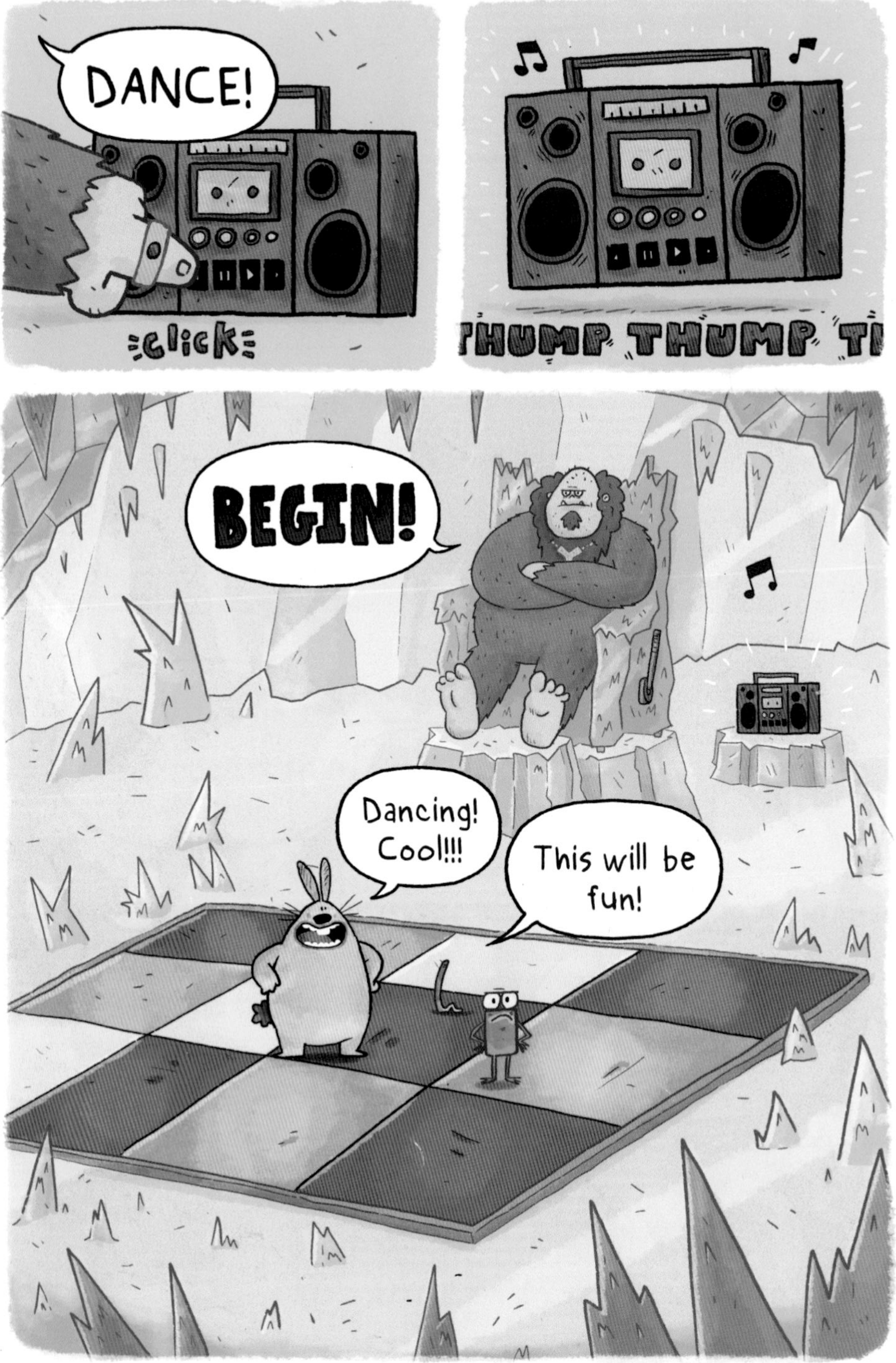
DANCE!
CLICK
THUMP THUMP
BEGIN!
Dancing! Cool!!!
This will be fun!

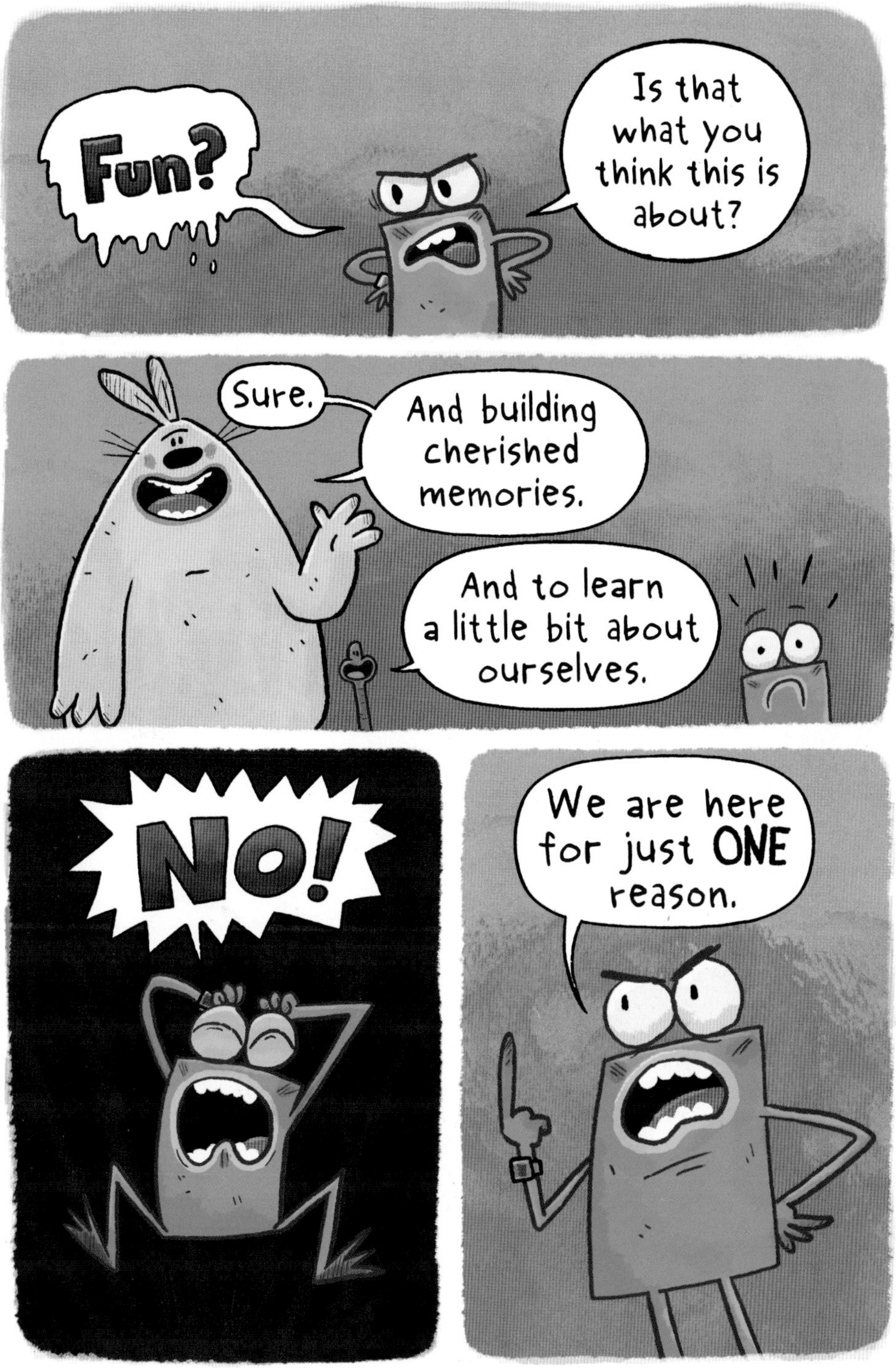
Fun?
Is that what you think this is about?
Sure.
And building cherished memories.
And to learn a little bit about ourselves.
NO!
We are here for just ONE reason.

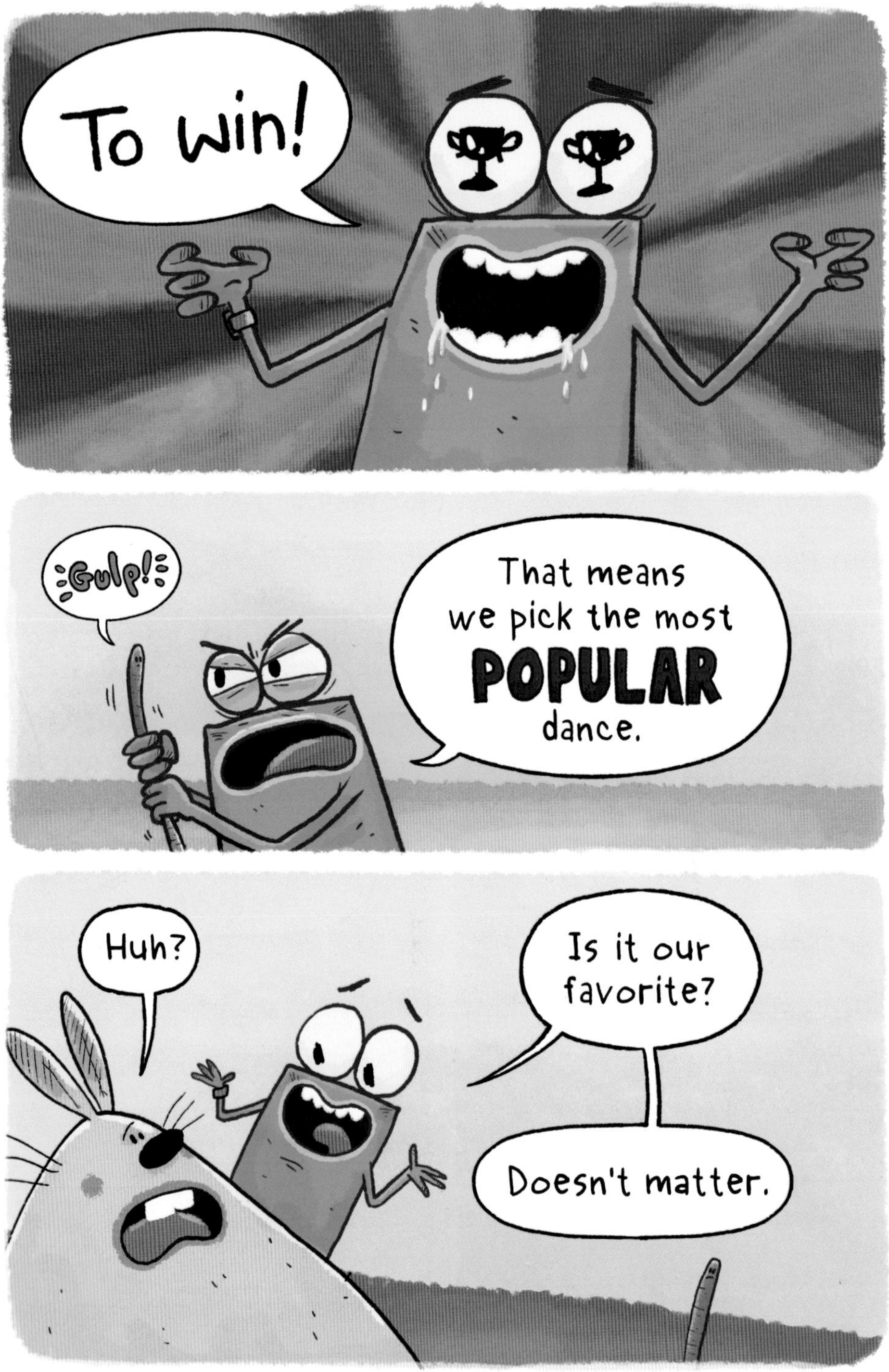
To win!
Gulp!
That means we pick the most POPULAR dance.
Huh?
Is it our favorite?
Doesn't matter.

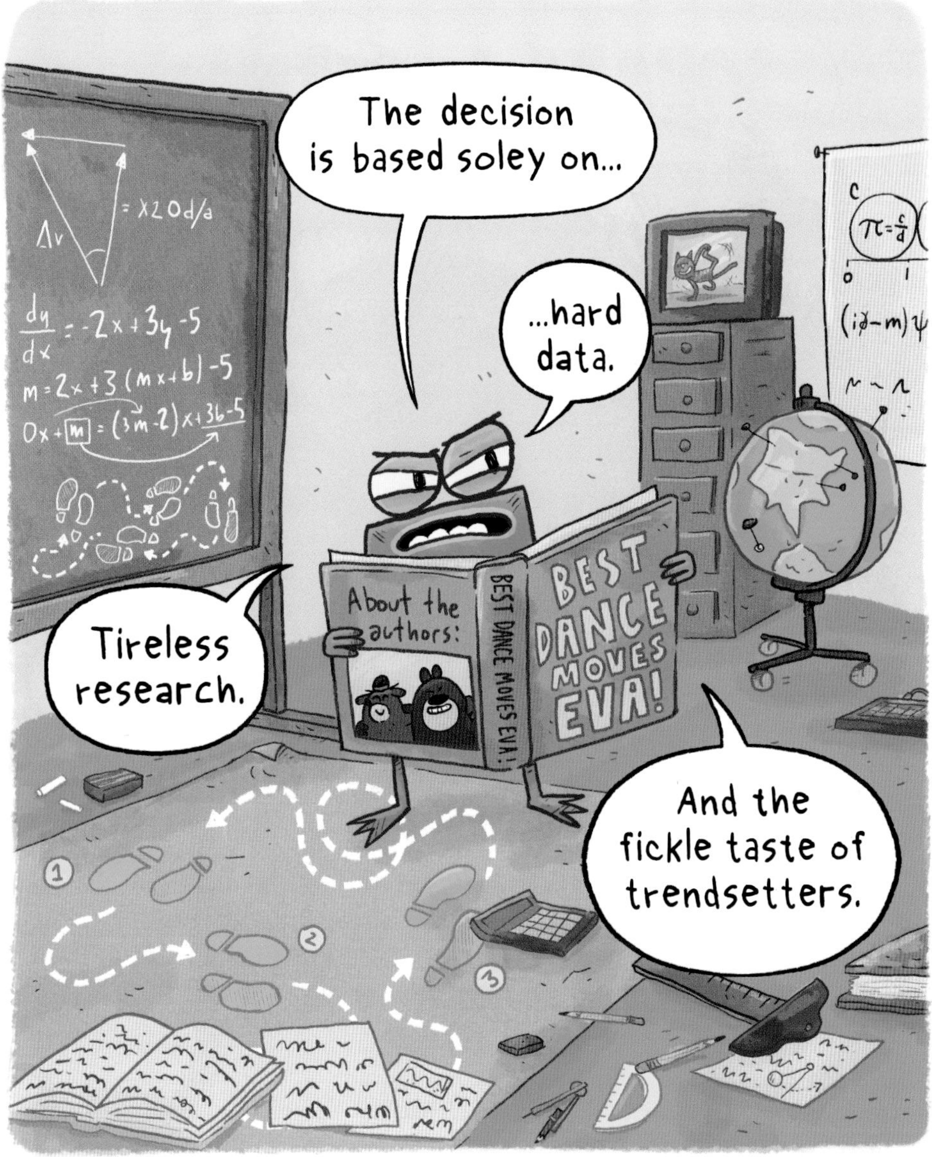
The decision is based soley on...
...hard data.
Tireless research.
And the fickle taste of trendsetters.
About the authors:
BEST DANCE MOVES EVA!
BEST DANCE MOVES EVA!

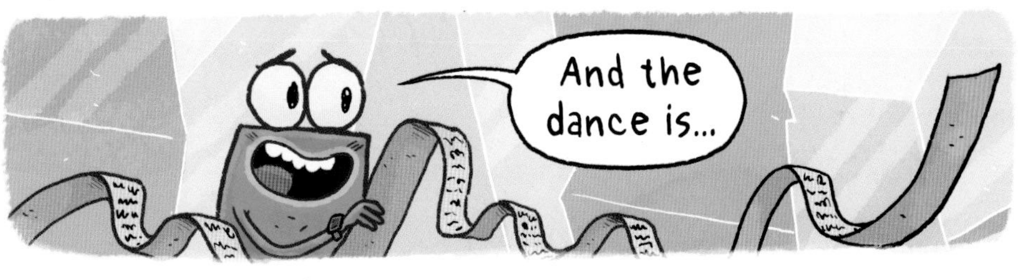
And the dance is...

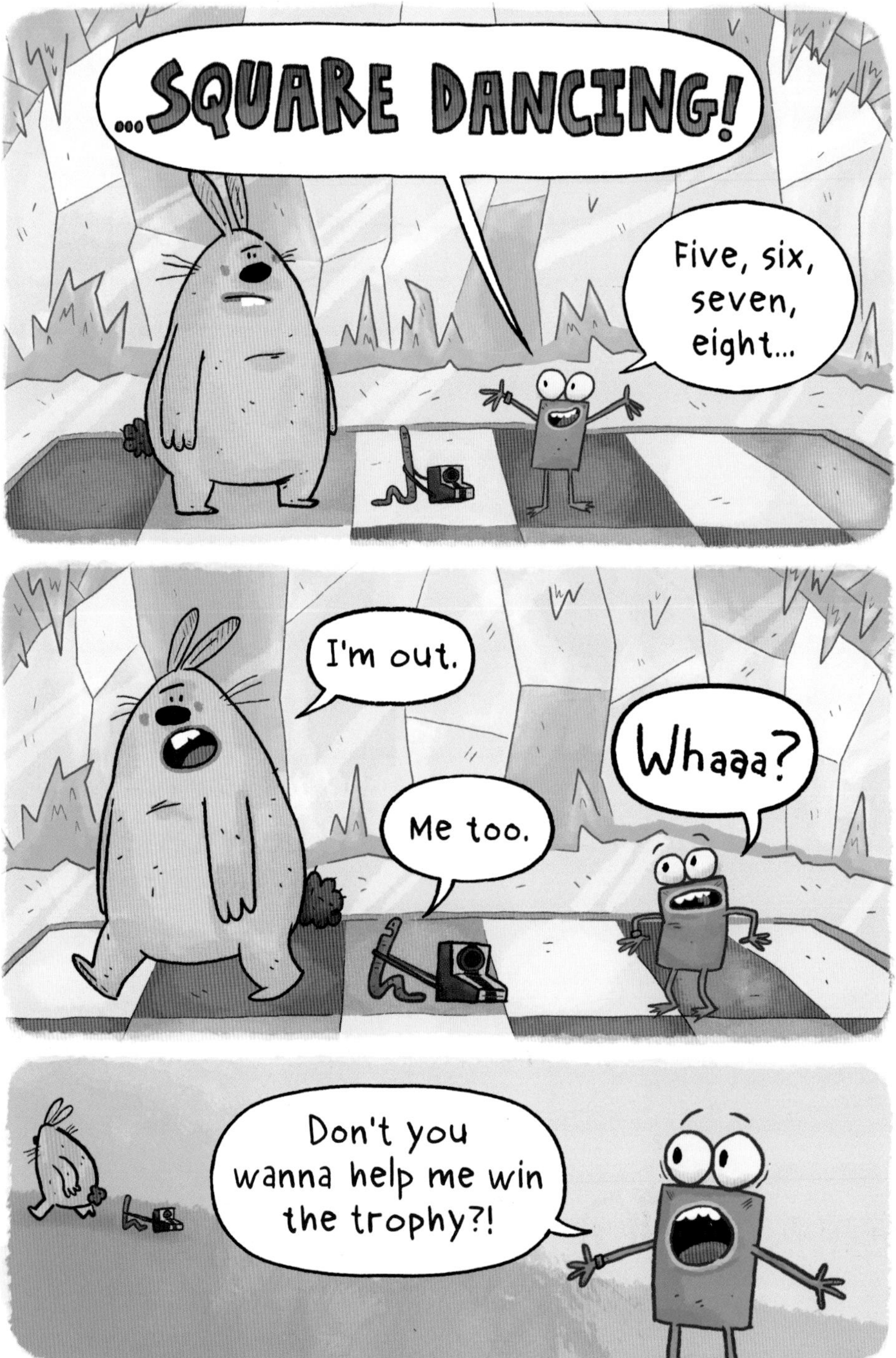
...SQUARE DANCING!
Five, six, seven, eight...
I'm out.
Whaaa?
Me too.
Don't you wanna help me win the trophy?!

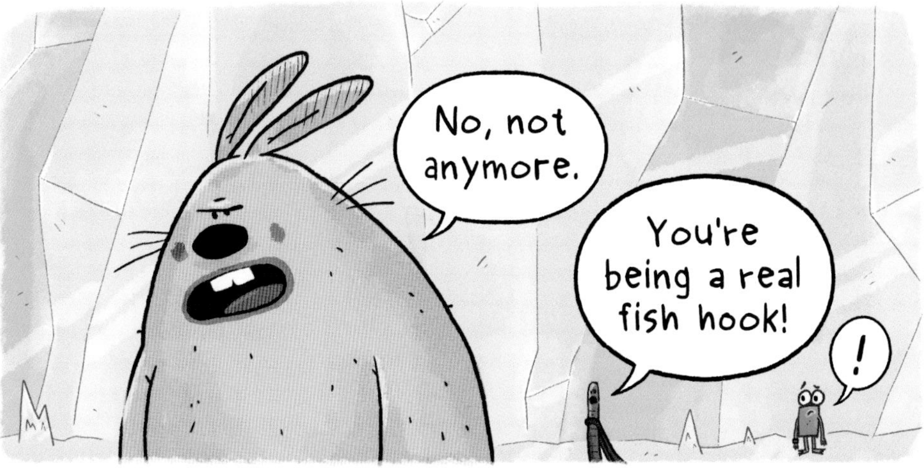
No, not anymore.
You're being a real fish hook!
!

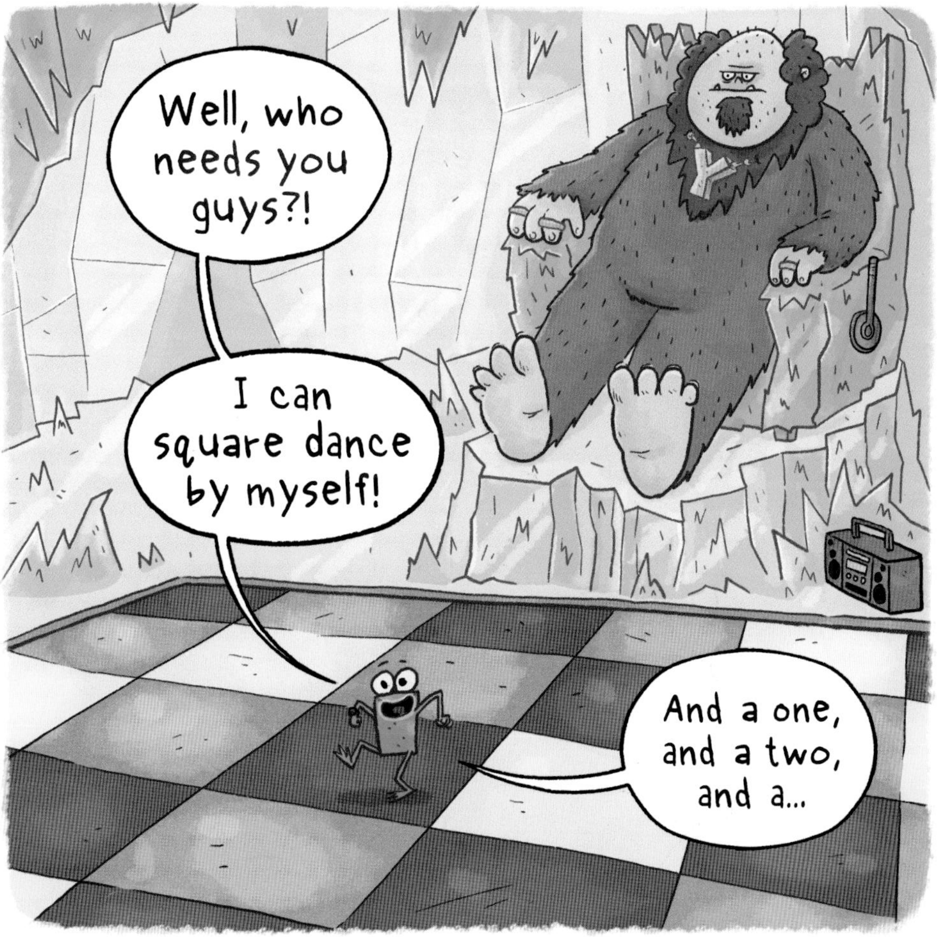
Well, who needs you guys?!
I can square dance by myself!
And a one, and a two, and a...

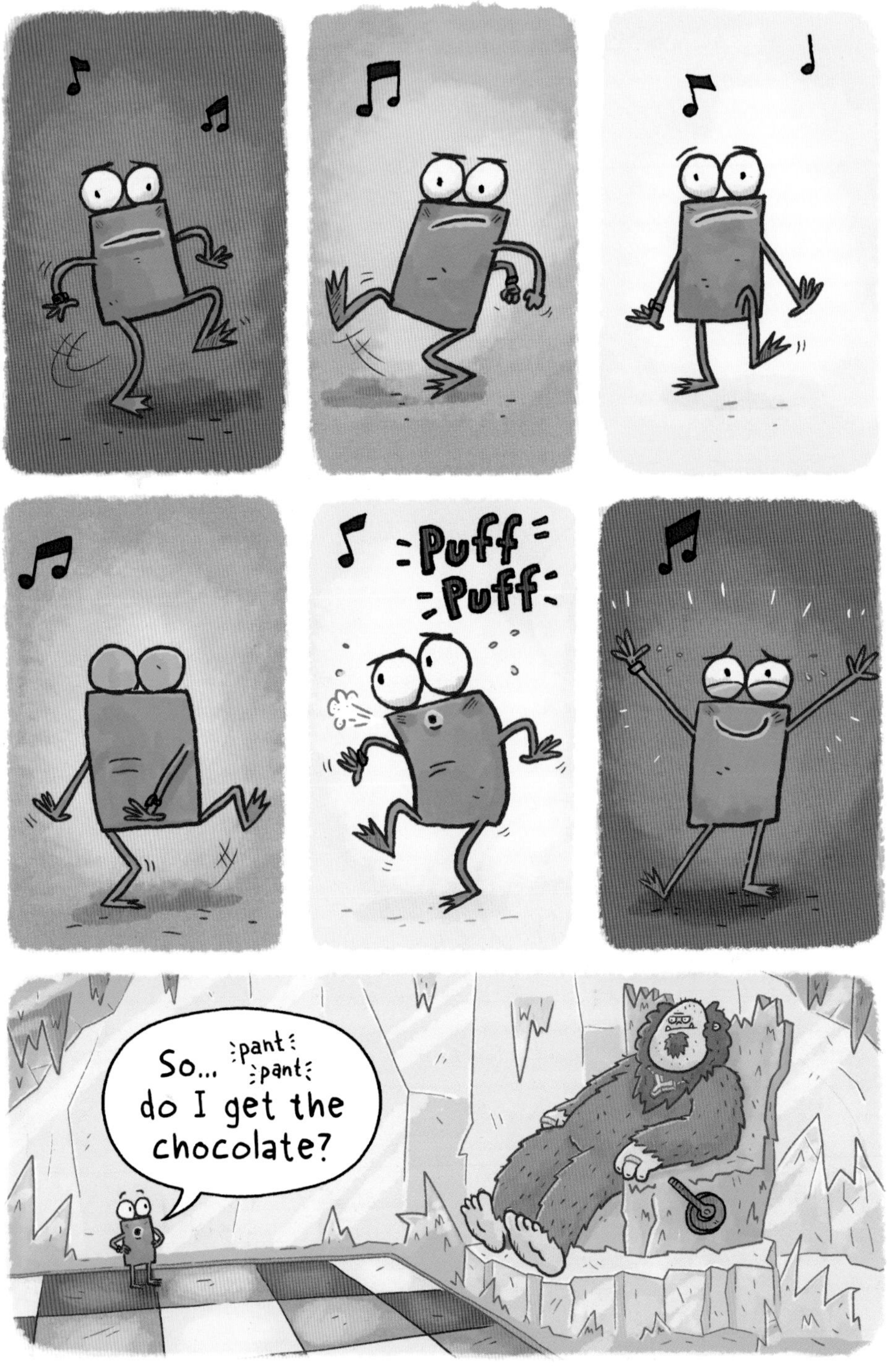
Puff
Puff
So... pant pant do I get the chocolate?

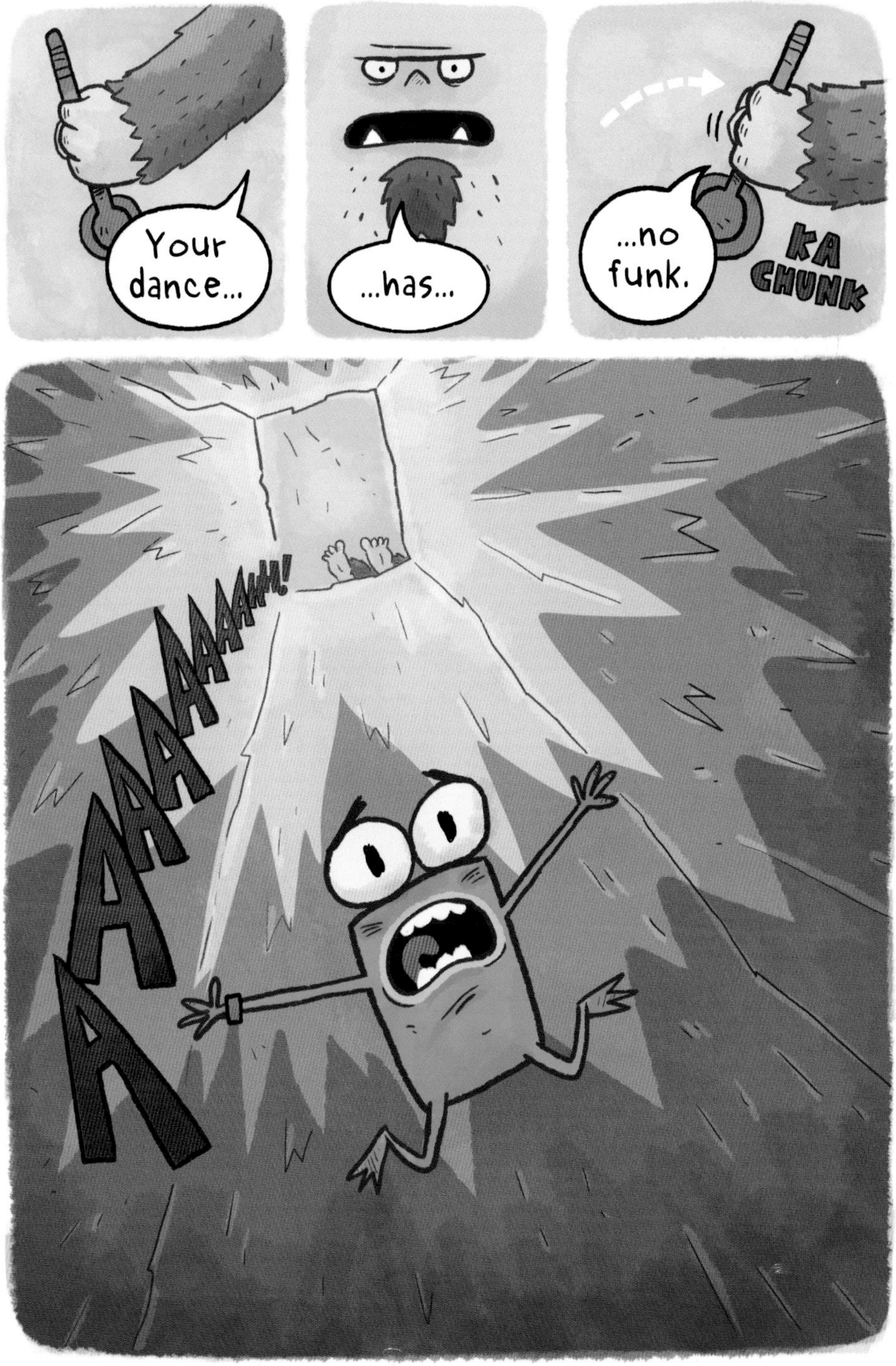
Your dance...
...has...
...no funk.
KA CHUNK
AAAAAAAAAAHH!

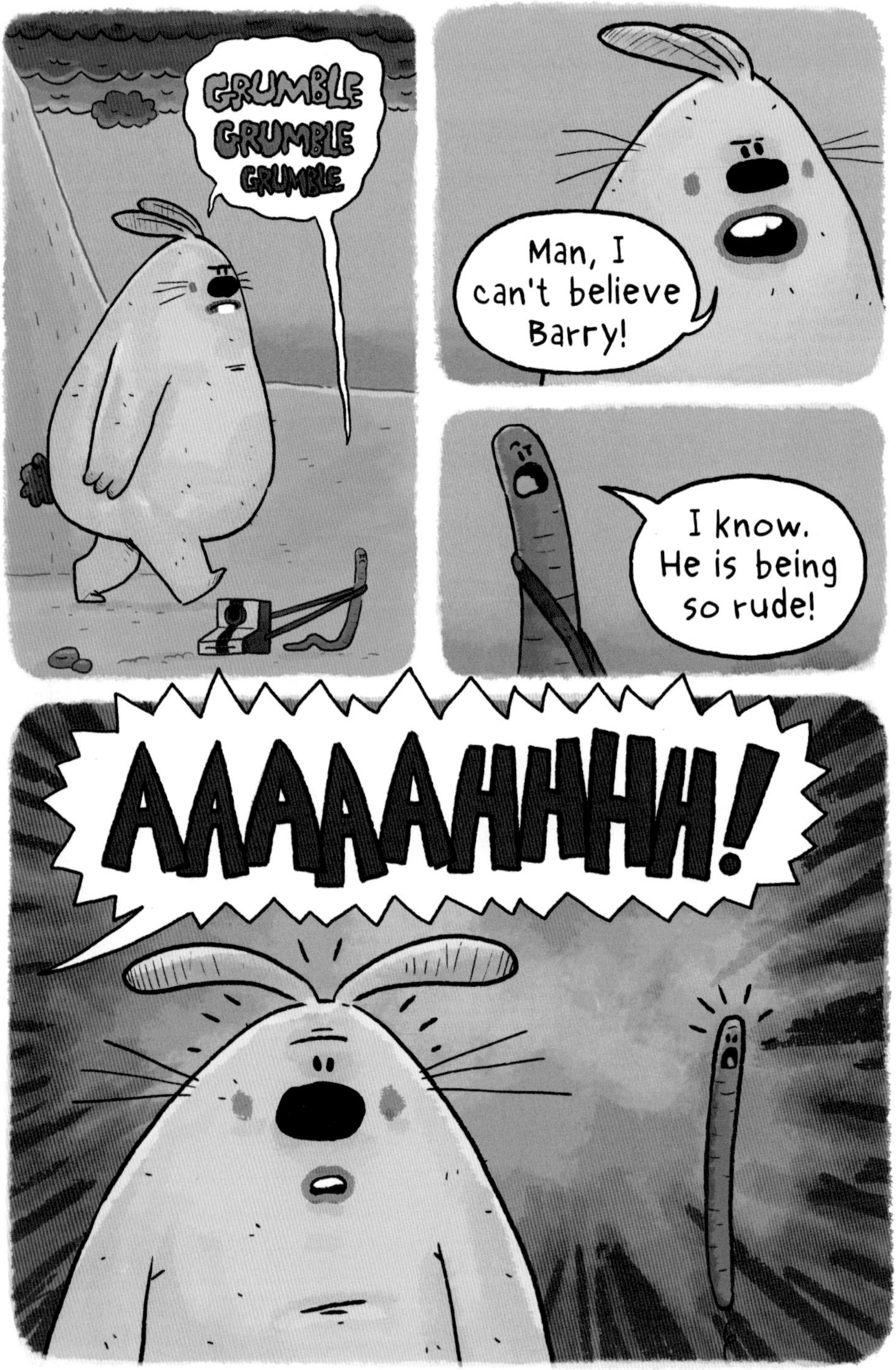
GRUMBLE GRUMBLE GRUMBLE
Man, I can't believe Barry!
I know. He is being so rude!
AAAAAHHHH!

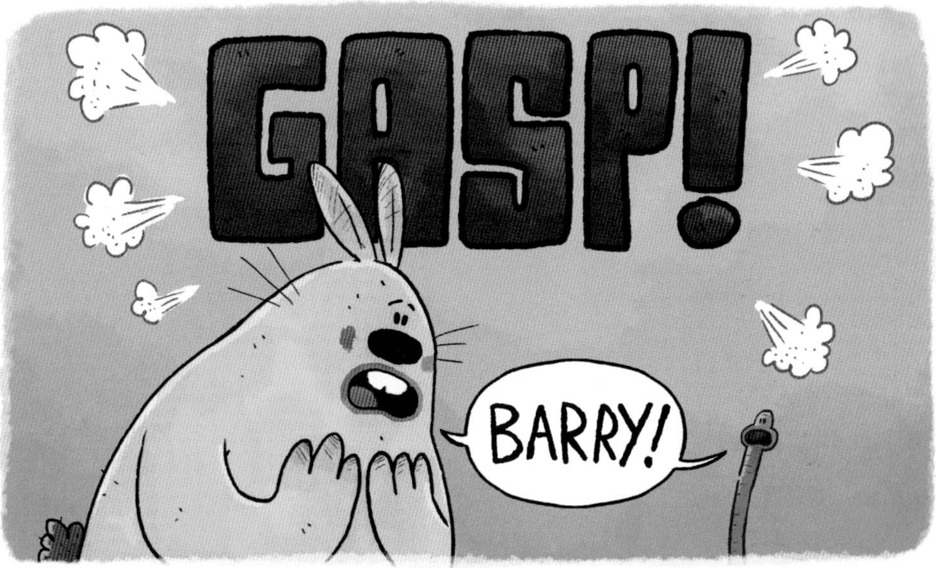
GASP!
BARRY!
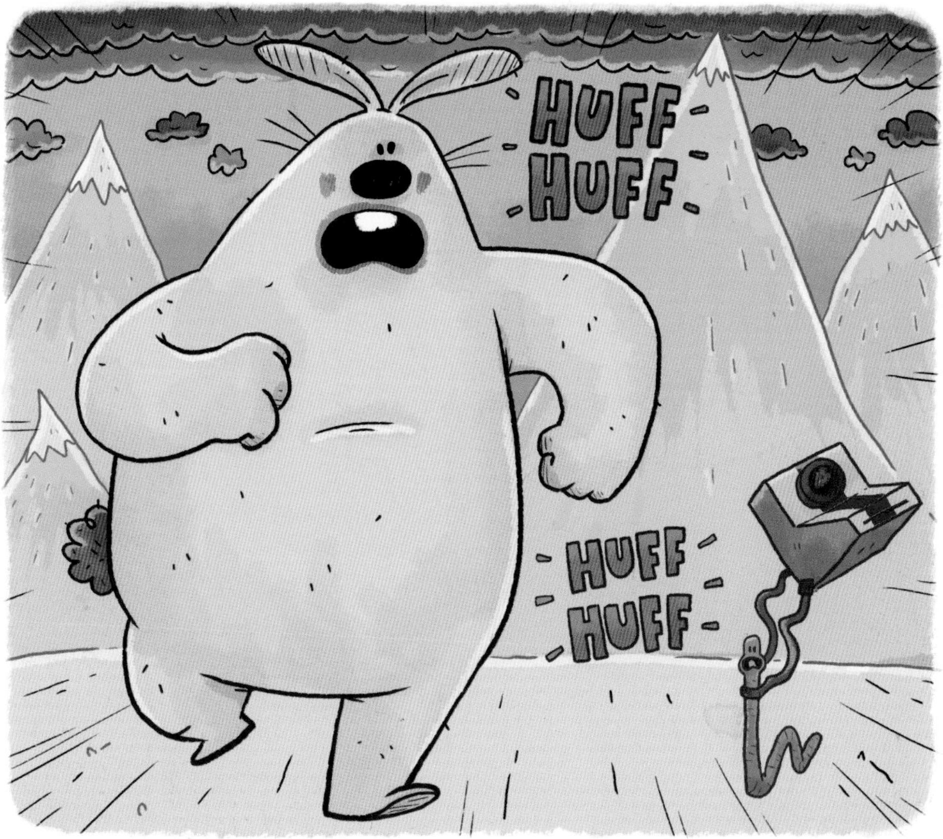
HUFF
HUFF
HUFF
HUFF

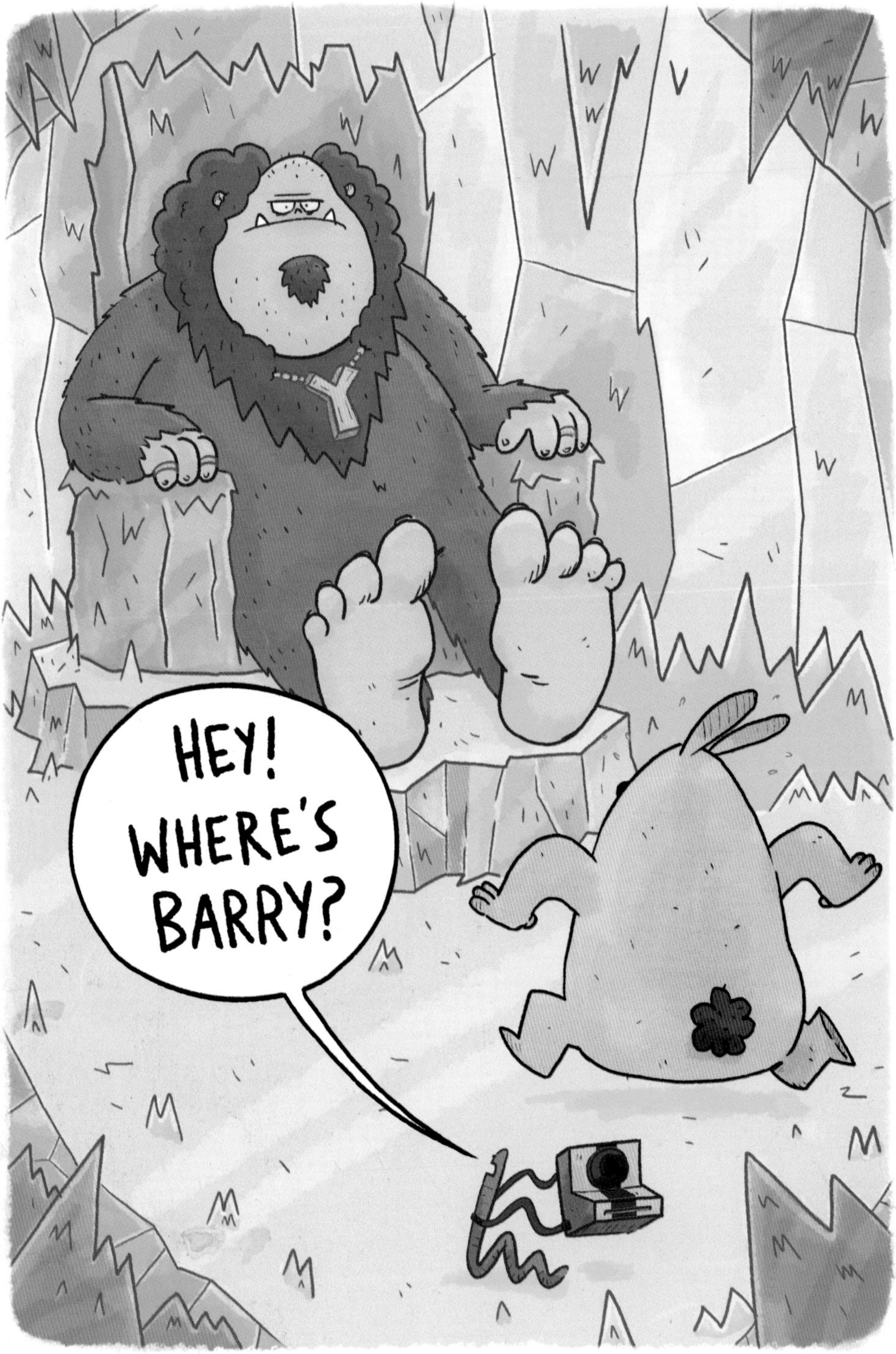
HEY! WHERE'S BARRY?

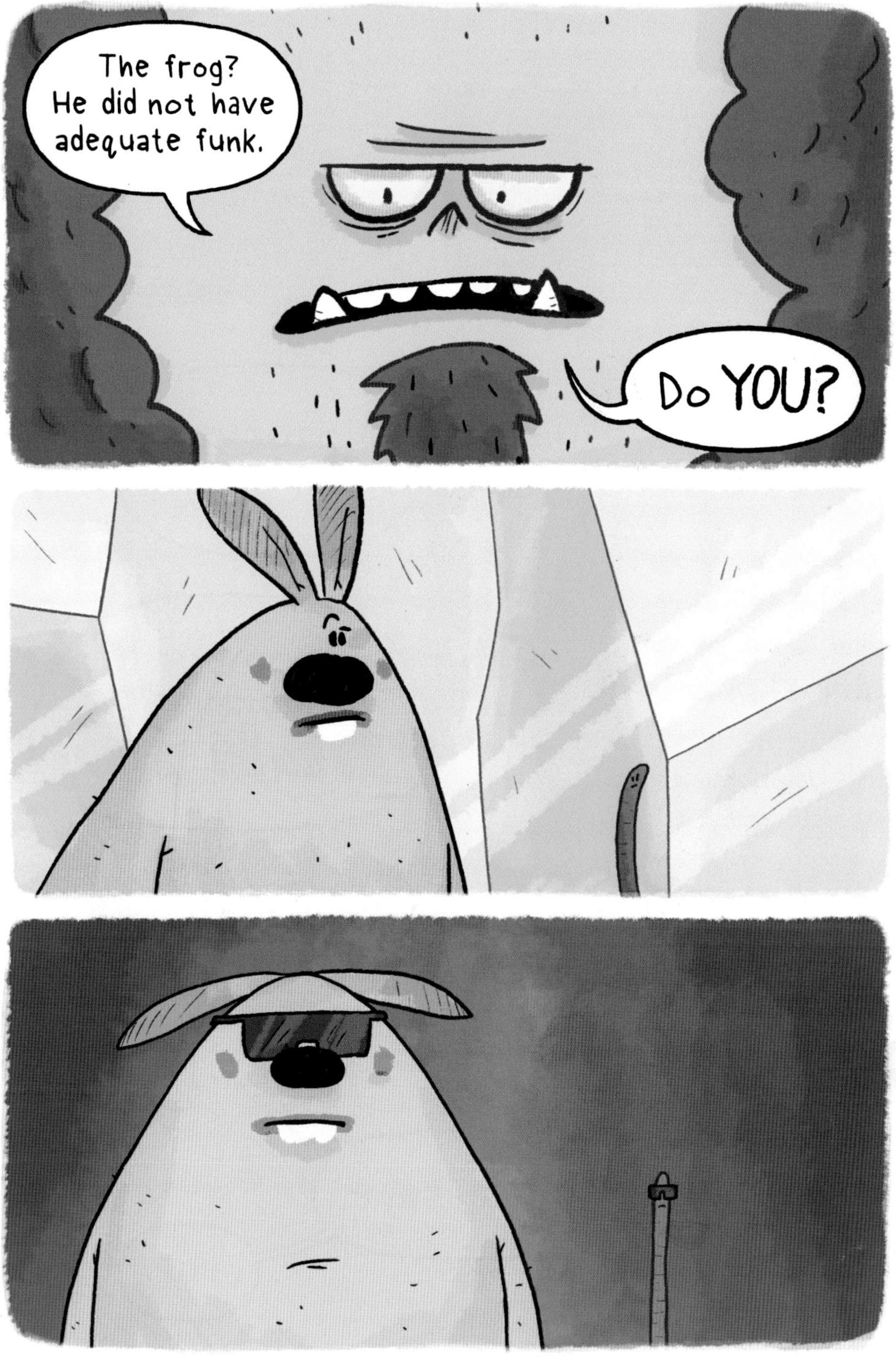
The frog? He did not have adequate funk.
Do YOU?

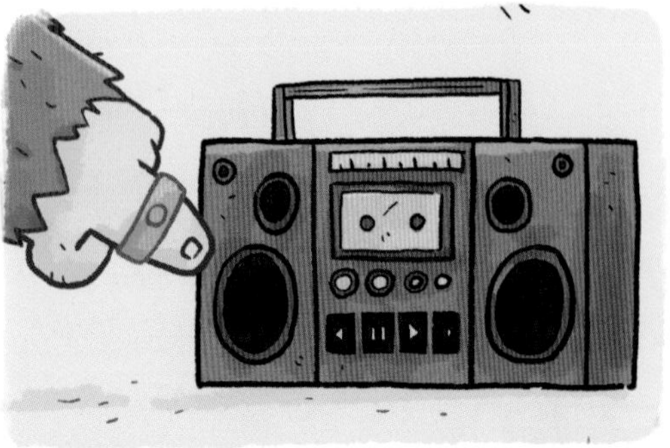

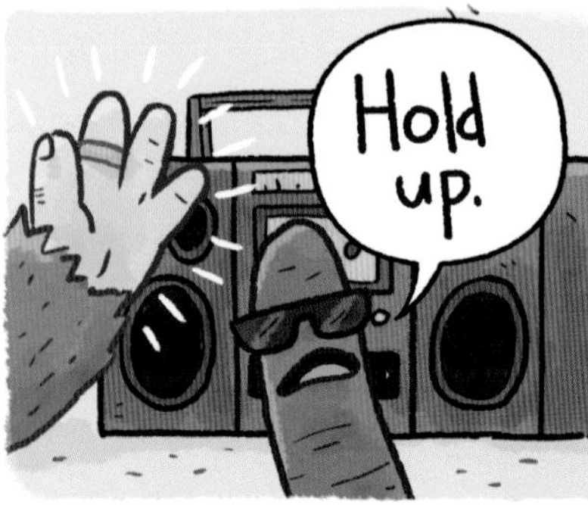
Hold up.

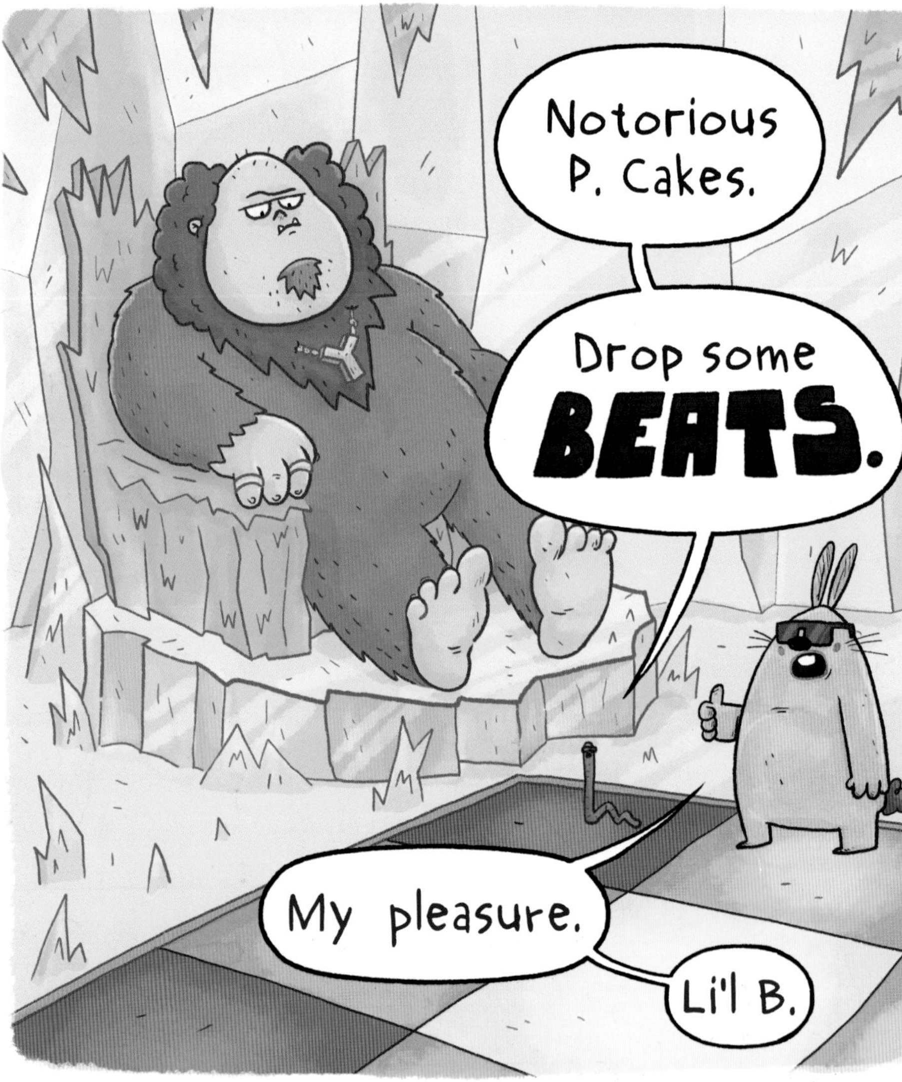
Notorious P. Cakes.
Drop some BEATS.
My pleasure.
Li'l B.

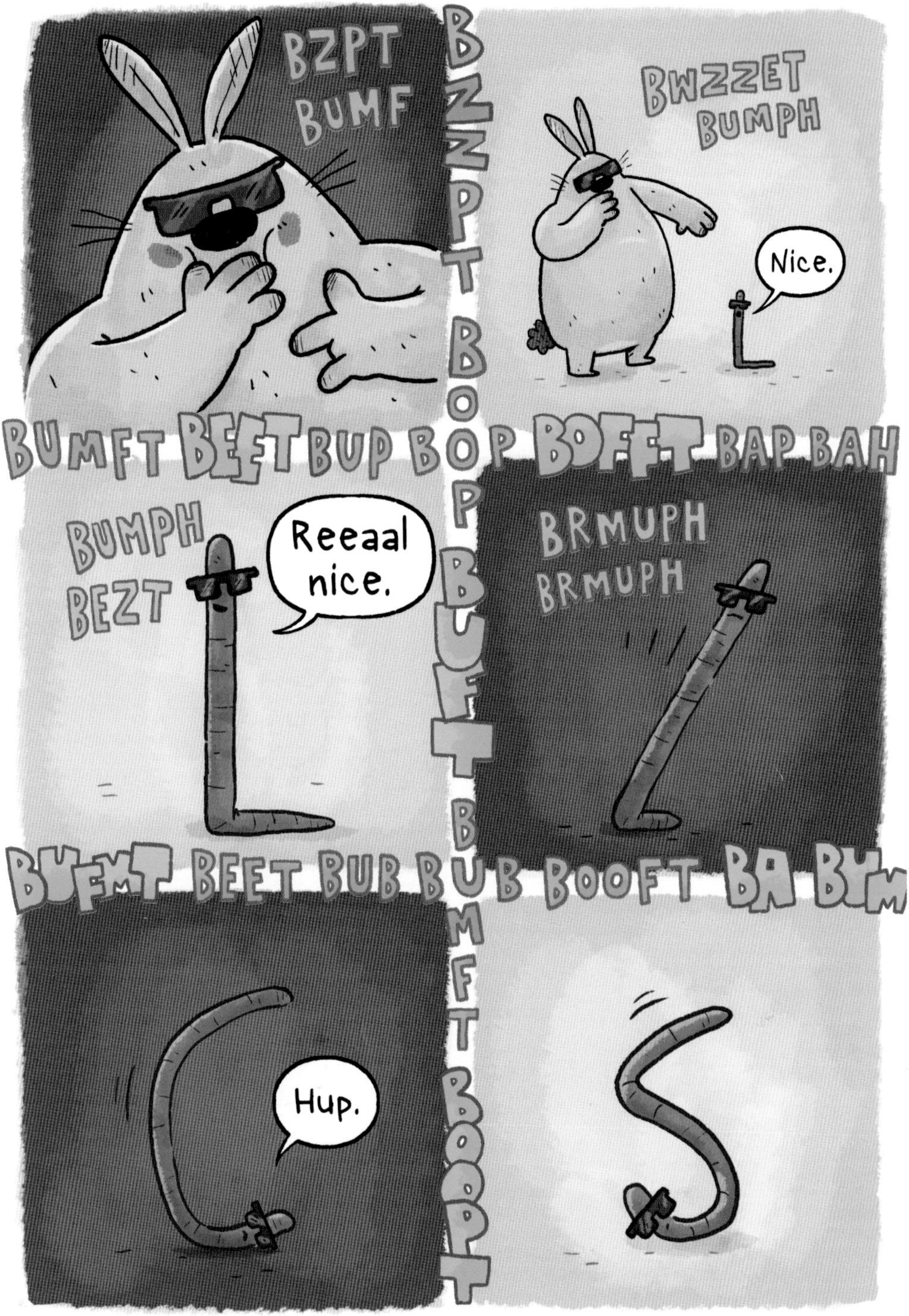
BZPT
BUMF
BZZPT
BOOP
BWZZET
BUMPH
Nice.
BUMFT BEET BUP BOP BOFFT BAP BAH
BUMPH
BEZT
Reeaal nice.
BUFT
BRMUPH
BRMUPH
BUFMT BEET BUB BUB BOOFT BA BUM
BUMFT
BOOPT
Hup.

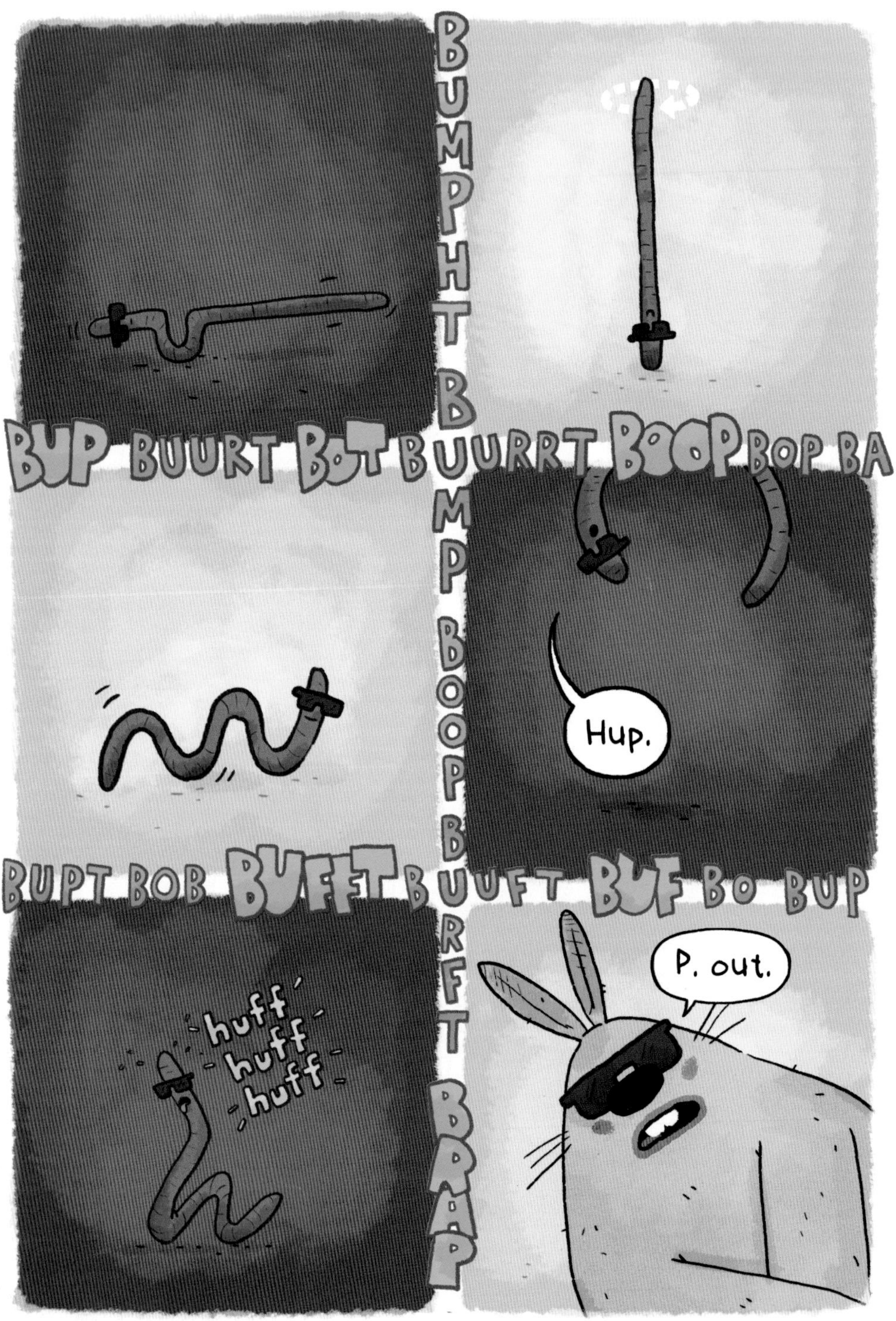
BUMPHHT
BUP BUURT BOT BUURRT BOOP BOP BA
BUMP
BOOP
Hup.
BUPT BOB BUFFT BUUFT BUF BO BUP
BURFT
huff huff huff
BRAP
P. out.

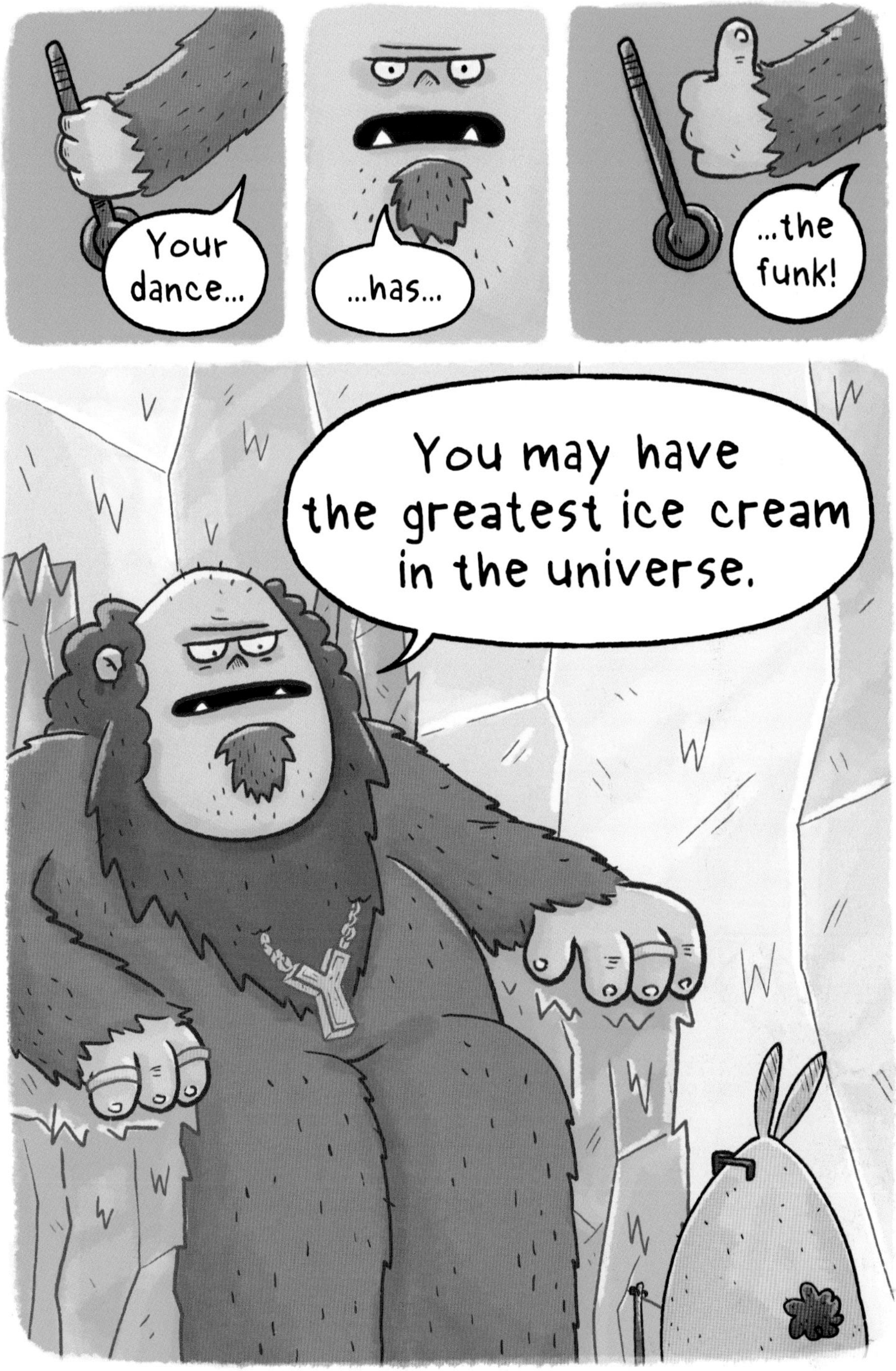
Your dance...
...has...
...the funk!
You may have the greatest ice cream in the universe.

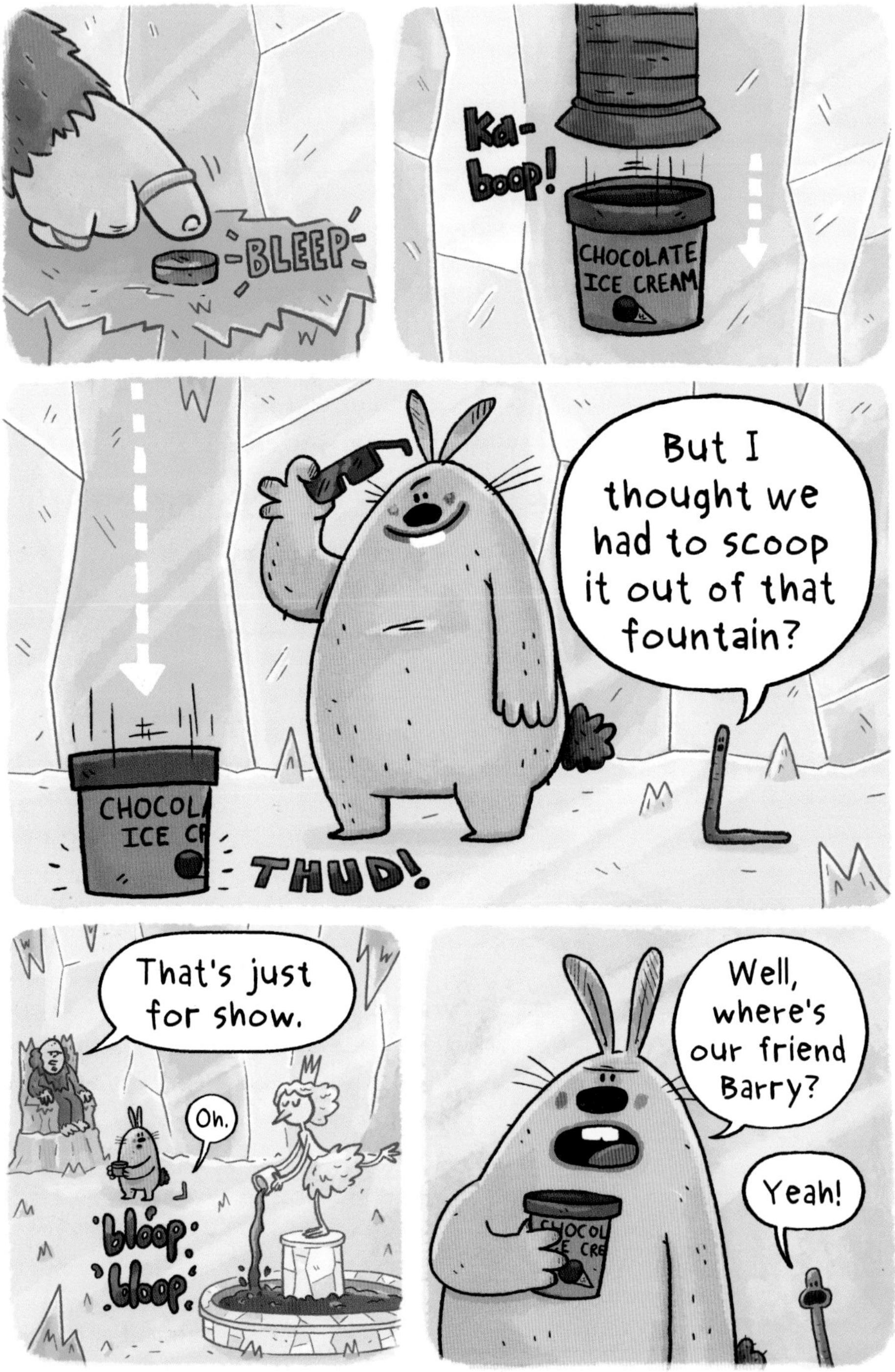
BLEEP
Ka-boop!
CHOCOLATE ICE CREAM
But I thought we had to scoop it out of that fountain?
CHOCOL ICE CR
THUD!
That's just for show.
Oh.
bloop bloop
Well, where's our friend Barry?
Yeah!

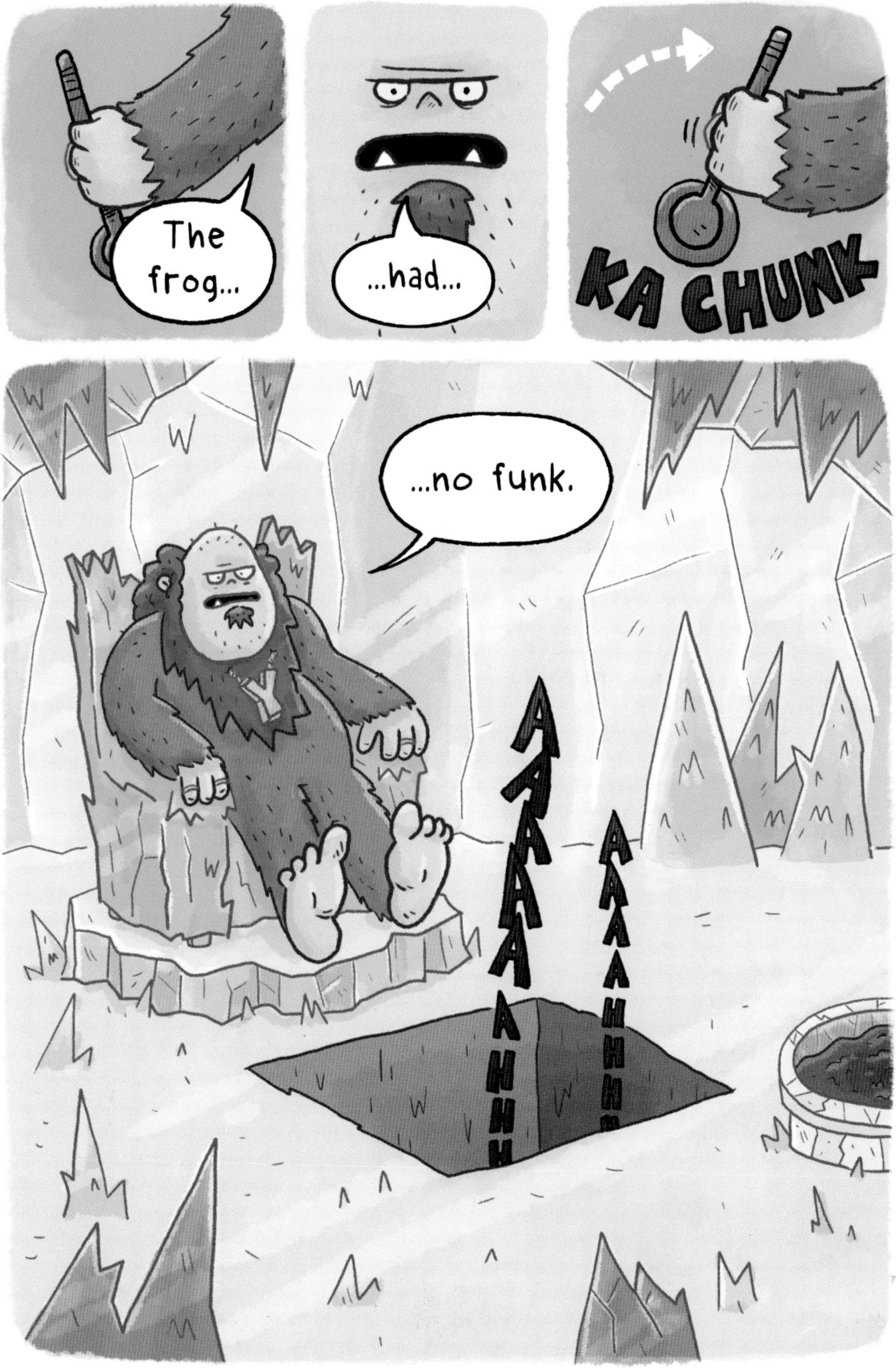
The frog...
...had...
KA CHUNK
...no funk.
AAAAAAAHHH
AAAAAAAHHHH

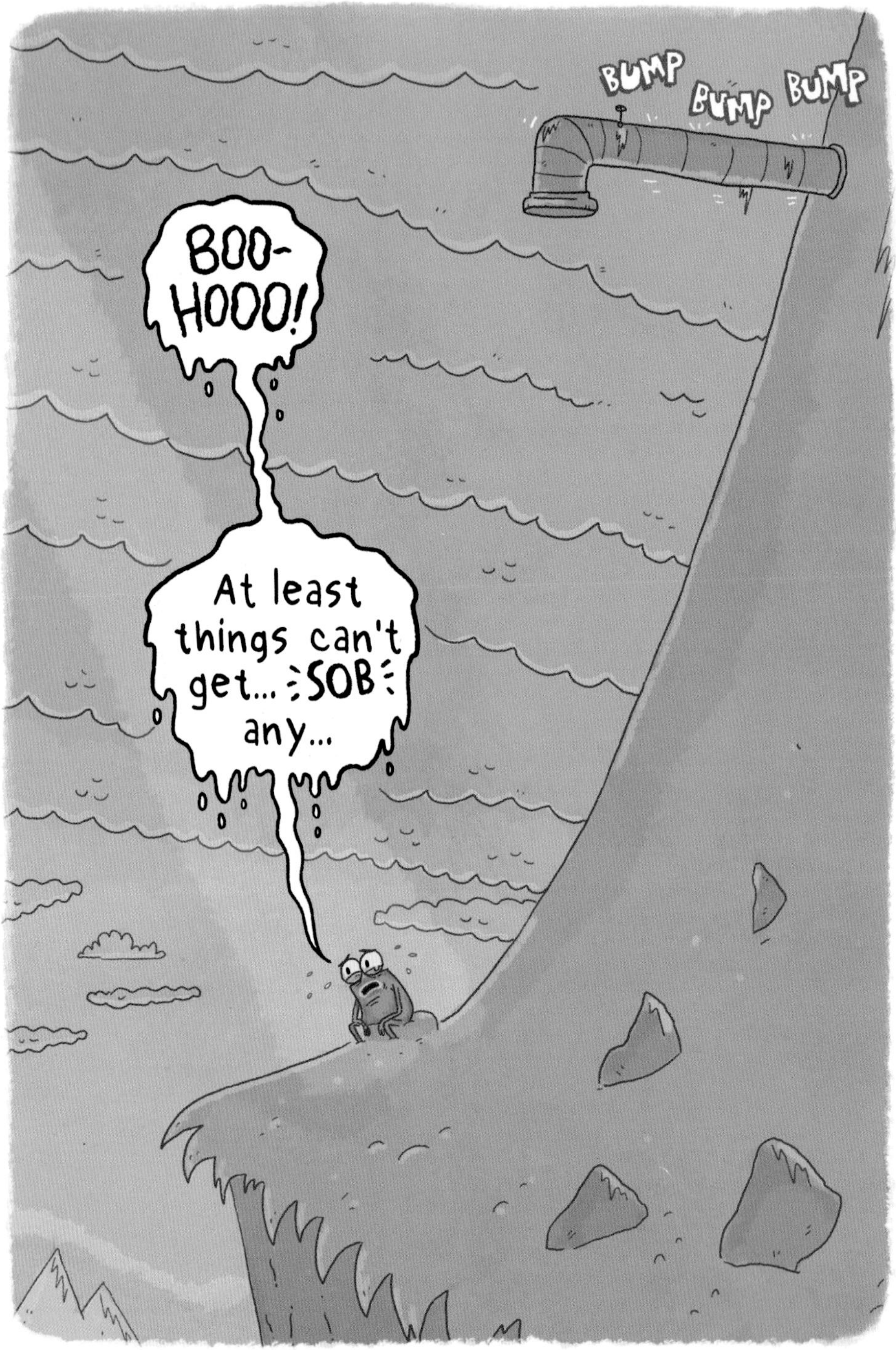
BUMP
BUMP BUMP
BOO-HOOO!
At least things can't get... SOB any...

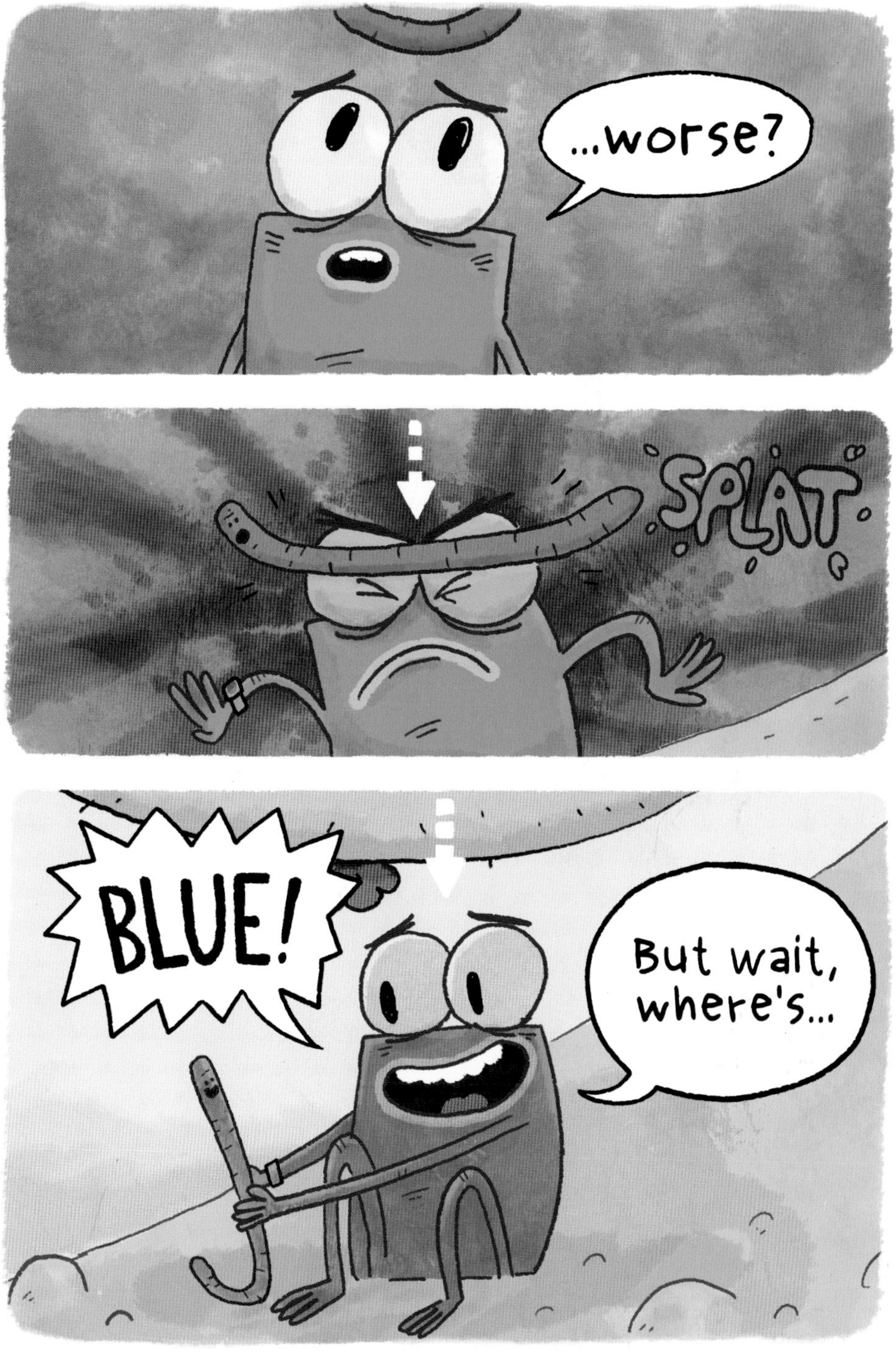
...worse?
SPLAT
BLUE!
But wait, where's...

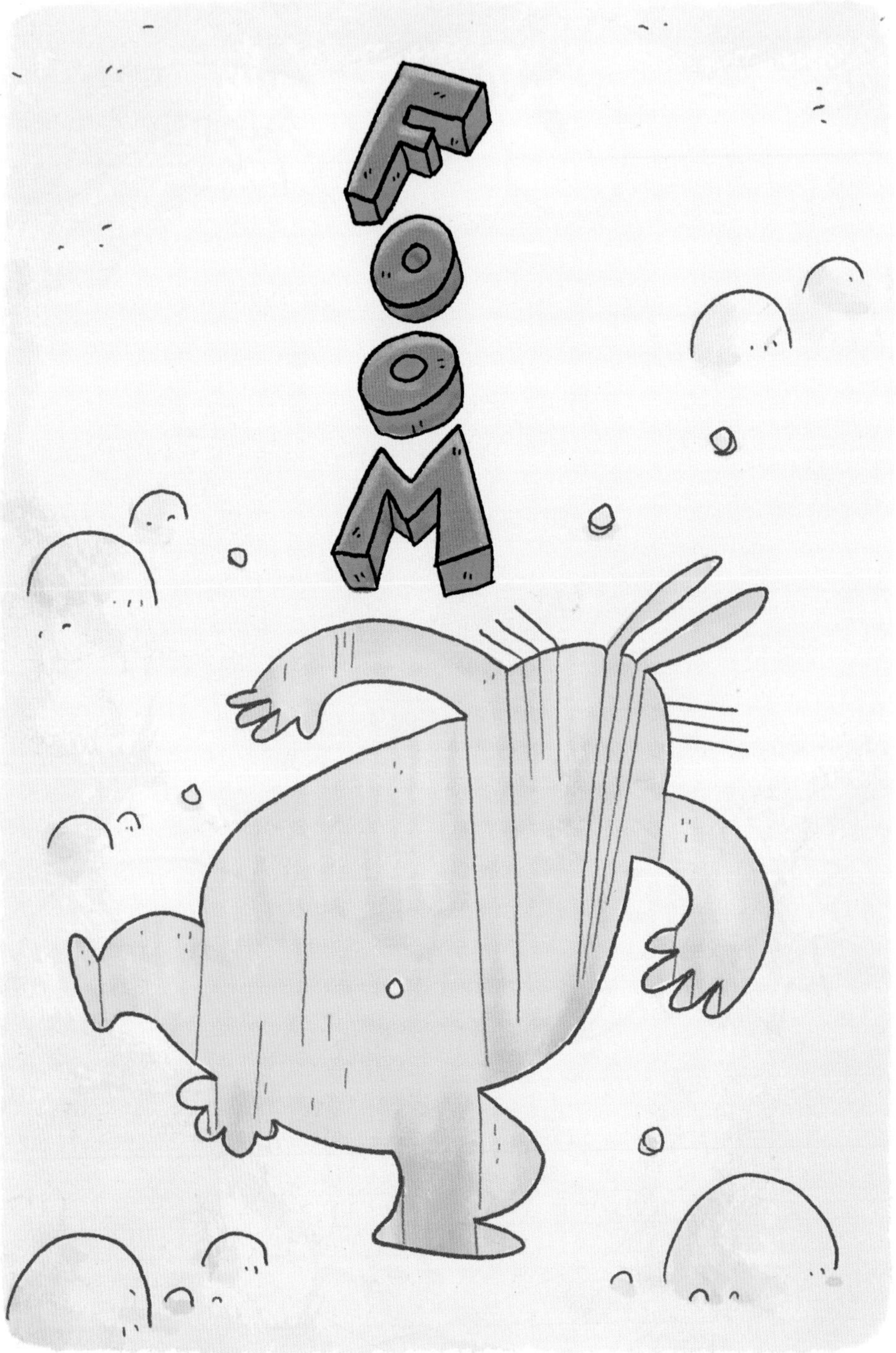
FOOM

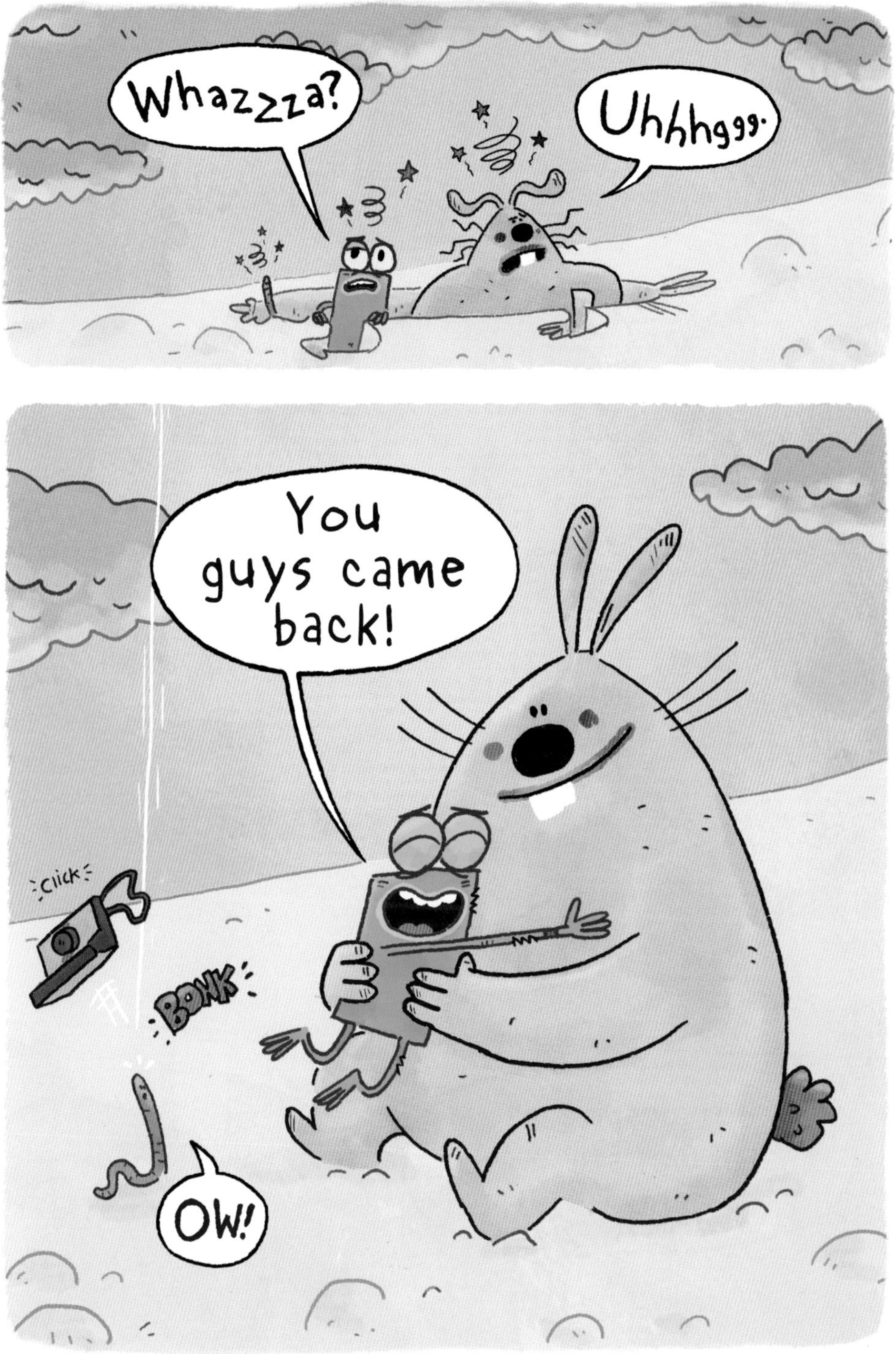
Whazzza?
Uhhhggg.
You guys came back!
CLICK
BONK
OW!

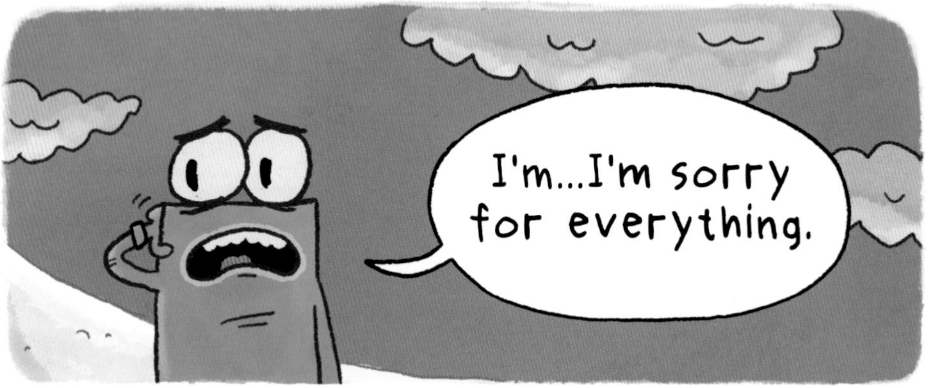
I'm...I'm sorry for everything.

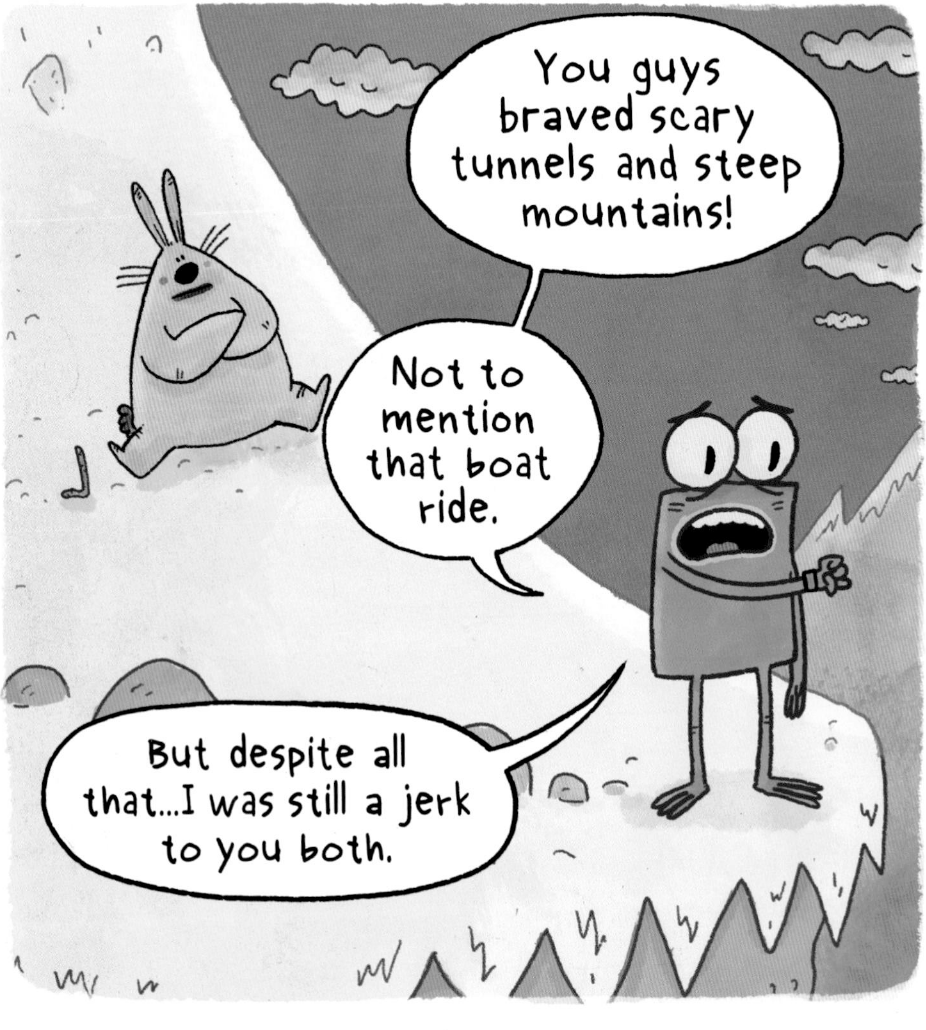
You guys braved scary tunnels and steep mountains!
Not to mention that boat ride.
But despite all that...I was still a jerk to you both.

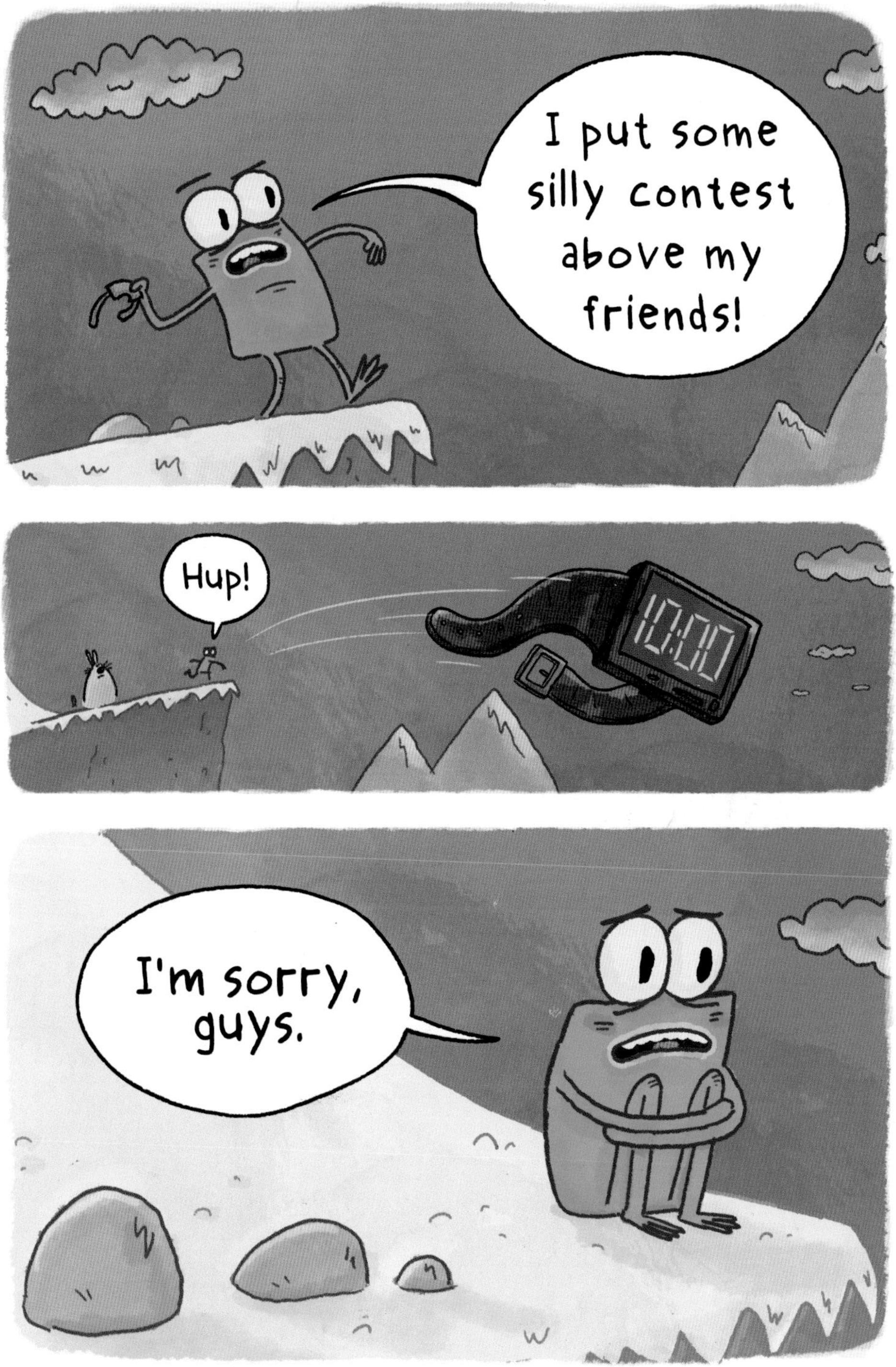
I put some silly contest above my friends!
Hup!
10:00
I'm sorry, guys.

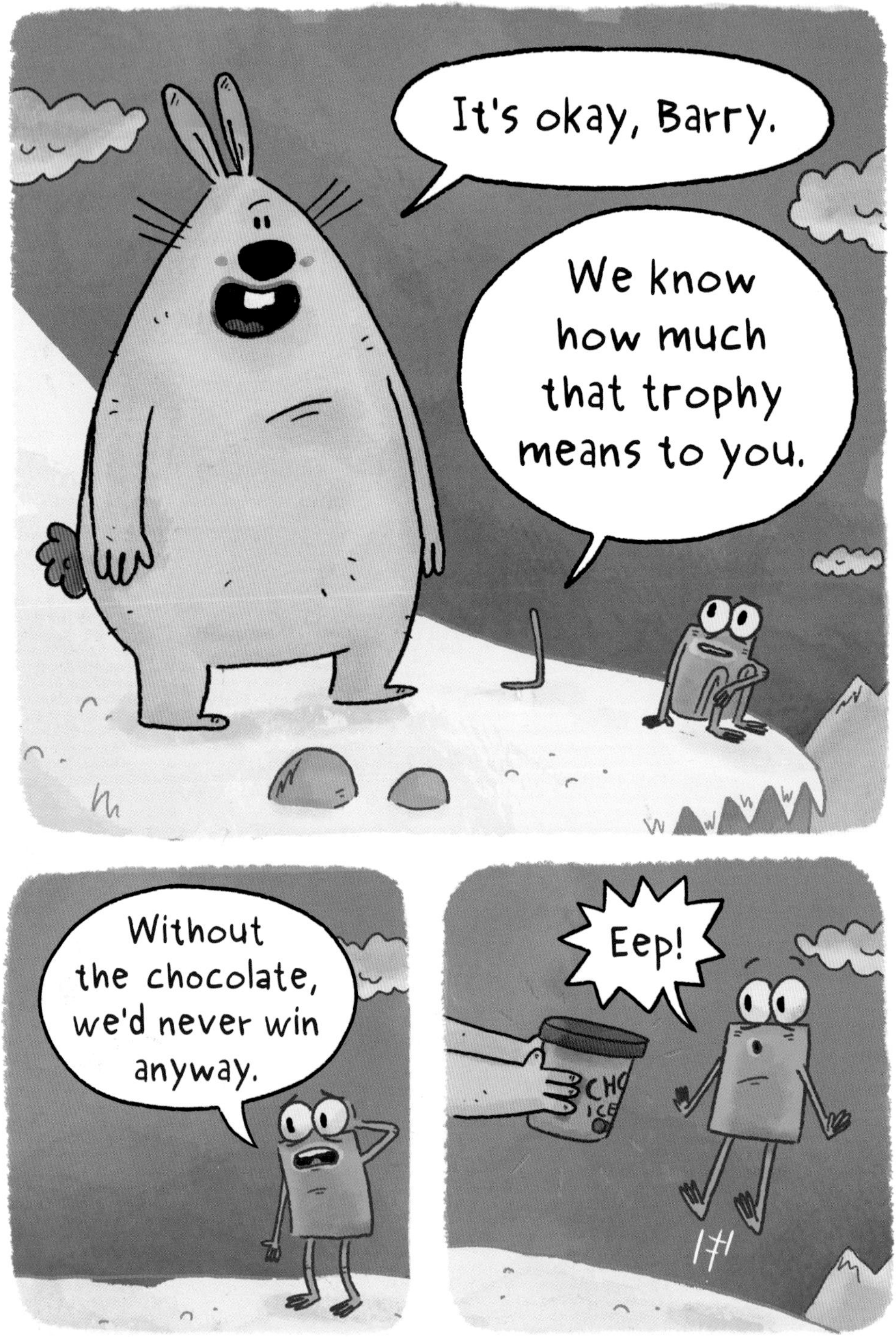
It's okay, Barry.
We know how much that trophy means to you.
Without the chocolate, we'd never win anyway.
Eep!
CHO ICE

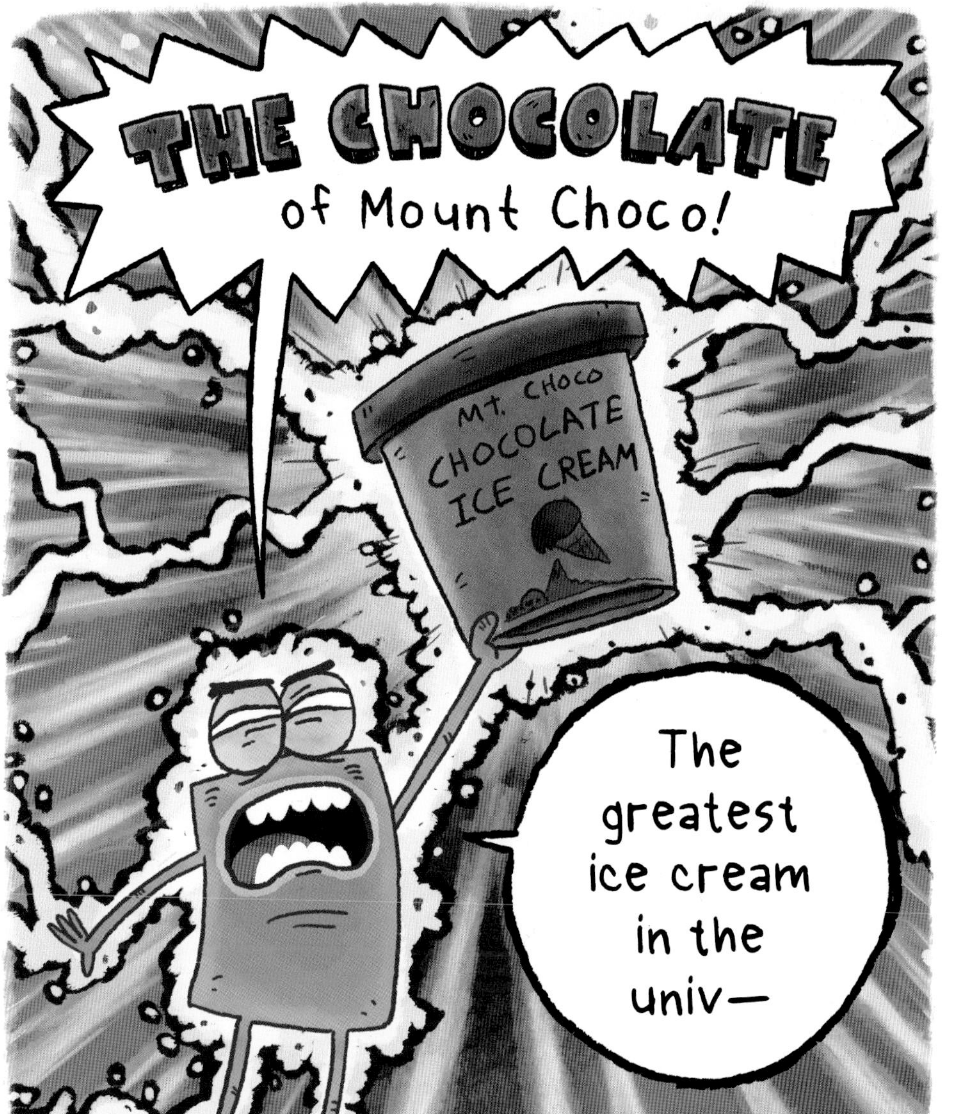
THE CHOCOLATE of Mount Choco!
MT. CHOCO CHOCOLATE ICE CREAM
The greatest ice cream in the univ—
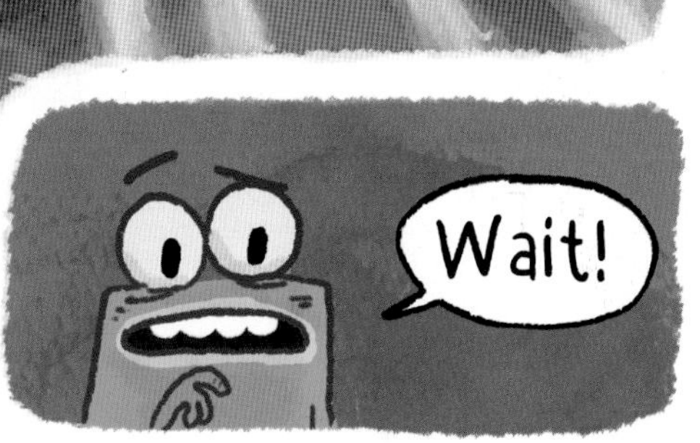
Wait!

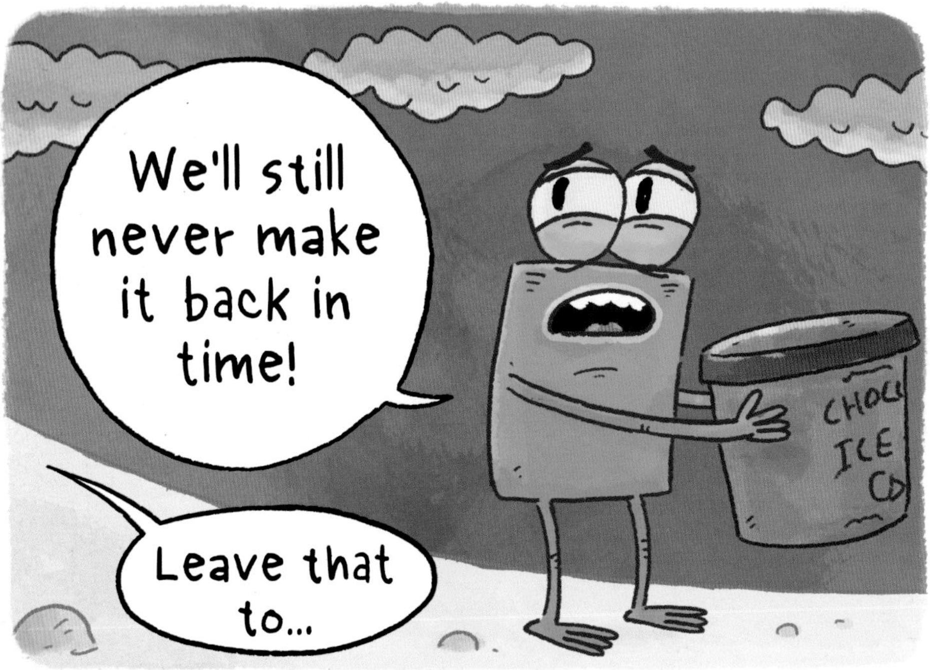
We'll still never make it back in time!
Leave that to...
CHOC ICE C

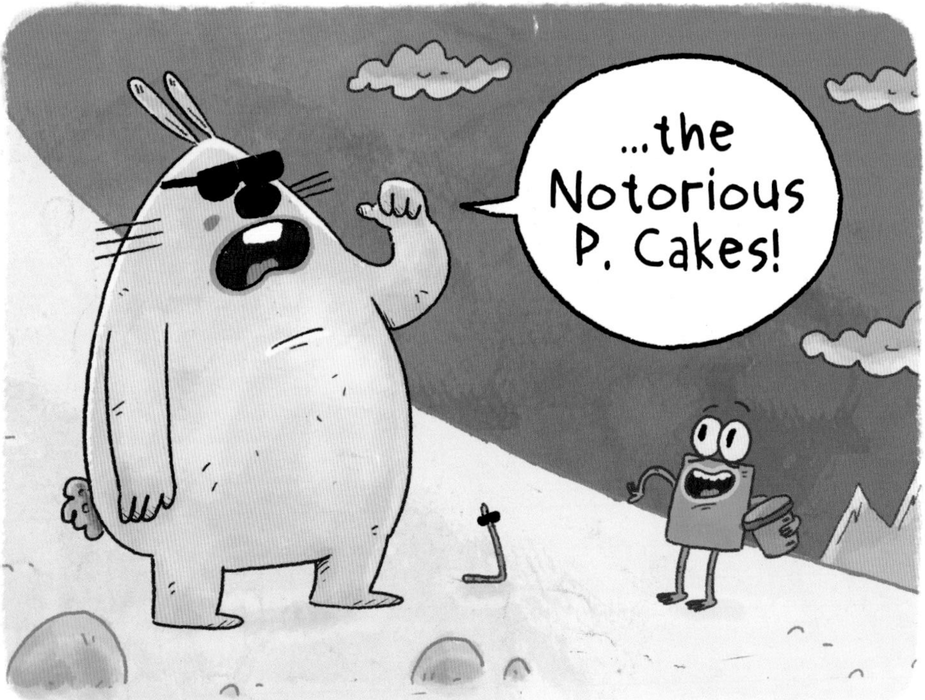
...the Notorious P. Cakes!

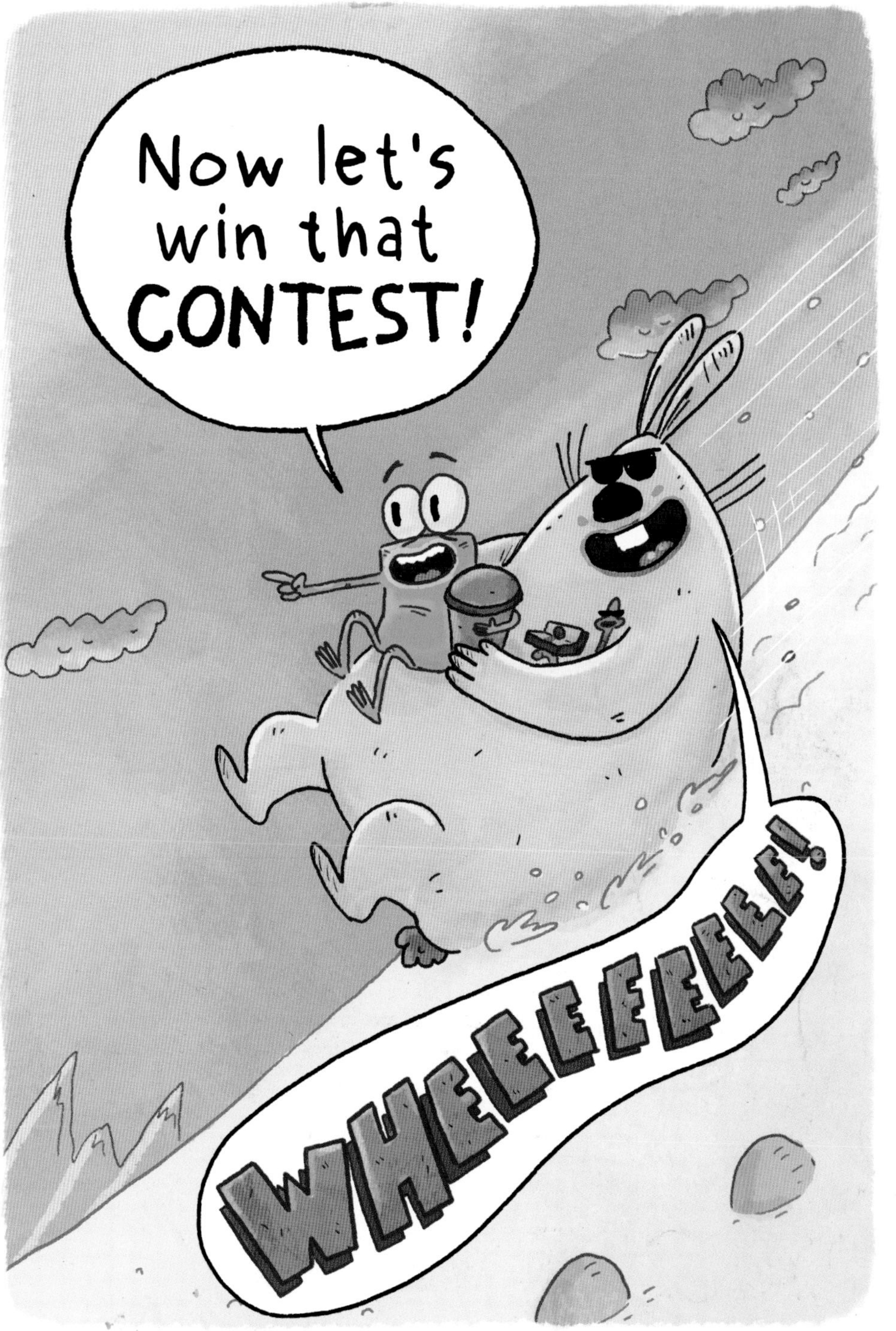
Now let's win that CONTEST!
WHEEEEEEEE!

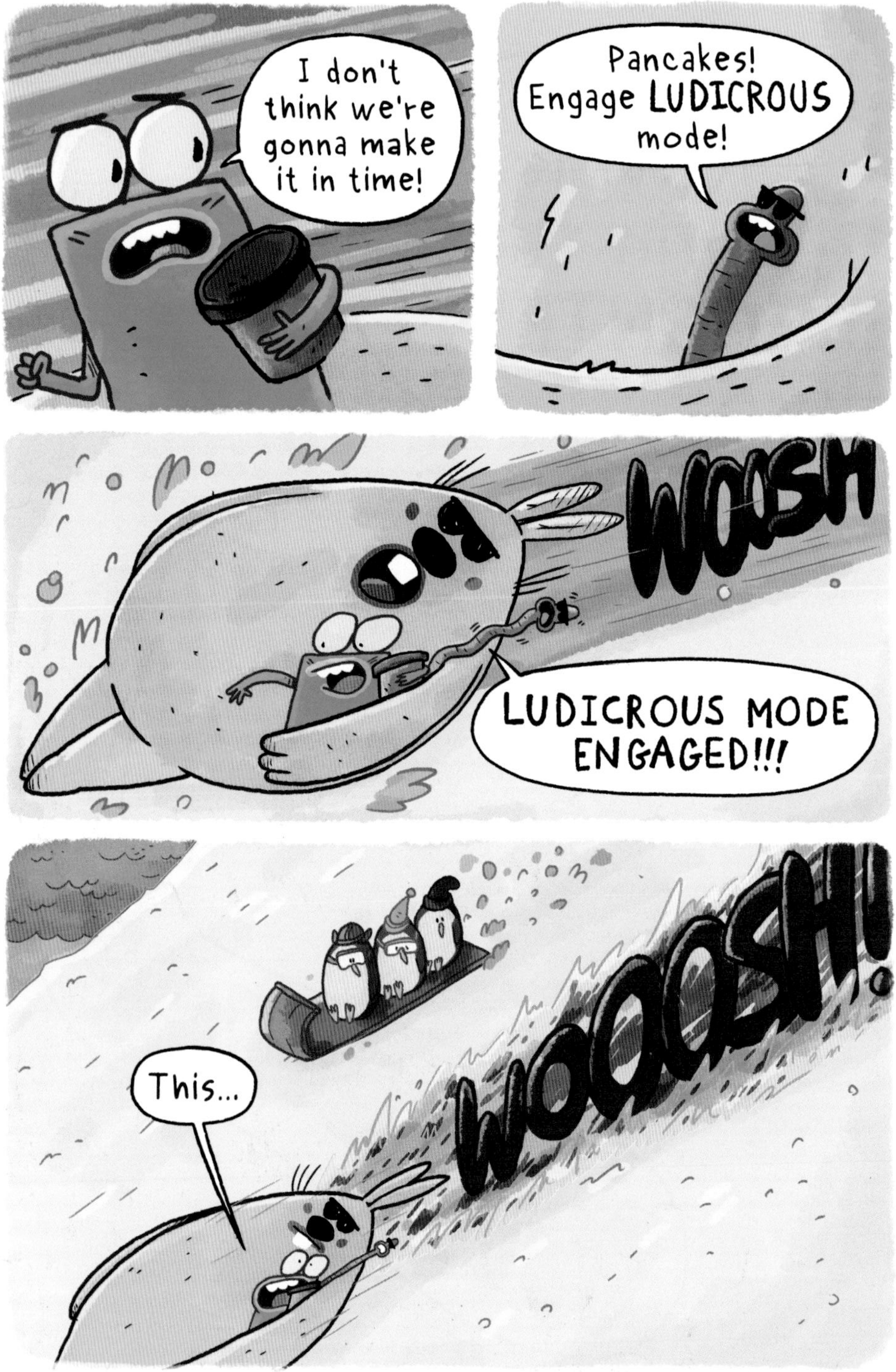

I don't think we're gonna make it in time!
Pancakes! Engage LUDICROUS mode!
WOOSH
LUDICROUS MODE ENGAGED!!!
WOOOSH!
This...

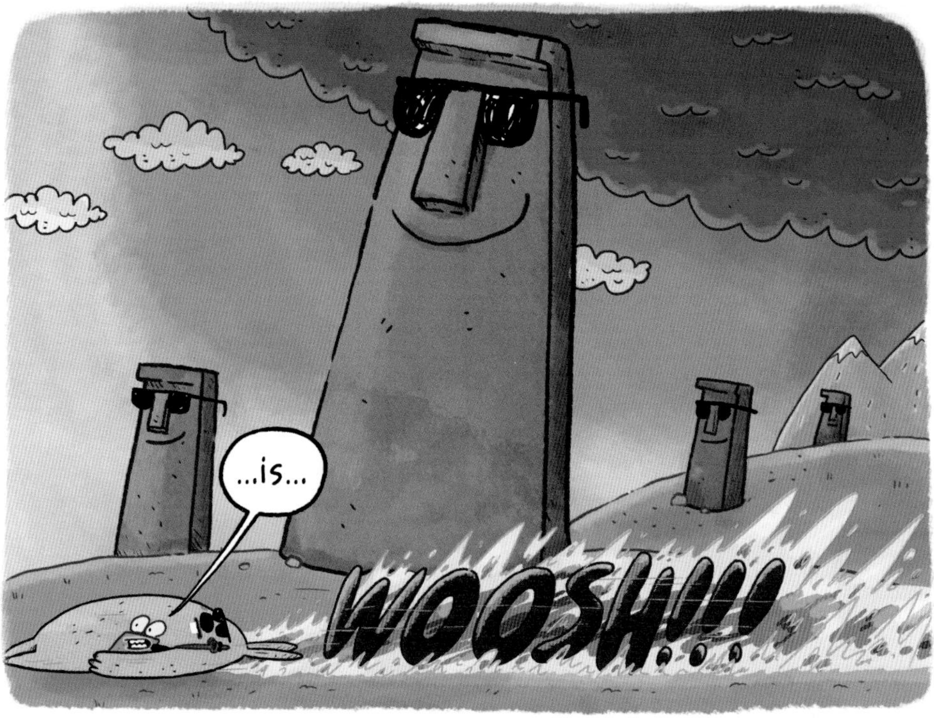
...is...
WOOSH!!!

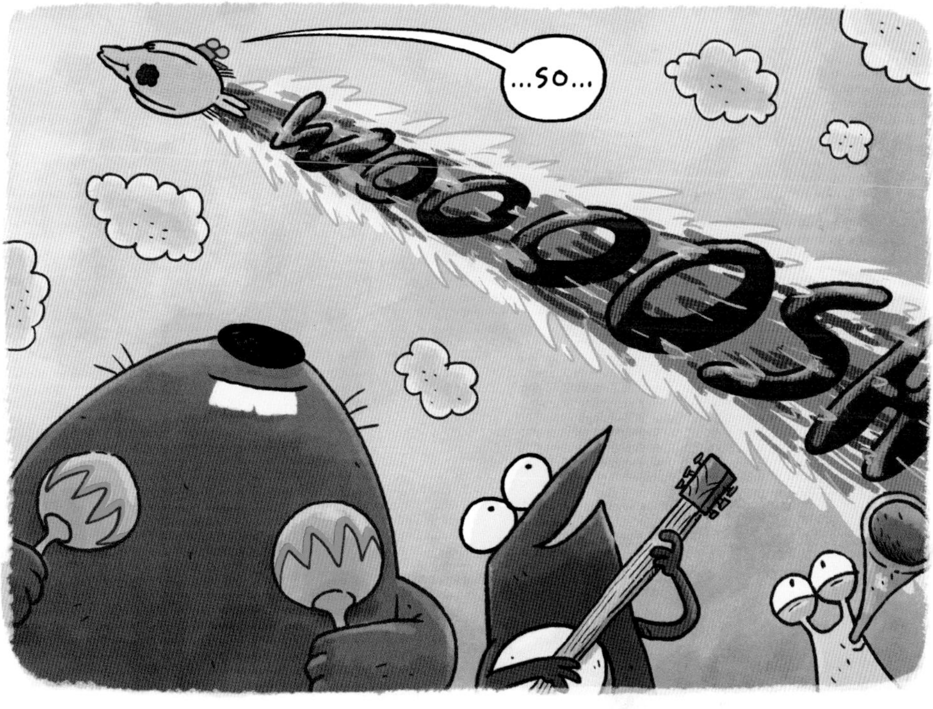
...so...
WOOOOOSH

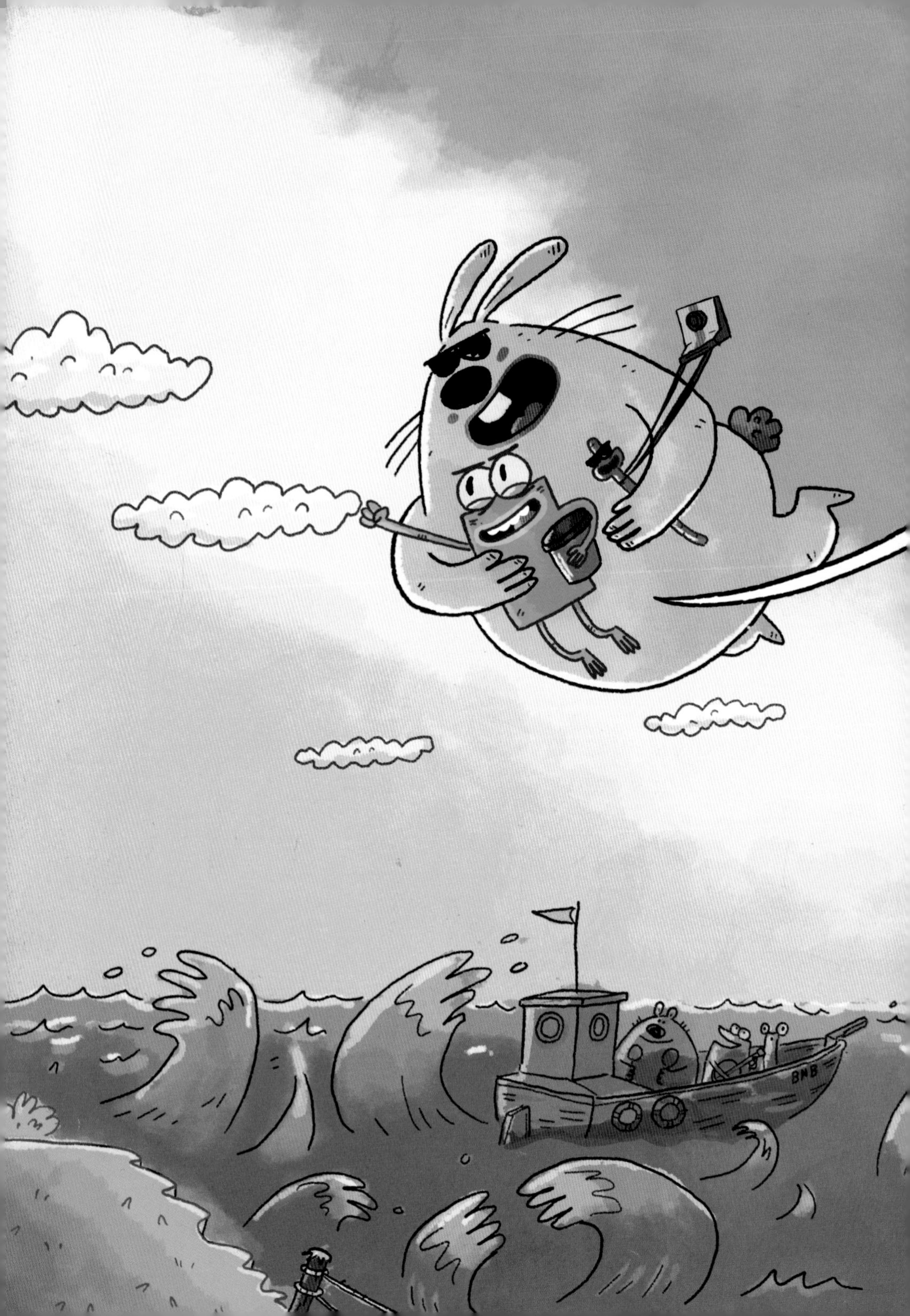
BNB

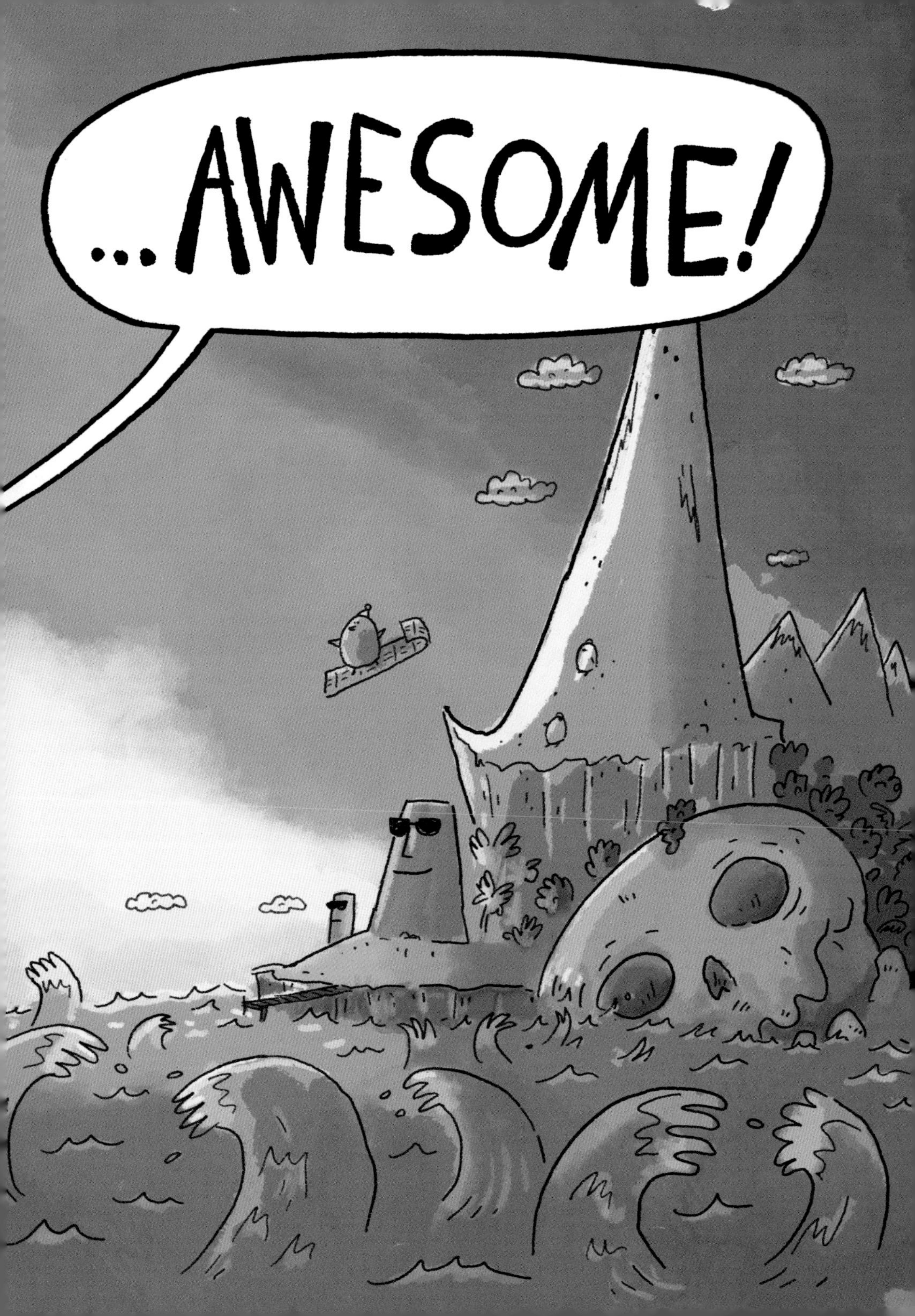
...AWESOME!

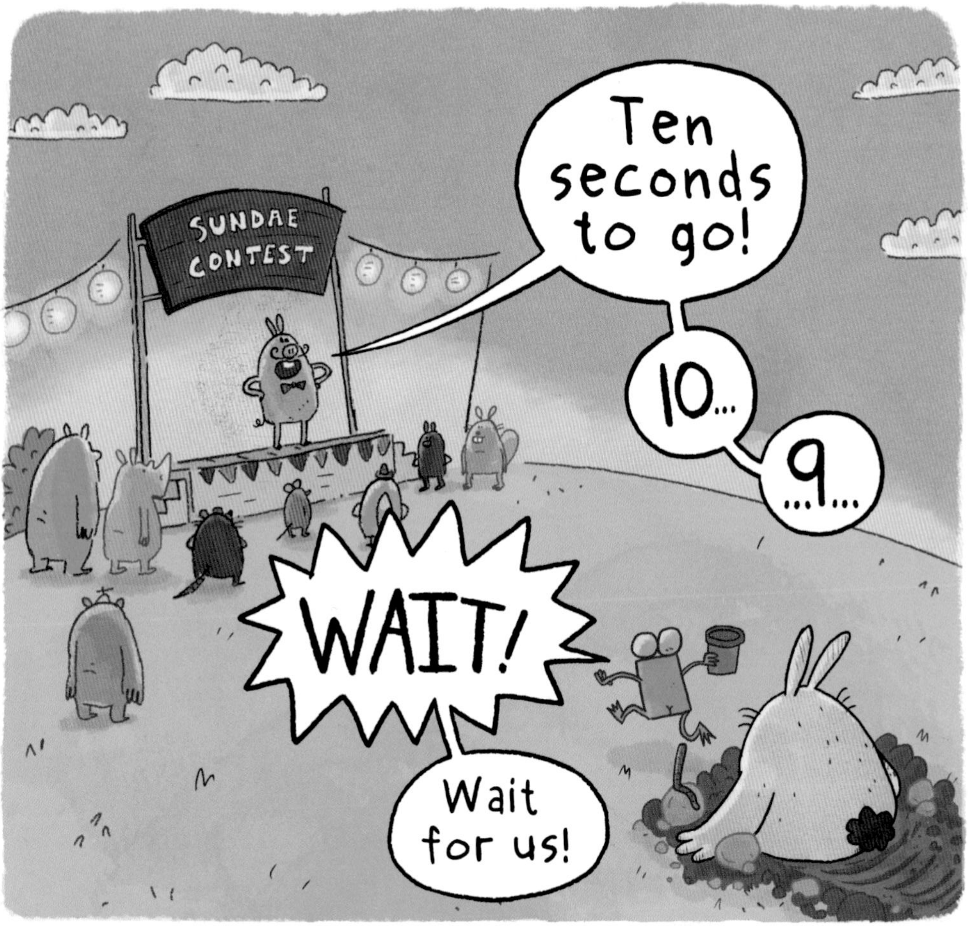
SUNDAE CONTEST
Ten seconds to go!
10...
...9...
WAIT!
Wait for us!

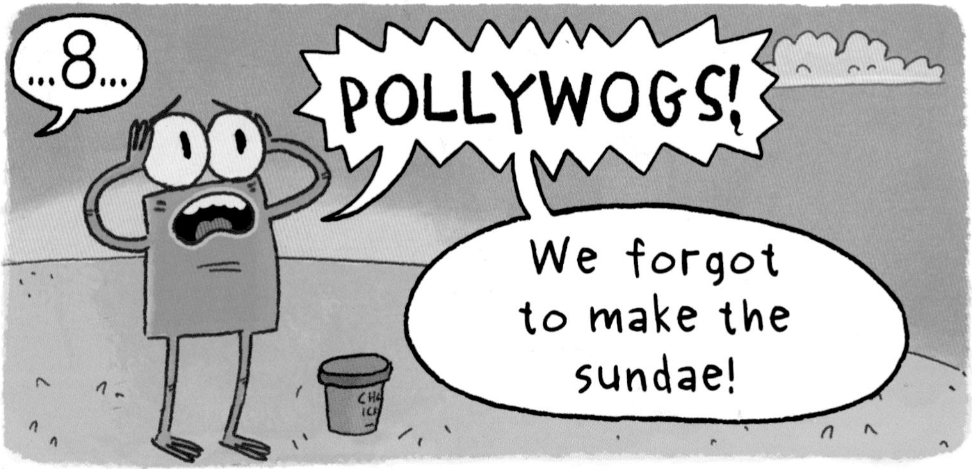
...8...
POLLYWOGS!
We forgot to make the sundae!

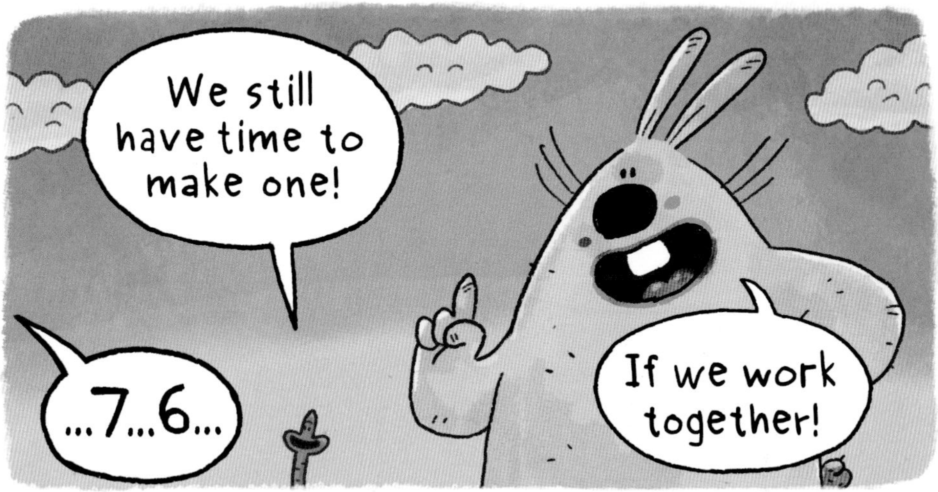
We still have time to make one!
...7...6...
If we work together!

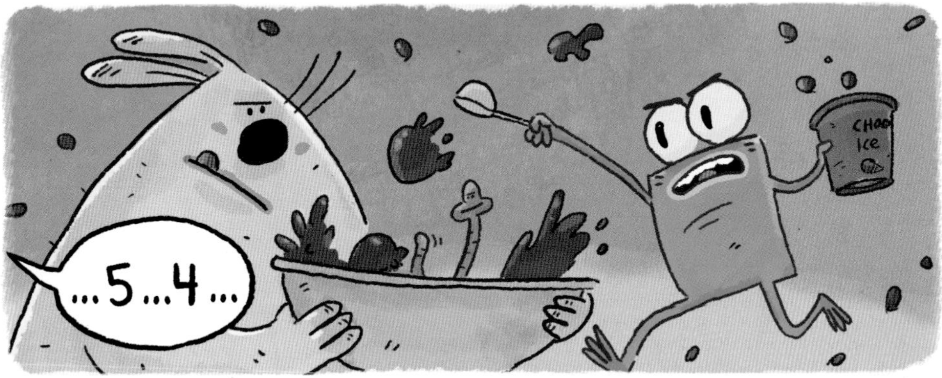
...5...4...

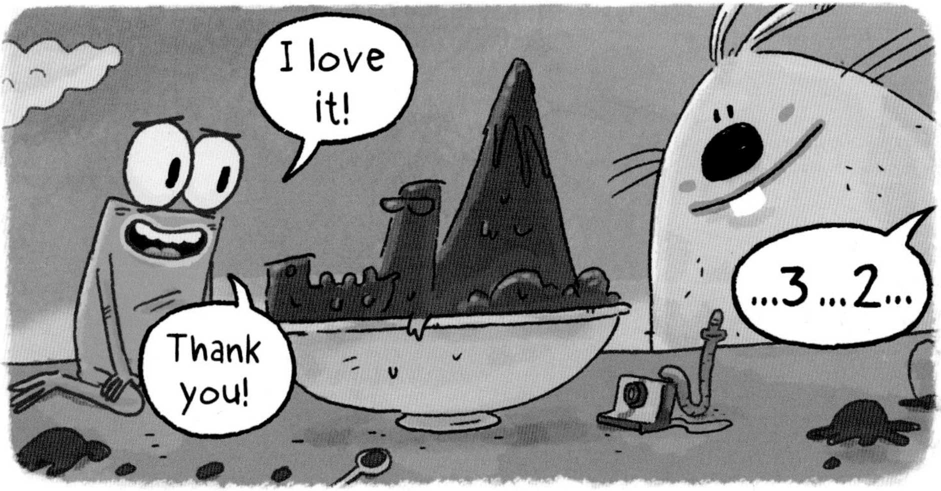
I love it!
Thank you!
...3...2...

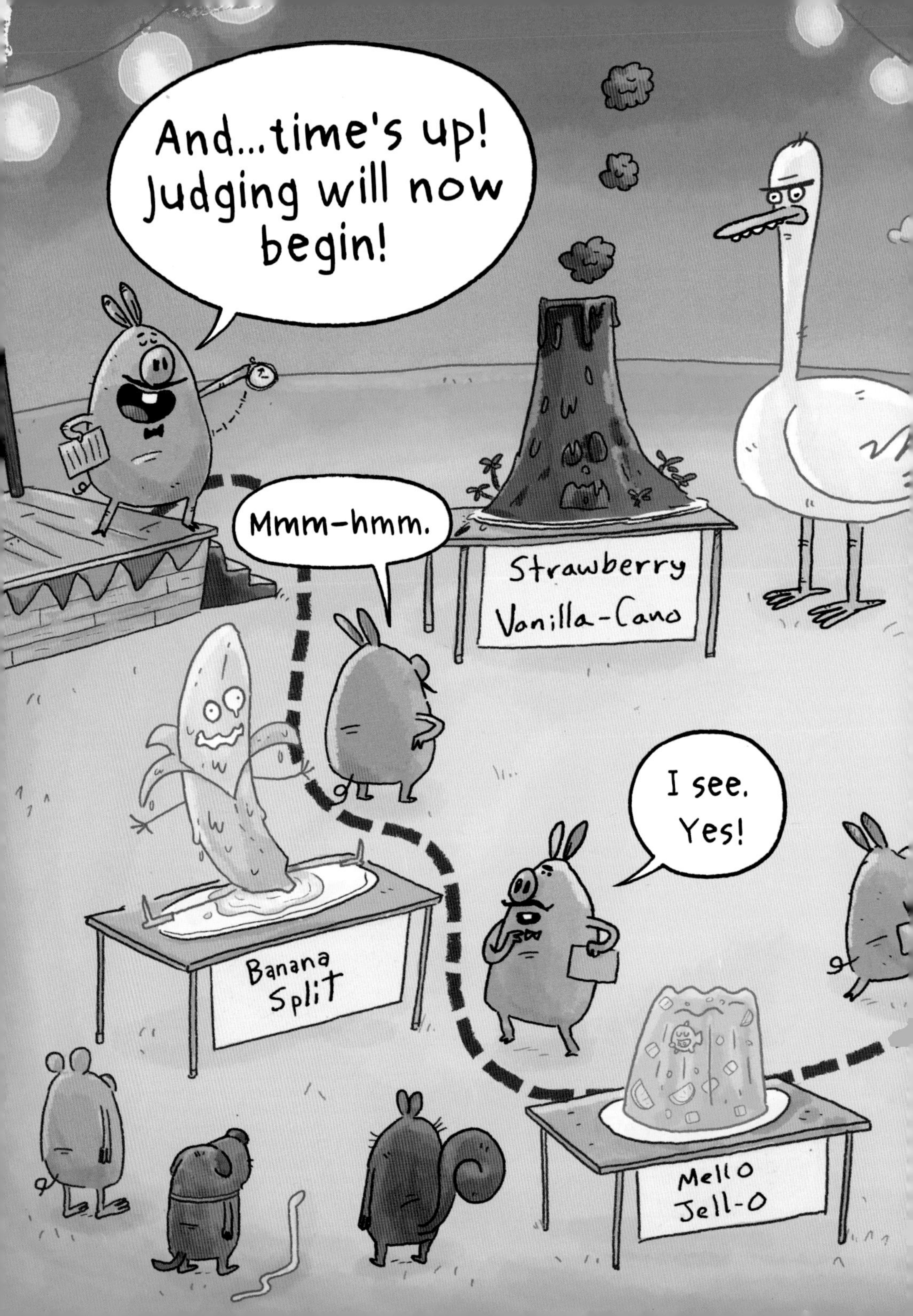
And...time's up! Judging will now begin!
Mmm-hmm.
Strawberry Vanilla-Cano
Banana Split
I see. Yes!
Mell O Jell-O

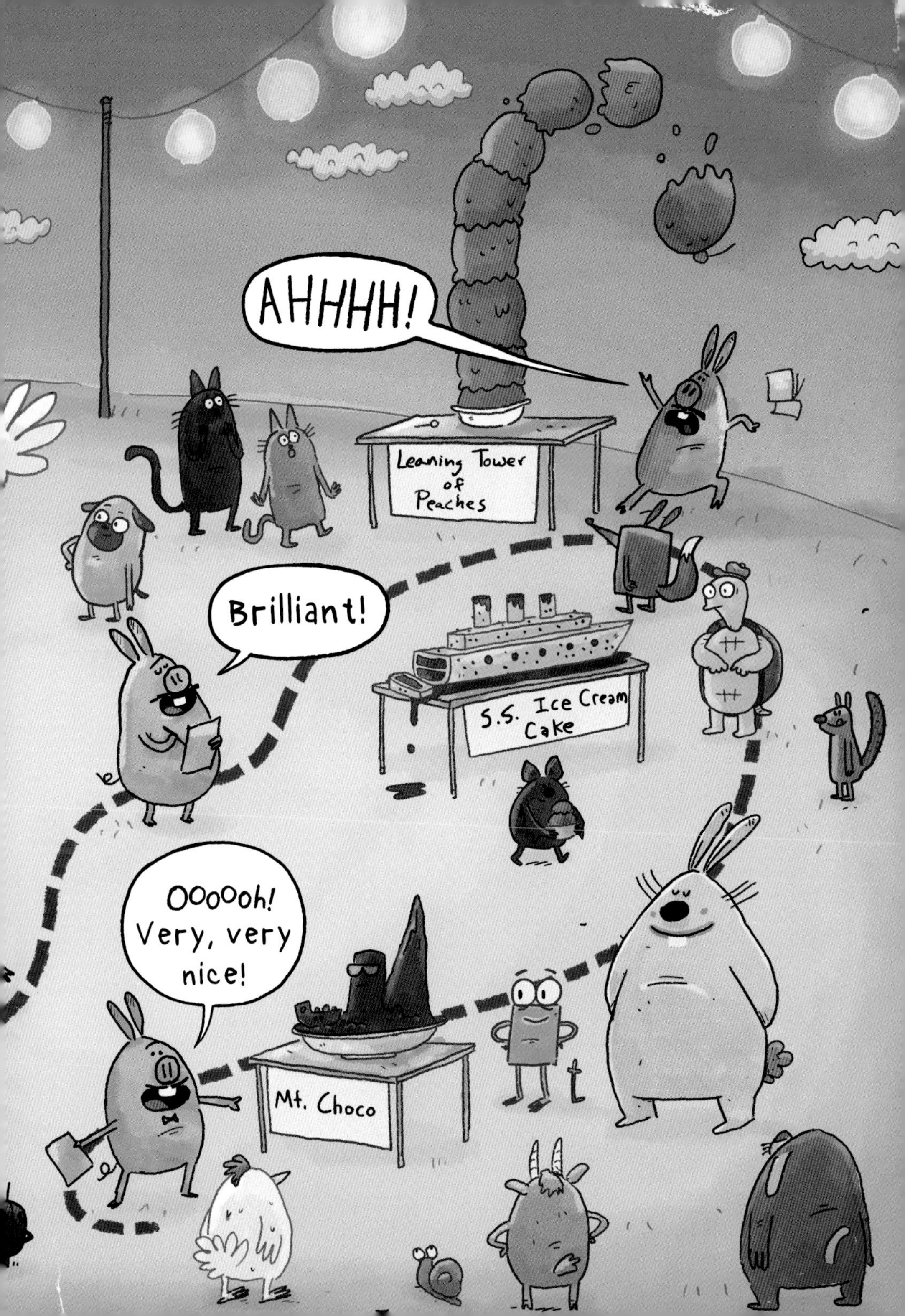
AHHHH!
Leaning Tower of Peaches
Brilliant!
S.S. Ice Cream Cake
Ooooooh! Very, very nice!
Mt. Choco

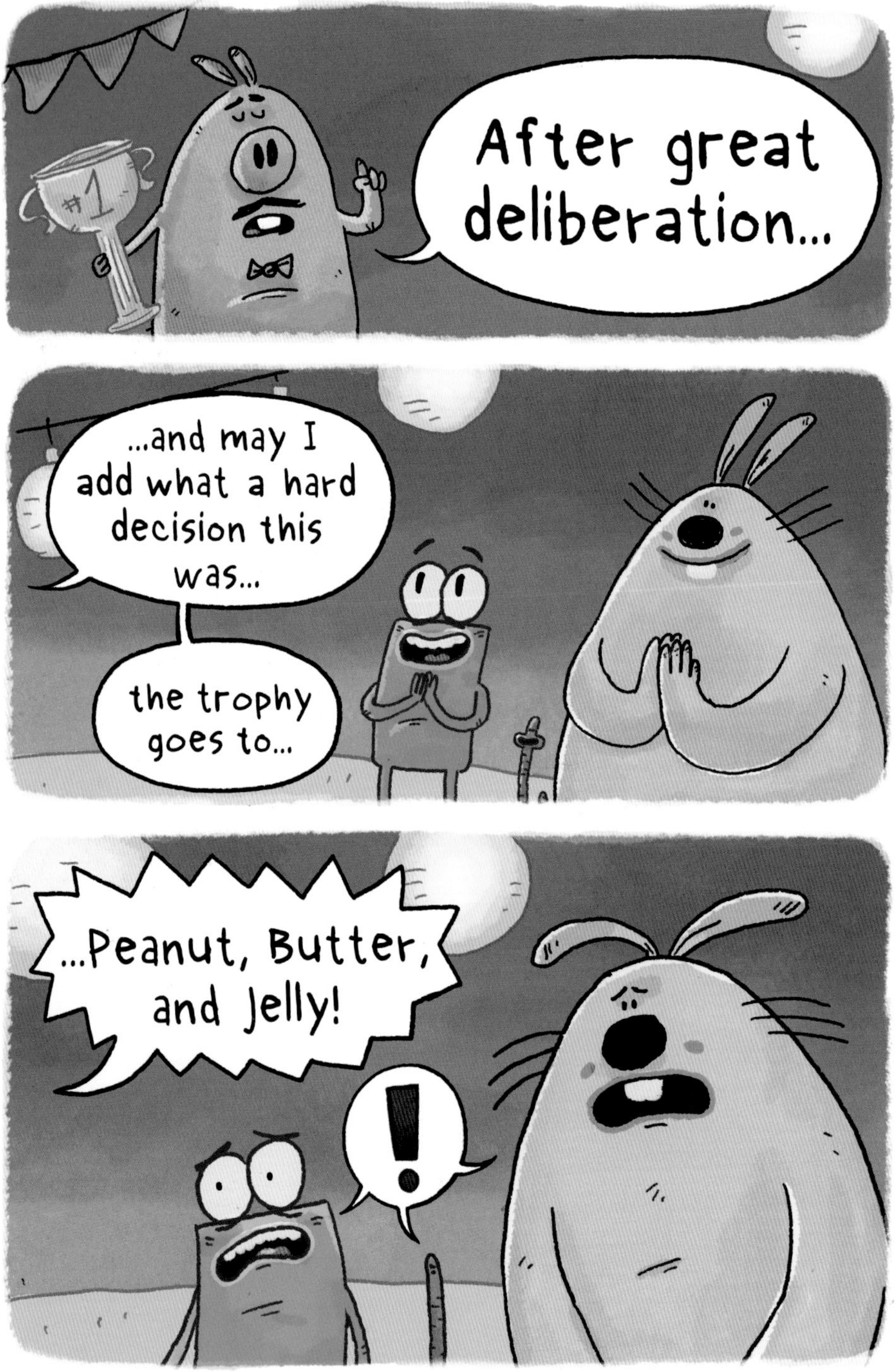
After great deliberation...
...and may I add what a hard decision this was...
the trophy goes to...
...Peanut, Butter, and Jelly!
!

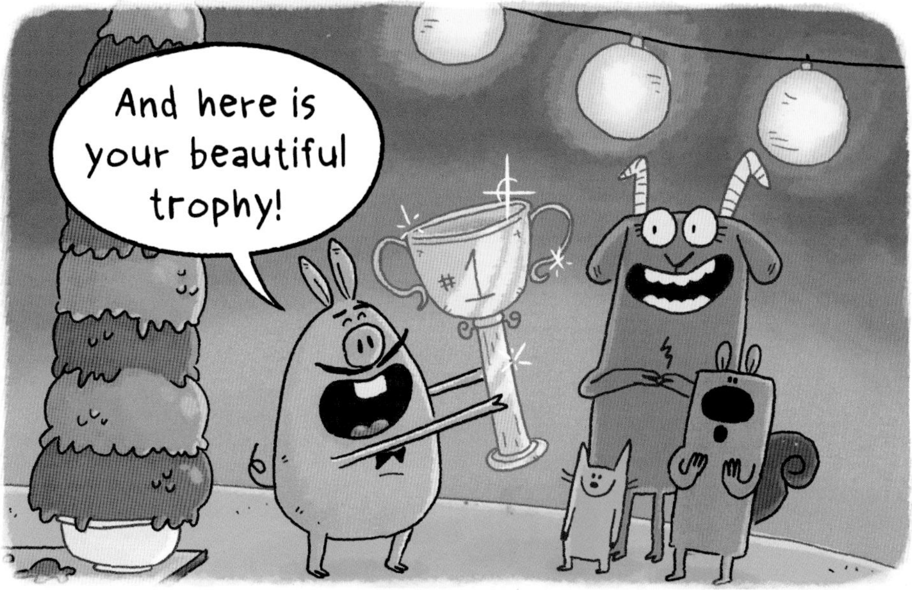
And here is your beautiful trophy!
#1

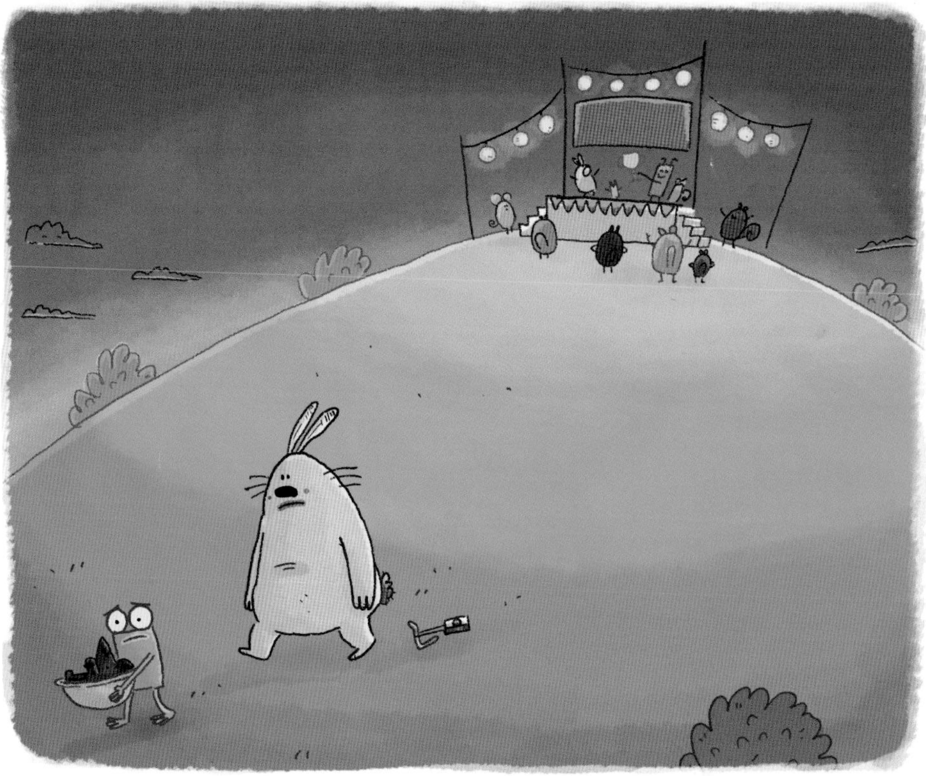

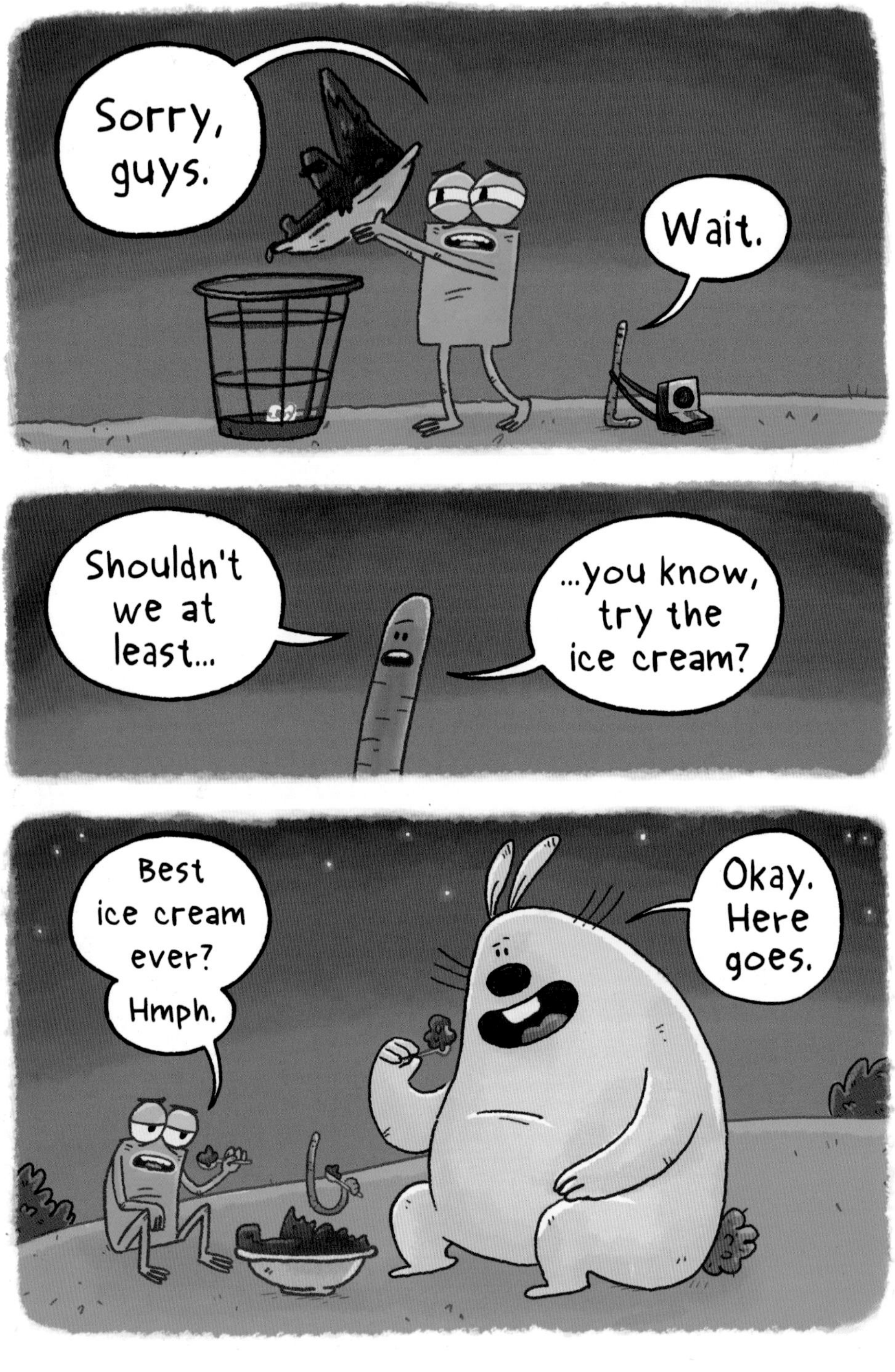
Sorry, guys.
Wait.
Shouldn't we at least...
...you know, try the ice cream?
Best ice cream ever?
Hmph.
Okay. Here goes.

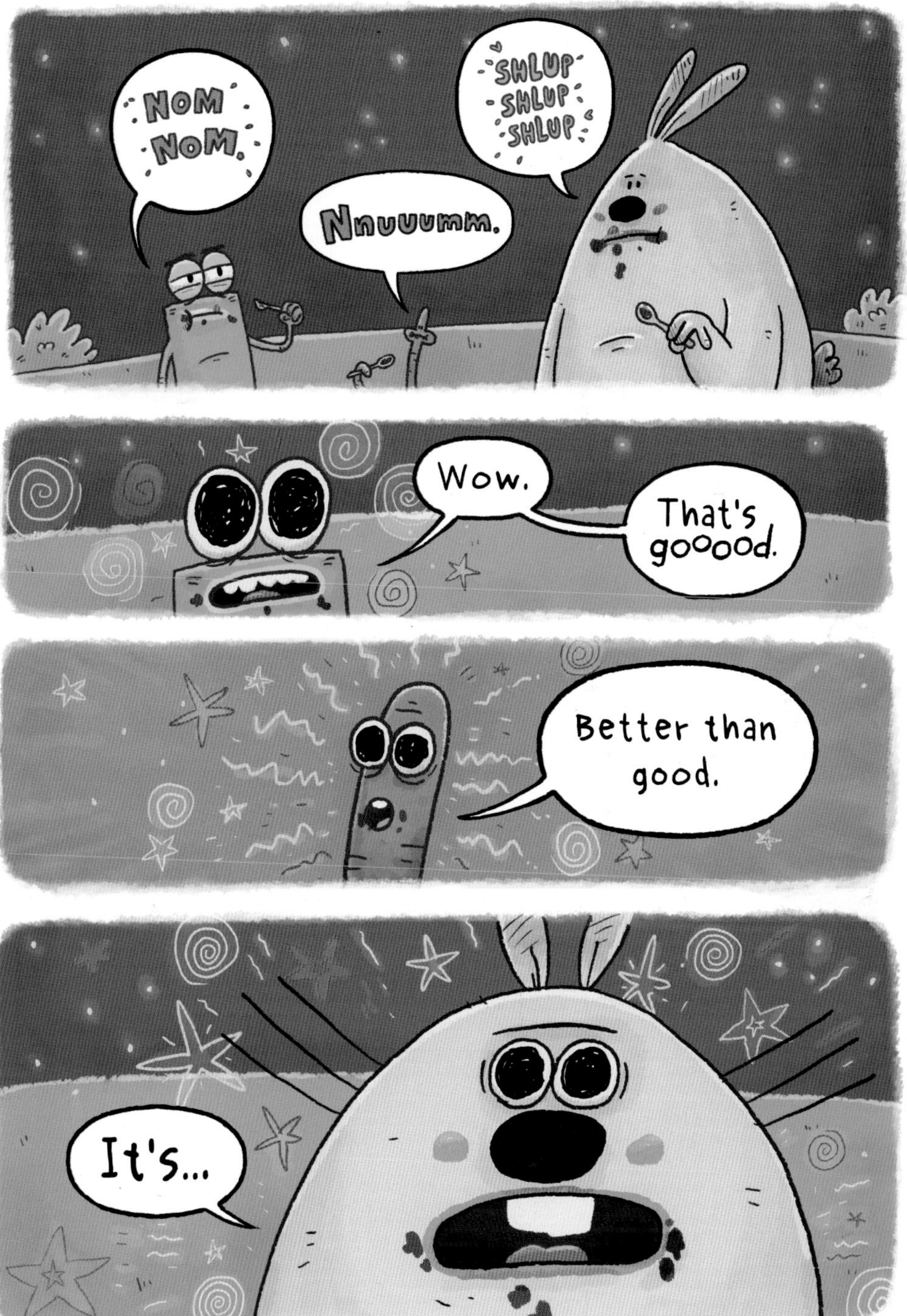
NOM NOM.
Nnuuumm.
SHLUP SHLUP SHLUP
Wow.
That's gooood.
Better than good.
It's...

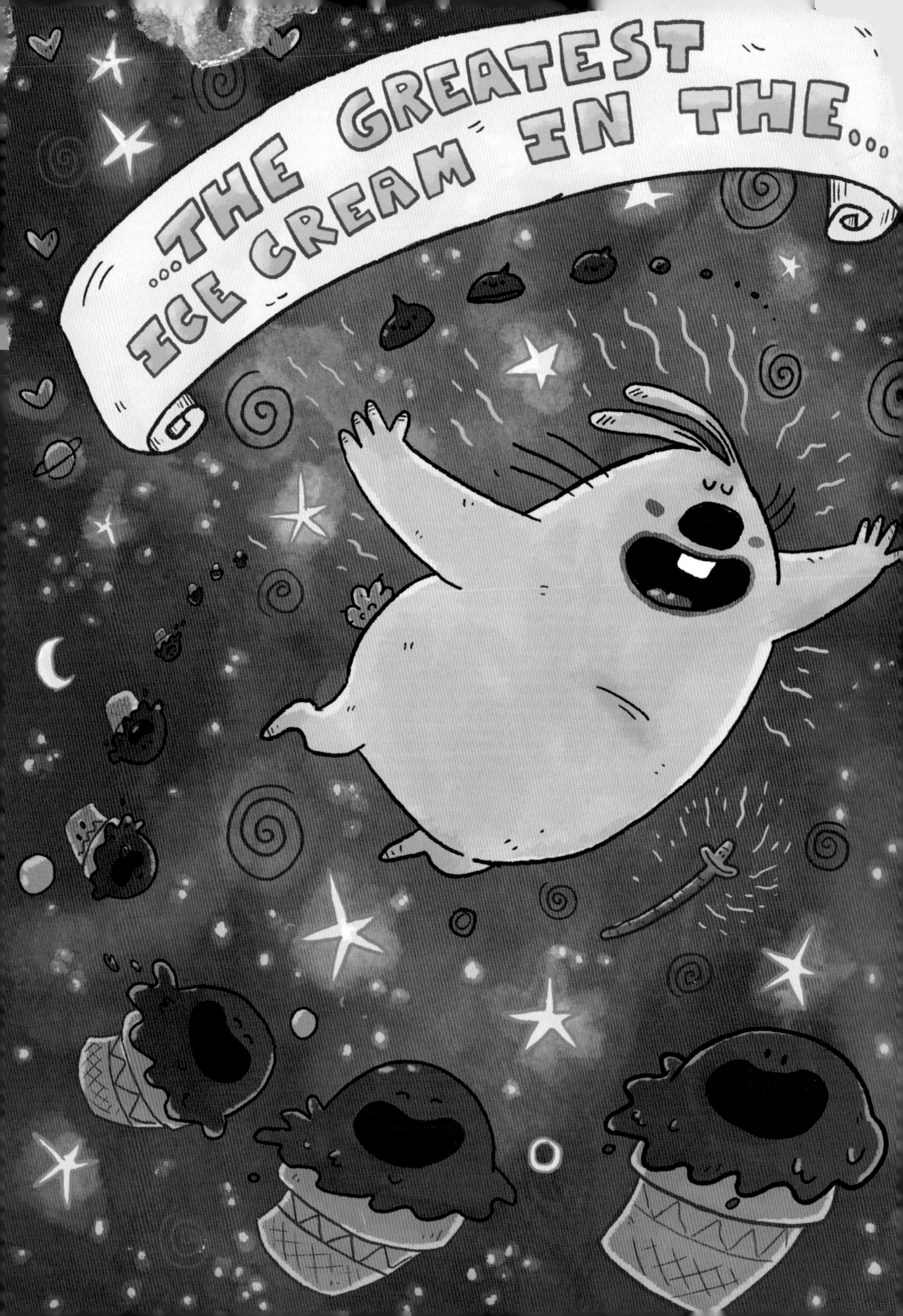
...THE GREATEST
ICE CREAM IN THE...

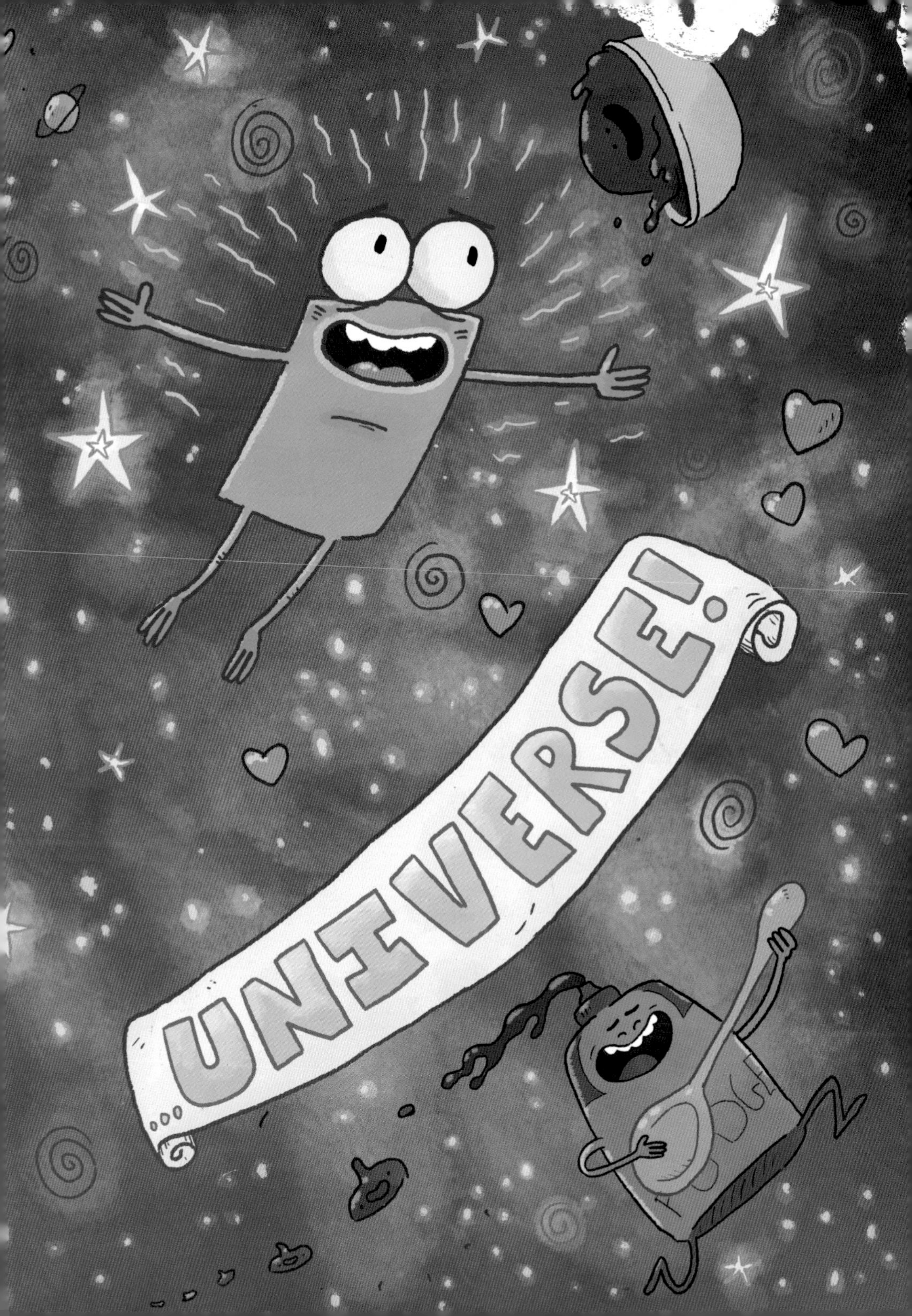

...UNIVERSE!

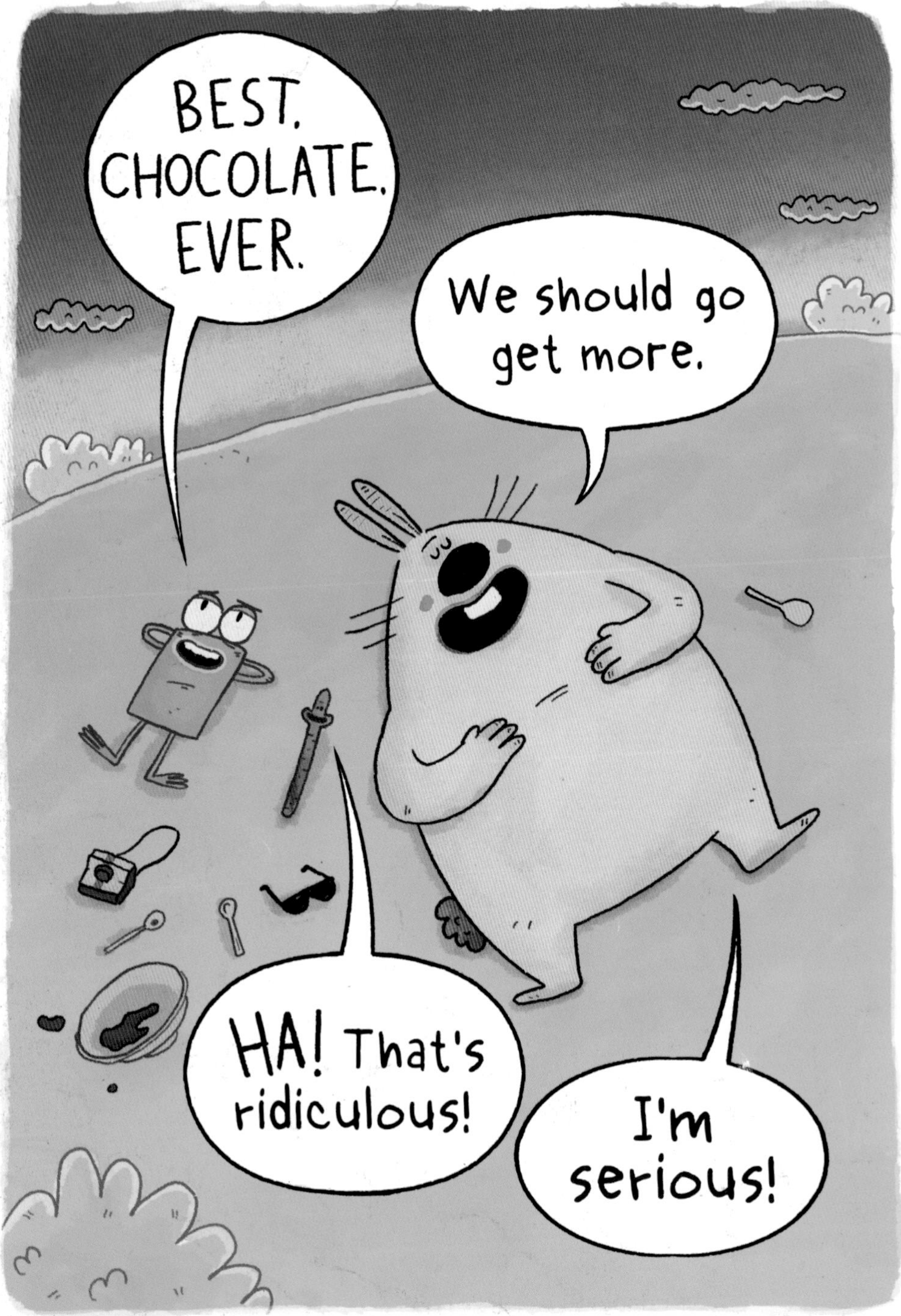
BEST. CHOCOLATE. EVER.
We should go get more.
HA! That's ridiculous!
I'm serious!

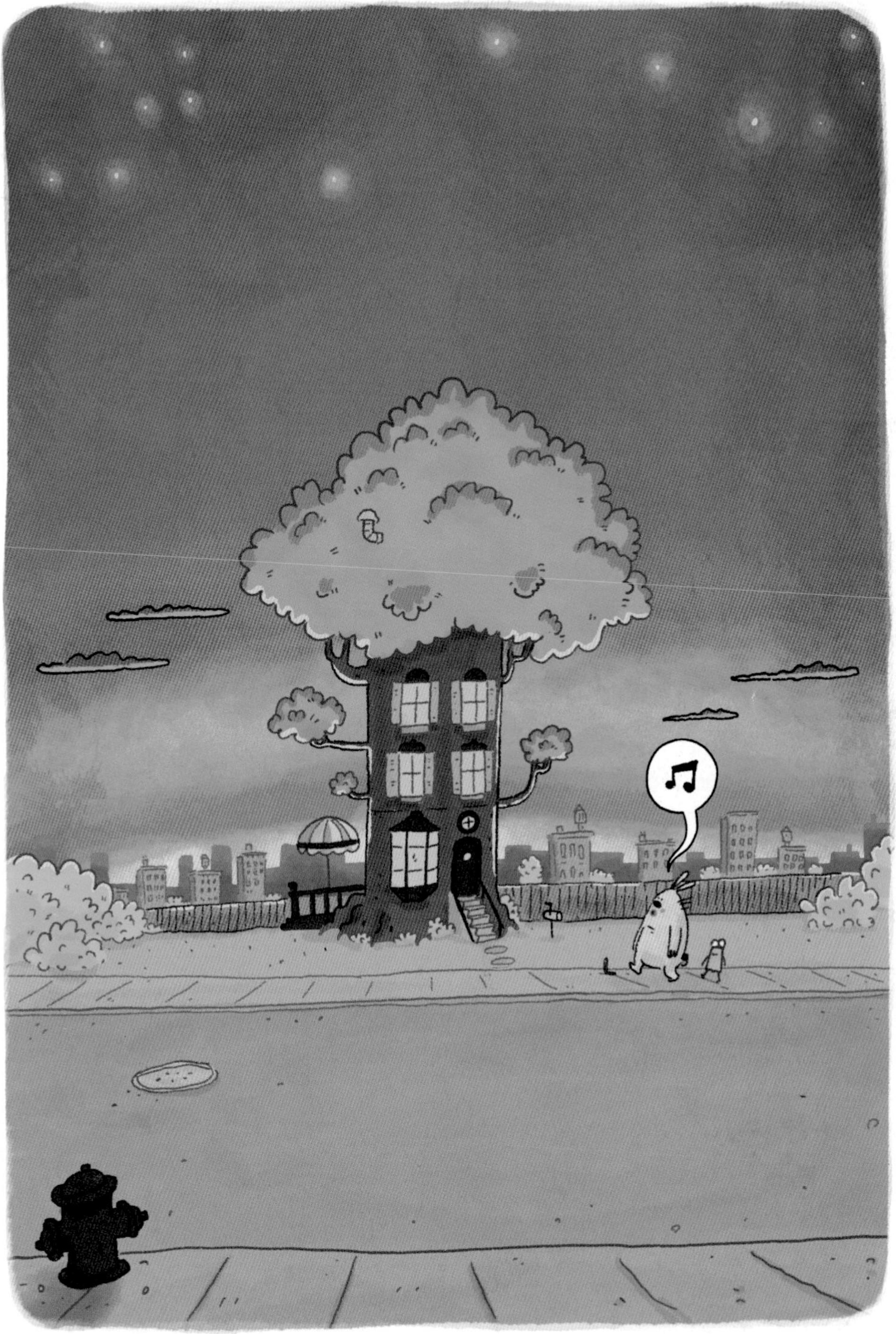

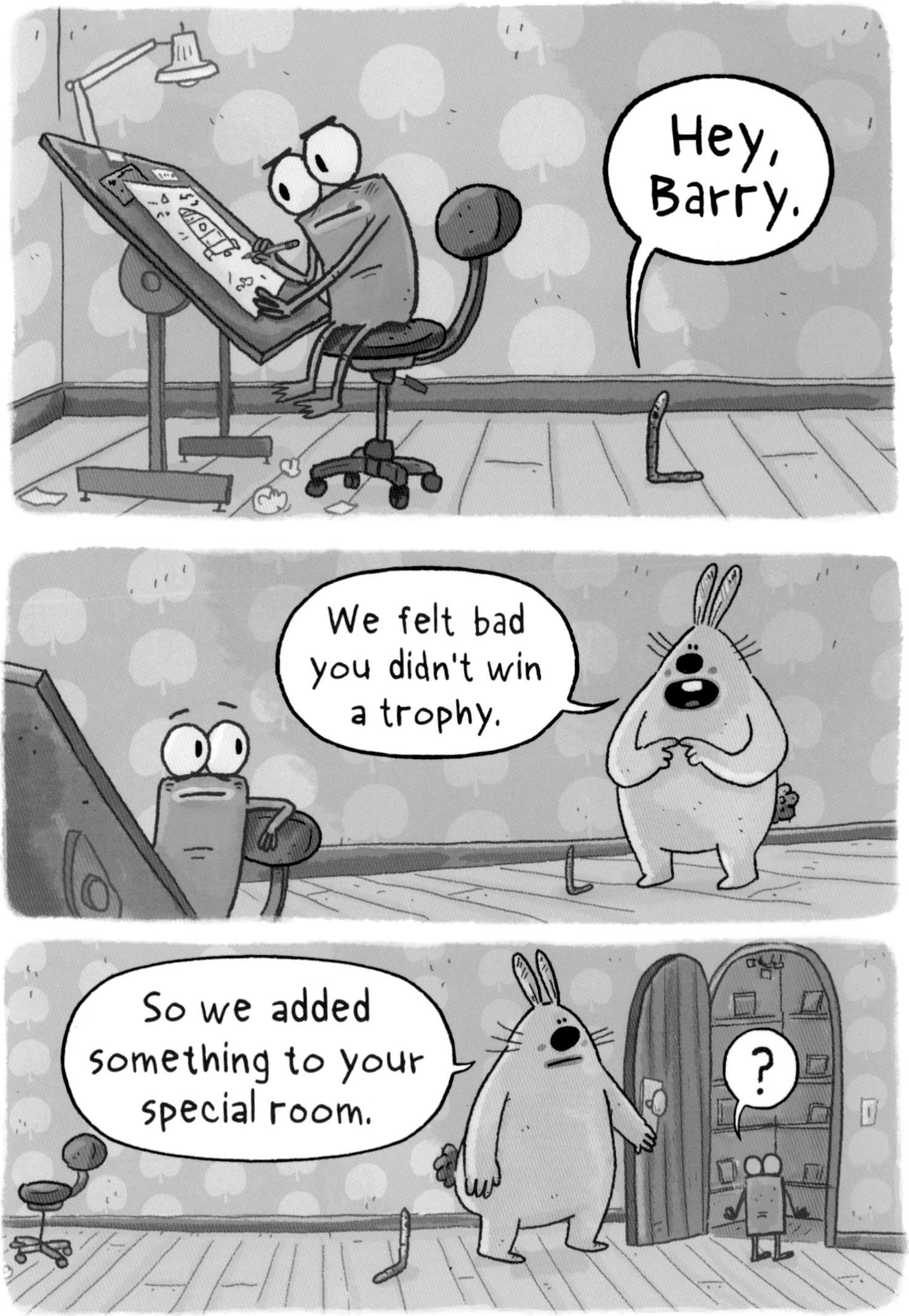
Hey, Barry.
We felt bad you didn't win a trophy.
So we added something to your special room.
?

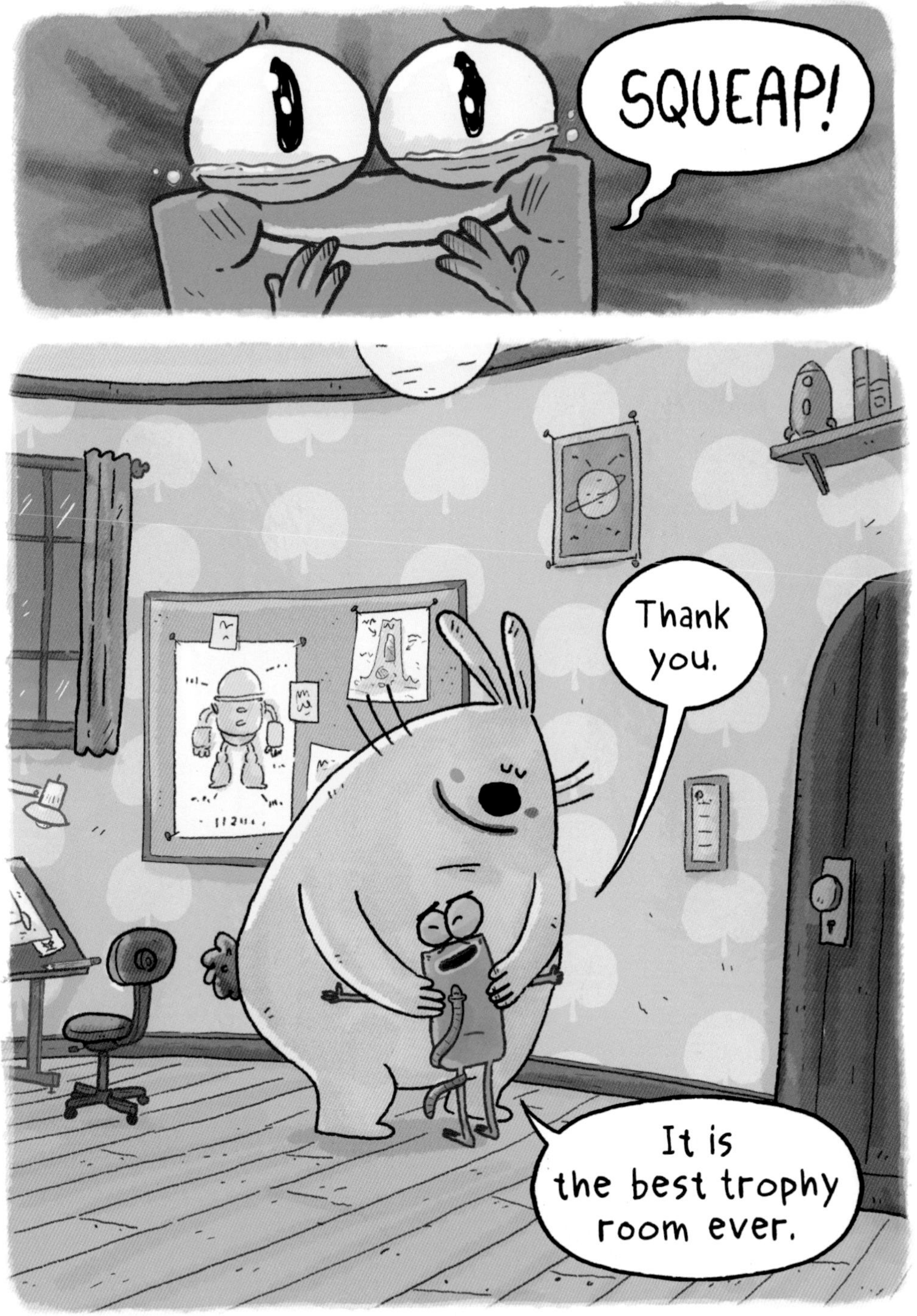
SQUEAP!
Thank you.
It is the best trophy room ever.

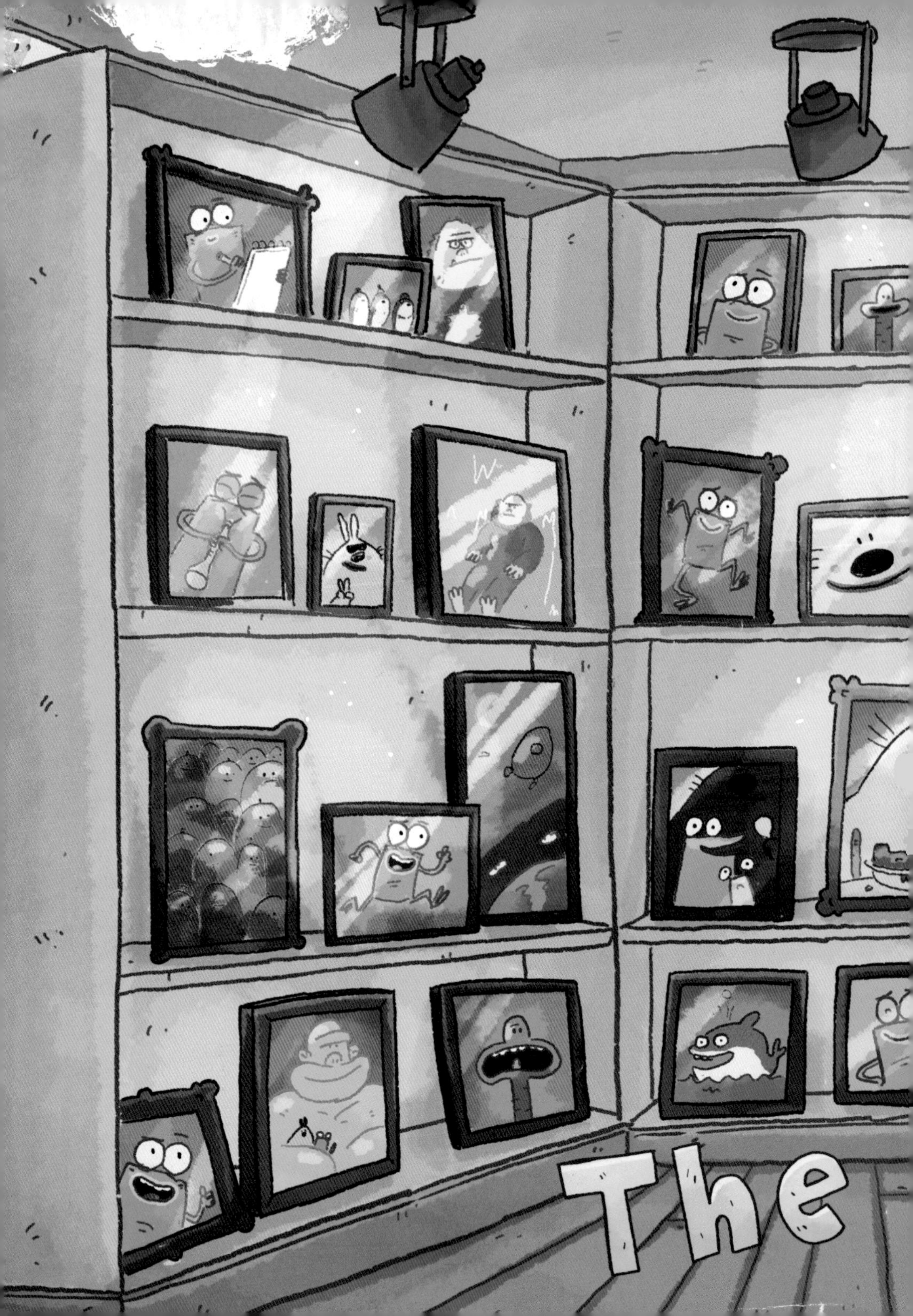
The

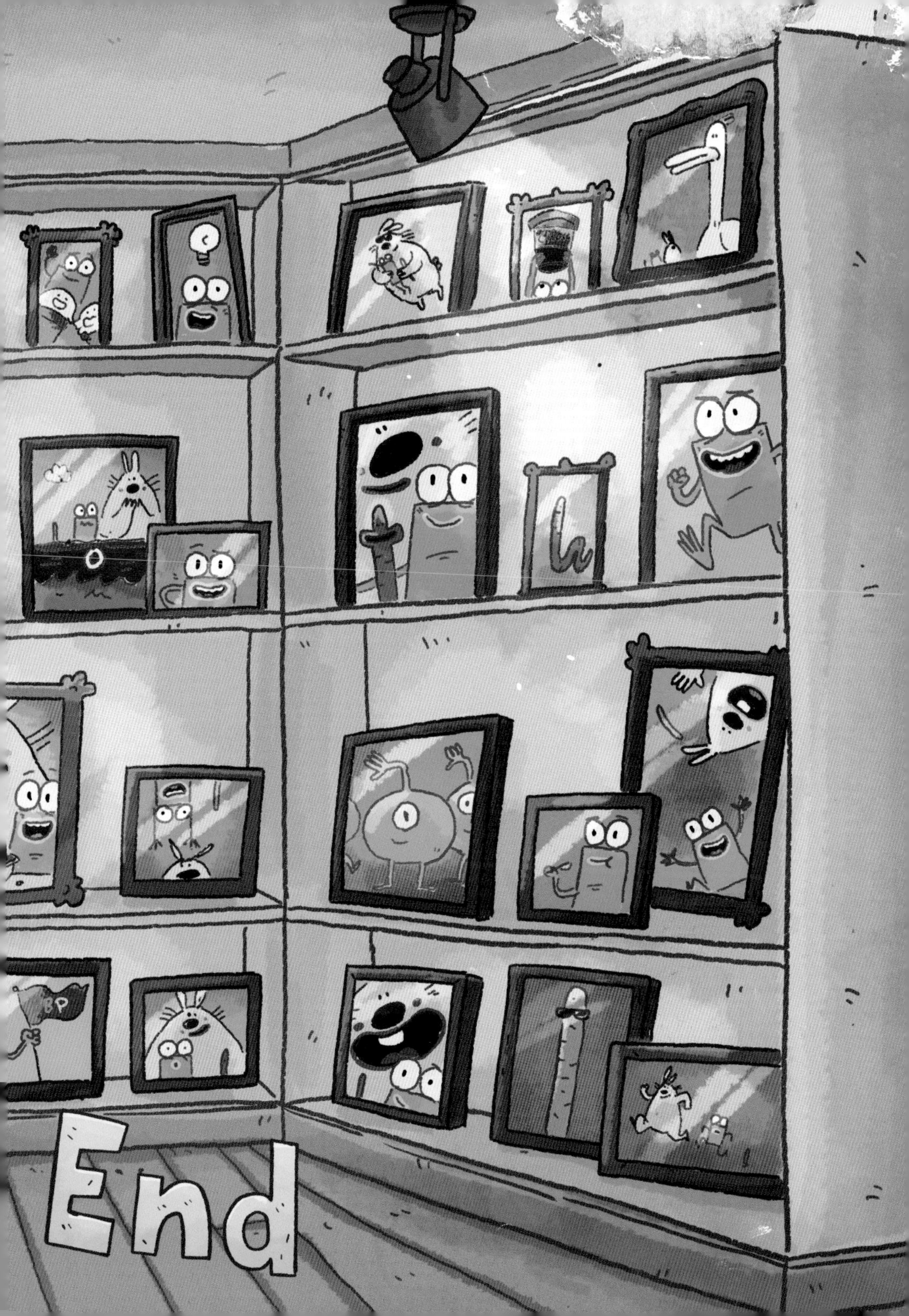
BP
End

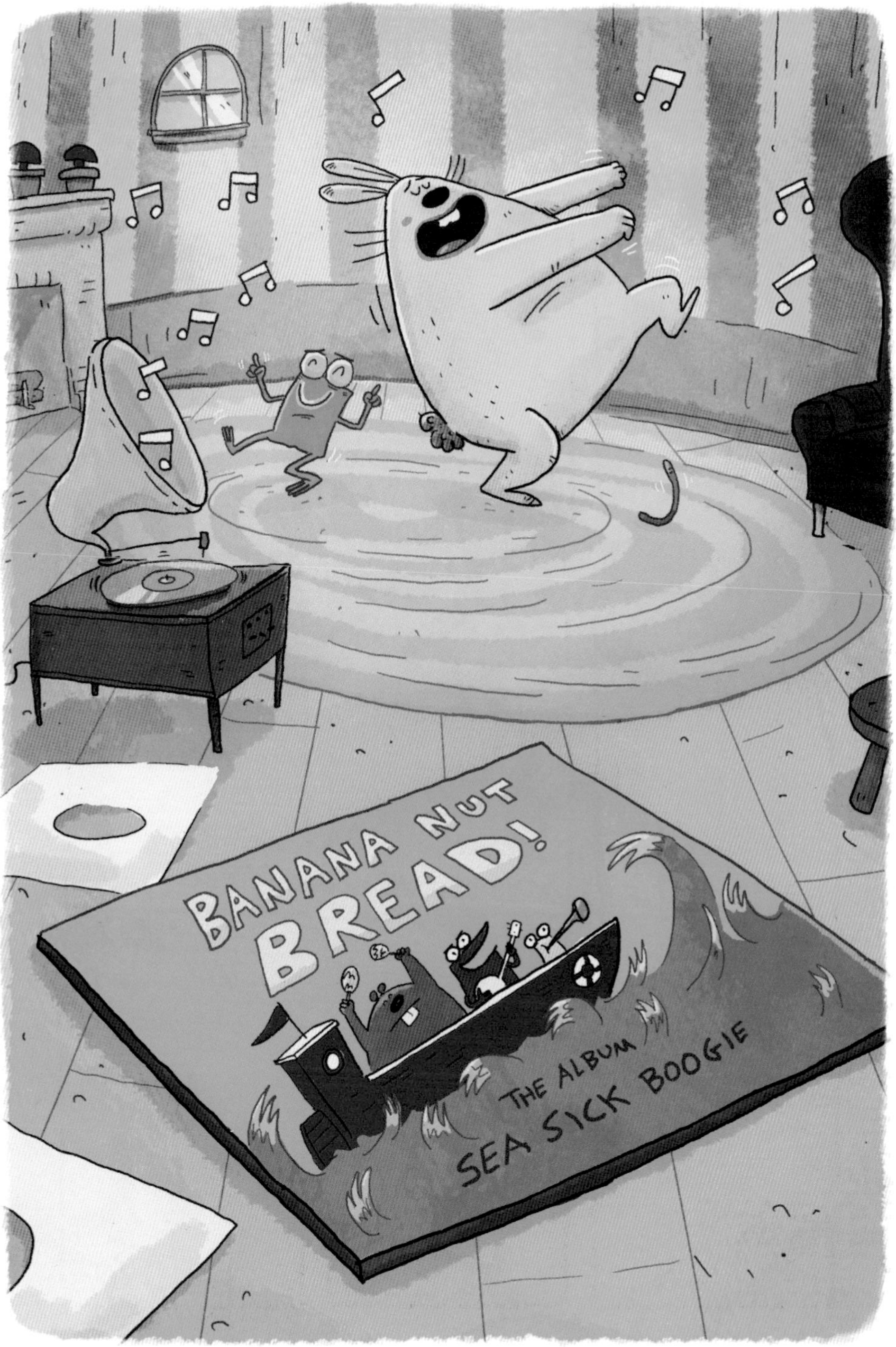
BANANA NUT
BREAD!
THE ALBUM
SEA SICK BOOGIE

BEST DANCE MOVES EVA:

THE FROGGY FANDANGO!

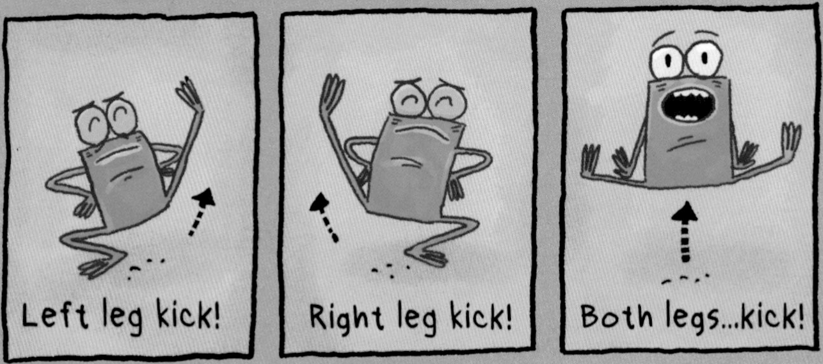
Left leg kick!
Right leg kick!
Both legs...kick!

THE RUNNING BUNNY!

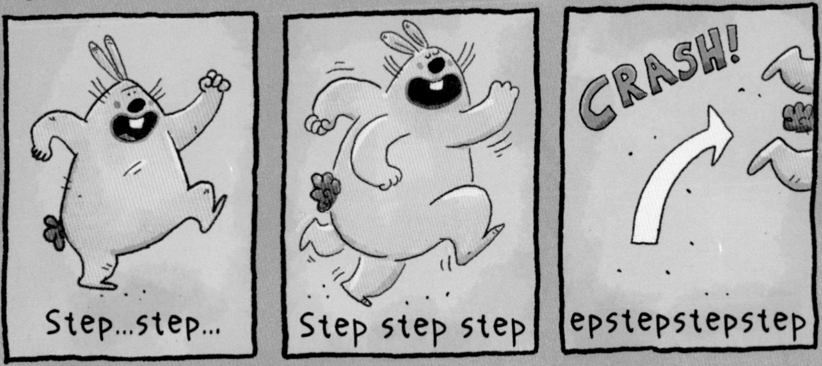
Step...step...
Step step step
CRASH!
epstepstepstep

THE TIRED WORM!

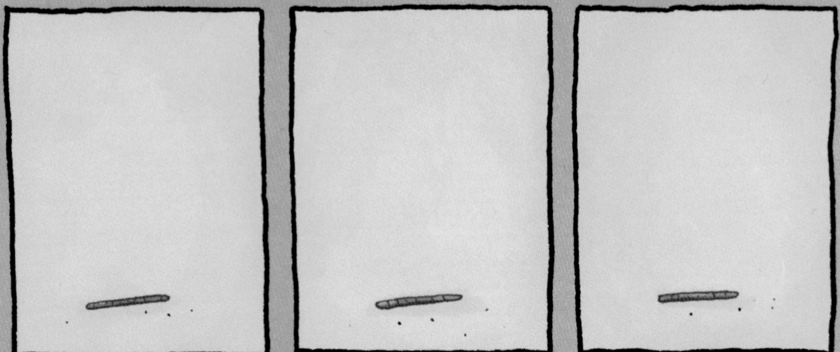

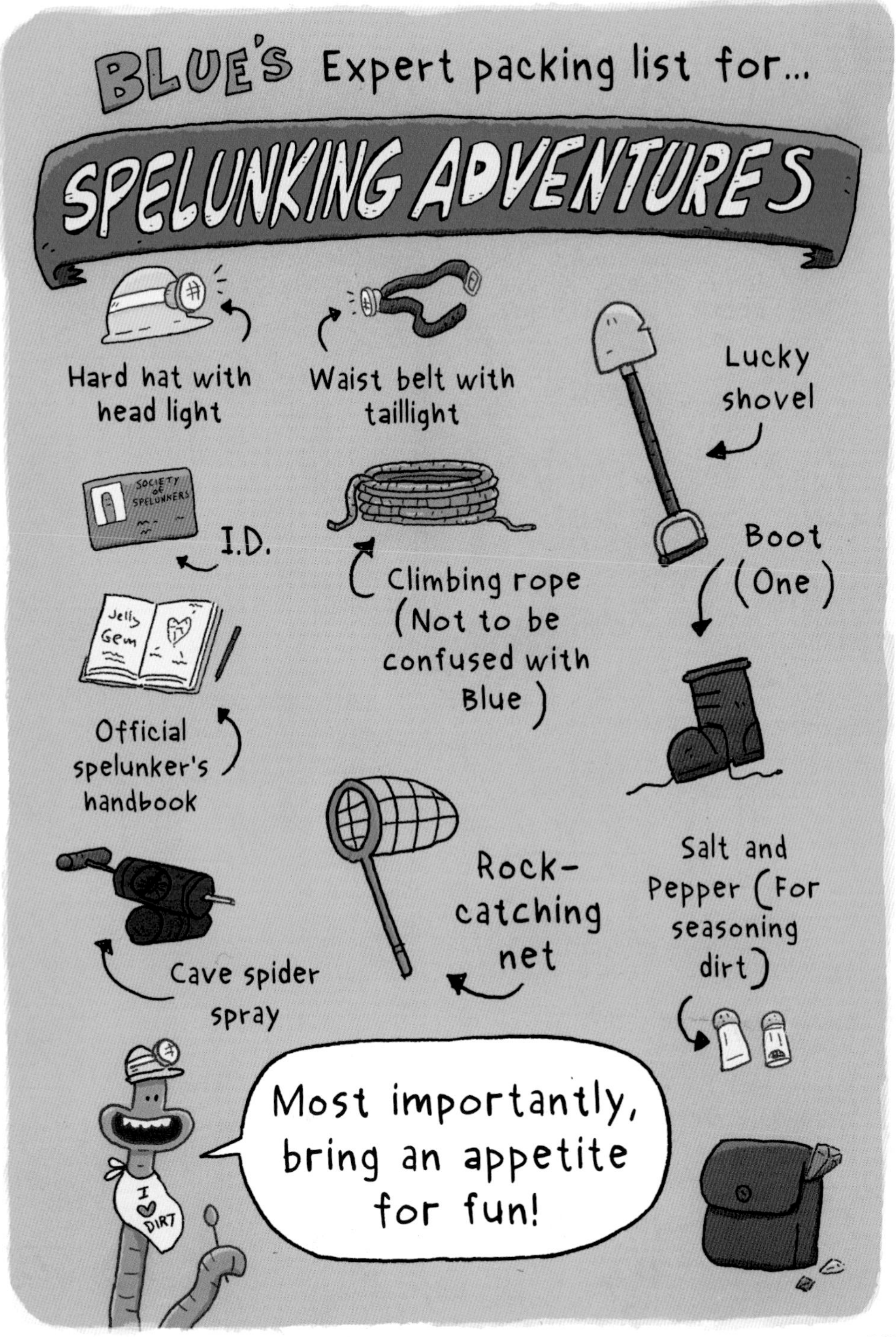
BLUE'S Expert packing list for...
SPELUNKING ADVENTURES
Hard hat with head light
Waist belt with taillight
Lucky shovel
SOCIETY OF SPELUNKERS
I.D.
Climbing rope (Not to be confused with Blue)
Boot (One)
Jelly Gem
Official spelunker's handbook
Rock-catching net
Salt and Pepper (For seasoning dirt)
Cave spider spray
Most importantly, bring an appetite for fun!
I DIRT

HOW TO MAKE A MINI COMIC!

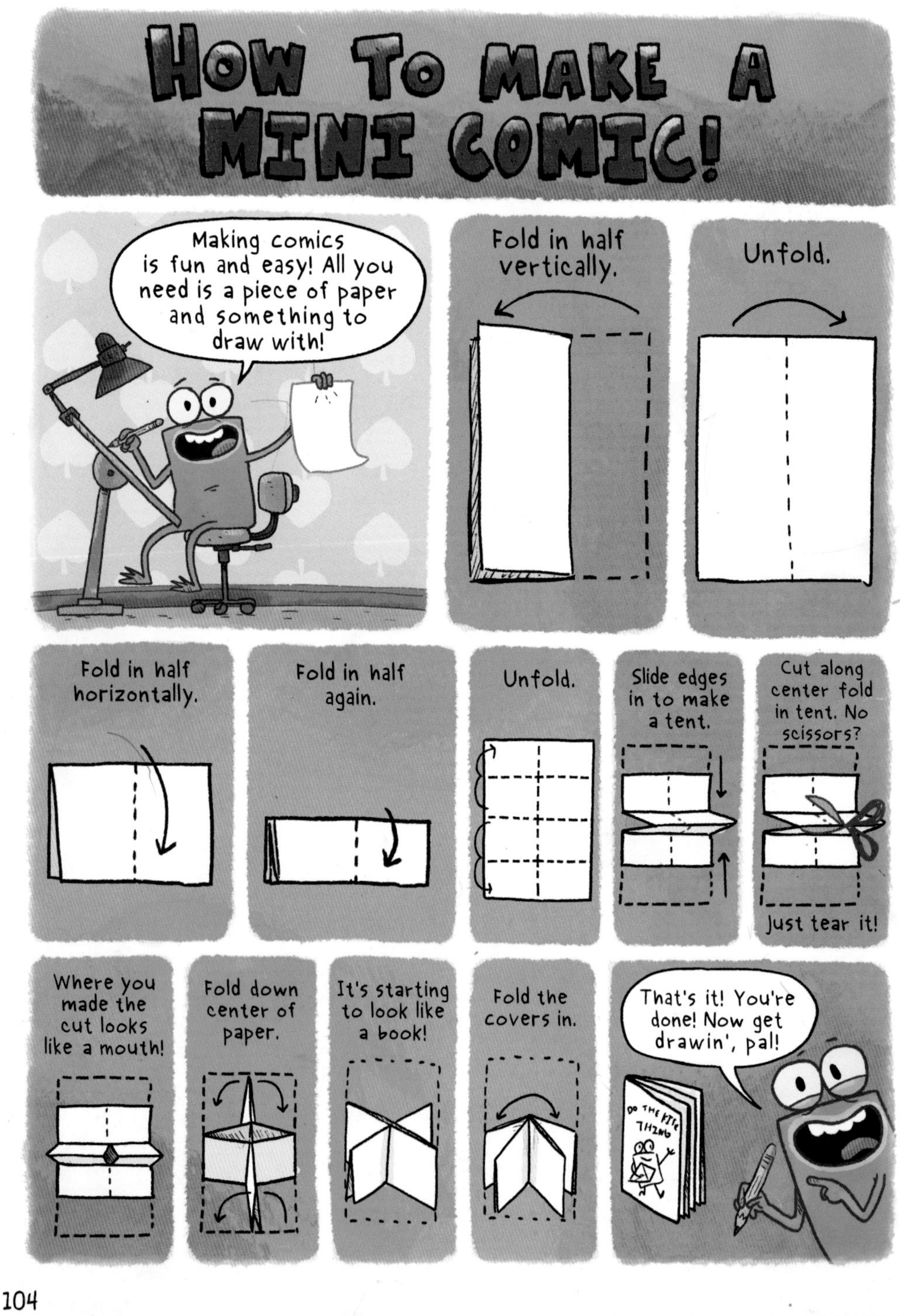
Making comics is fun and easy! All you need is a piece of paper and something to draw with!
Fold in half vertically.
Unfold.
Fold in half horizontally.
Fold in half again.
Unfold.
Slide edges in to make a tent.
Cut along center fold in tent. No scissors?
Just tear it!
Where you made the cut looks like a mouth!
Fold down center of paper.
It's starting to look like a book!
Fold the covers in.
That's it! You're done! Now get drawin', pal!

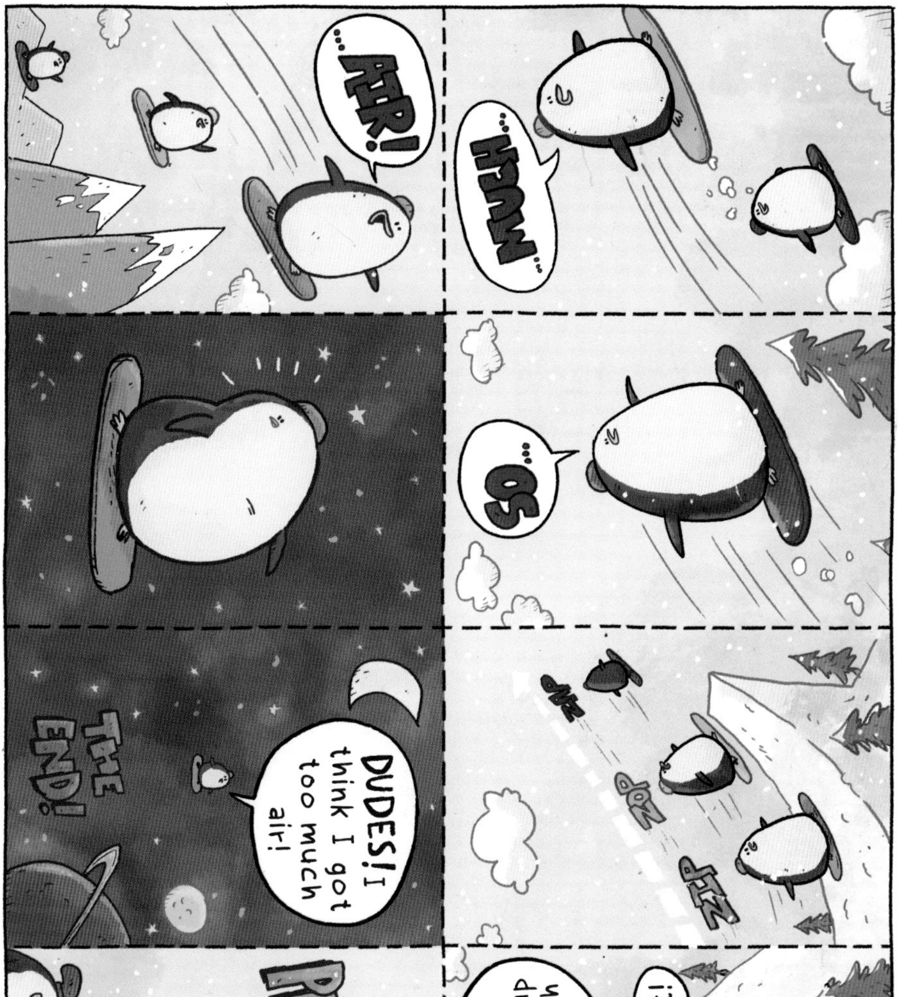
Front cover
3 PENGUINS IN SO MUCH AIR!!!
Page 1
Let's all hit that jump for so much air!
Sweet!
Fer sher.
Page 2
Page 3
SO...
Page 4
...MUCH...
Page 5
...AIR!
Page 6
Page 7
DUDES! I think I got too much air!
THE END!

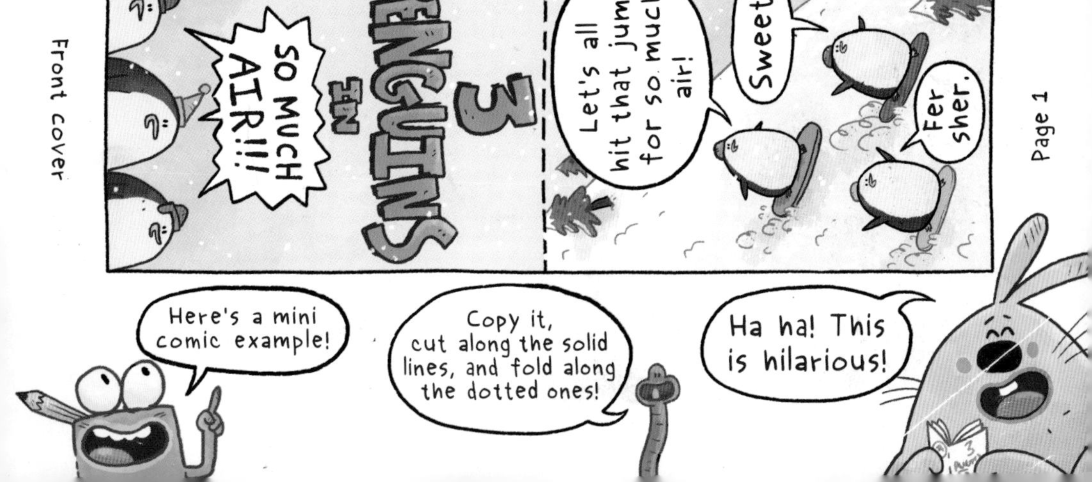
Here's a mini comic example!
Copy it, cut along the solid lines, and fold along the dotted ones!
Ha ha! This is hilarious!

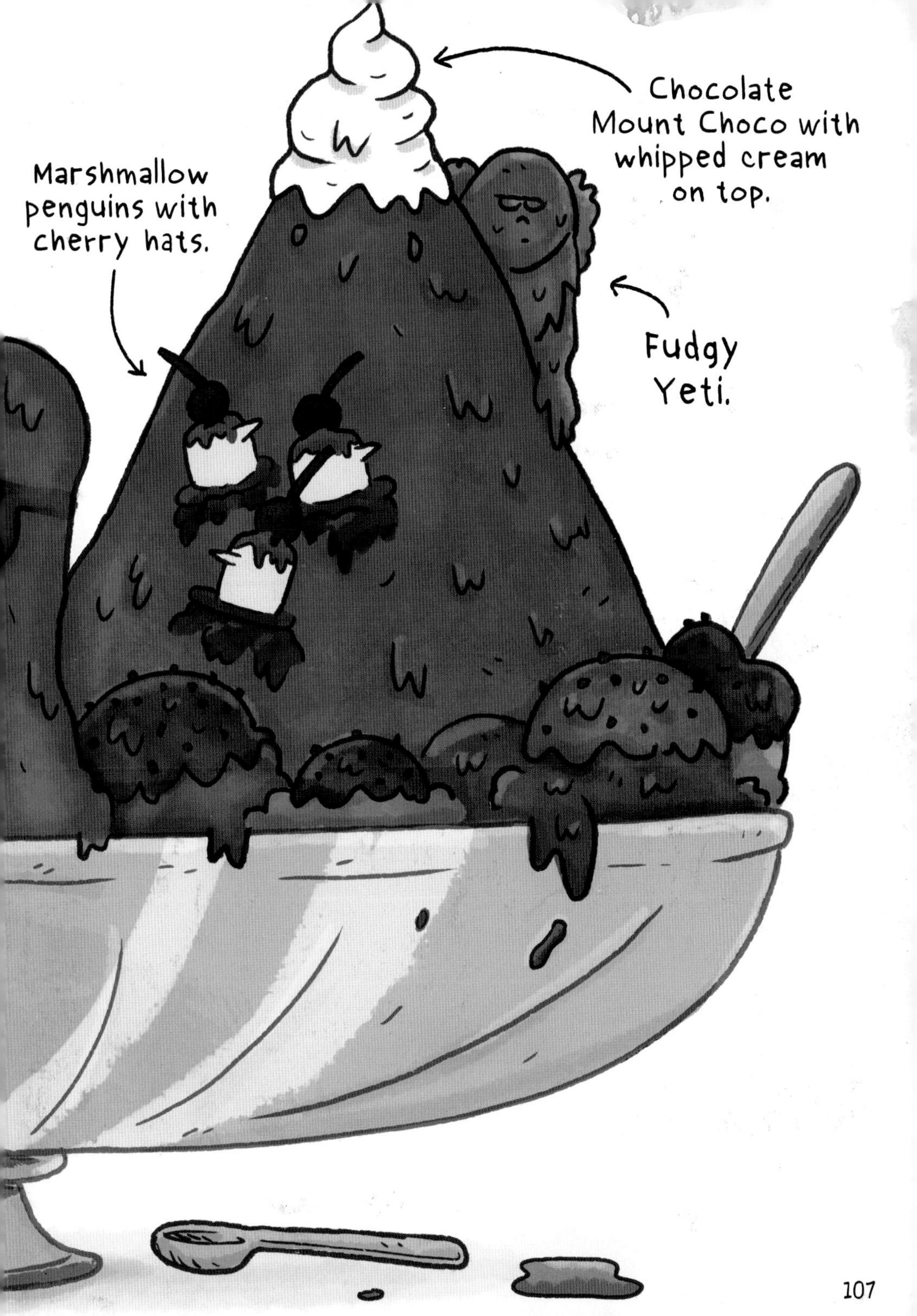
Chocolate Mount Choco with whipped cream on top.
Marshmallow penguins with cherry hats.
Fudgy Yeti.

About the Authors

Jason

Dan

Dan & Jason go back. Waaaaay back. They got their start drawing and writing stories in what feels like the early Jurassic period, also known as the '90s, when they were making comics in the back of their high school art room. Annnnnd they never stopped!

The acclaimed cartooning duo live, breathe, and eat comics and animation. *Danger on Mount Choco* is their third Blue, Barry & Pancakes book. They love writing and drawing these stories more than anything else in the whole wide world, and they really hope you like reading them. Dan and Jason make everything together! They think it, write it, draw it, mix it, bake it, and serve it together. Just like Blue, Barry, and Pancakes, they're best friends!

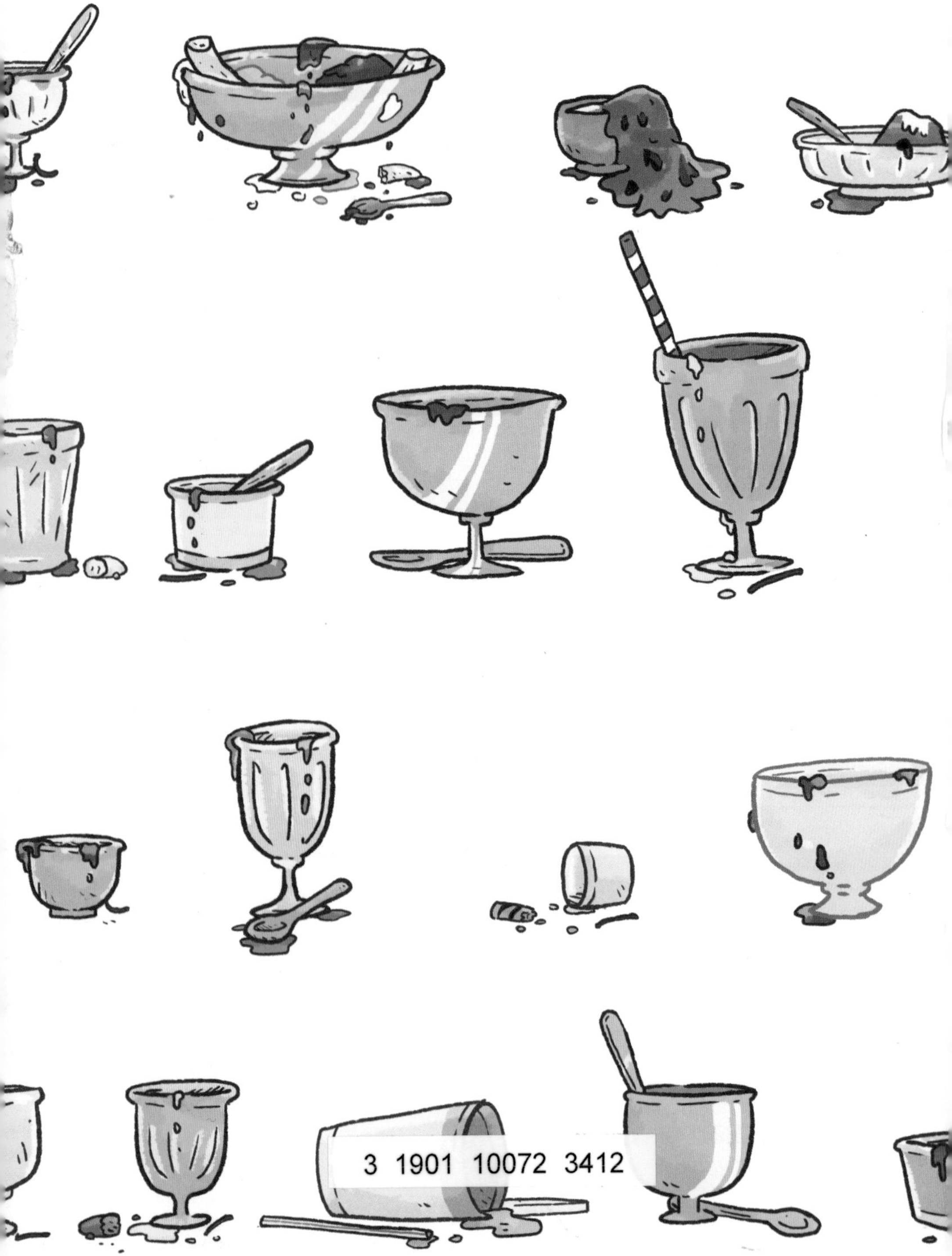